蔡志忠 / 编绘

[美] 拉思杰博士 等 / 译

觉者的法音　智慧的语言

佛陀说·法句经

SAYINGS OF BUDDHA · DHARMA SUTRA

The indoctrination of consciousness
The language of wisdom

中国出版集团

现代出版社

图字：01-2006-1447

图书在版编目（C I P）数据

佛陀说·法句经 / 汉英对照：蔡志忠编绘；（美）拉思杰（Rathje,W.L.）等译.
-- 北京：现代出版社,2013.10
（蔡志忠漫画中国传统文化经典）
ISBN 978-7-5143-1872-2

Ⅰ.①佛… Ⅱ.①蔡… ②拉… Ⅲ.①漫画—连环画
—作品集—中国—现代 Ⅳ.① J228.2

中国版本图书馆 CIP 数据核字（2013）第 240733 号

蔡志忠漫画中国传统文化经典：中英文对照版

佛陀说·法句经

作　　者	蔡志忠　编绘
	［美］拉思杰博士 等译
责任编辑	袁　涛
出版发行	现代出版社
地　　址	北京市安定门外安华里 504 号
邮政编码	100011
电　　话	010-64267325　010-64245264（兼传真）
网　　址	www.1980xd.com
电子信箱	xiandai@cnpitc.com.cn
印　　刷	三河市南阳印刷有限公司
开　　本	710×1000　1 / 16
印　　张	18.5
版　　次	2013 年 11 月第 1 版　2015 年 4 月第 3 次印刷
书　　号	ISBN 978-7-5143-1872-2
定　　价	36.00 元

目录
contents

佛陀说
SAYINGS OF BUDDHA

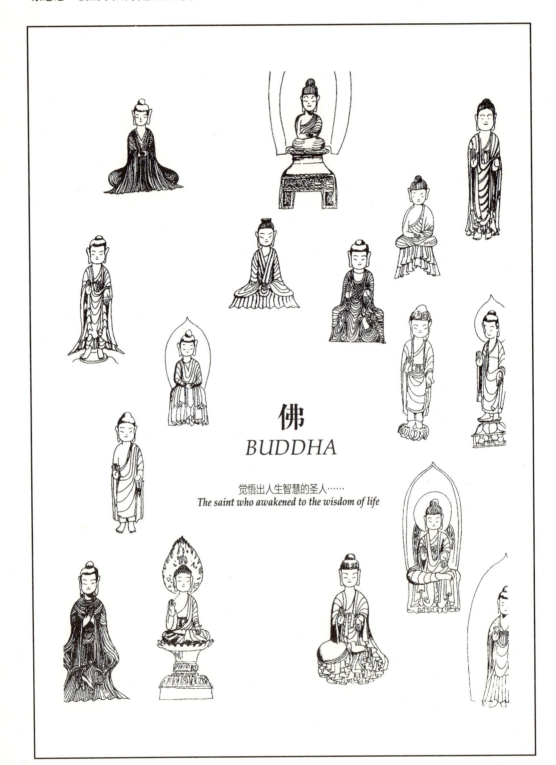

佛
BUDDHA

觉悟出人生智慧的圣人……
The saint who awakened to the wisdom of life

《智度论二》曰："佛名为觉，于一切无明睡眠中最初觉故，名为觉。"
According to the Second Treatise on the Philosophy of the Measurement of Wisdom:
"Buddha means awakened. Among all who sleep in delusion, a Buddha is the first one to be awakened to the Essential Universal Truths. This is why the Buddha is defined as being awakened."

一切众生断三界烦恼果报尽者，名为"佛"。
All living beings who can eliminate worries arising from all realms of manifestations and end the cycle of reincarnation are named Buddha.

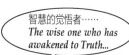

智慧的觉悟者……
The wise one who has awakened to Truth...

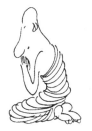

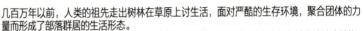

几百万年以前，人类的祖先走出树林在草原上讨生活，面对严酷的生存环境，聚合团体的力量而形成了部落群居的生活形态。

人，由草原生活慢慢地演变为定居洞穴、山谷，乃至最后到平原，形成乡村与城市的社会结构；生存方式也由逐水草而居、猎食鸟兽进化为畜牧与务农。

由于畜牧业与农业社会中忙的时候很忙，空闲的时间也很多，因此，智慧的人们便开始发展出艺术与哲学思想。

佛，是智慧的觉悟者之义。这些智慧的觉悟者们觉悟了什么呢？他们觉悟出了：

人与时空的关系、人生的意义和时空宇宙的本质。

Millions of years ago, our human ancestors walked out of the forests to make a living on the grasslands. Facing harsh environments, humans gathered group force by living in communities and forming the tribal lifestyle.

From living on the grasslands, humans slowly evolved into permanent residence in caves and valleys, and eventually on the plains where they formed the social structure of villages and cities. Their lifestyles also evolved from hunter-gatherers to herding animals and agriculture.

Both animal herding and agricultural societies involved a lot of both hard work and leisure time. Therefore, intelligent humans started developing arts and philosophies.

Buddha means the one who is awakened and wise. What did these wise ones awaken to? They were awakened to the following Truths:

The relationship among humans, time and space;

The meaning of life;

The true nature of time, space and the universe.

佛陀
SAKYAMUNI BUDDHA
如来十号之一
One of the ten titles of "Ultimate Essence Arriving"

《智度论二》曰："佛陀，秦言智者。有常无常等一切诸法，菩提树下了了觉知，故名佛陀。"

约在公元前五六五年，今尼泊尔境内迦毗罗卫国净饭王的儿子乔答摩·悉达多（*Cautama Sidhartha*）降生了。七天之后母亲去世。悉达多自幼多愁善感，受传统婆罗门教育，常感世事无常，于二十九岁出家，先随沙门思潮的两位大师阿罗逻·迦罗摩（*Arada Kalama*）和郁陀迦·罗摩子（*Udraka Ramaputra*）学习禅定，后又自行苦修六年，最后在菩提树下悟道成佛。

According to the Second Treatise on the Philosophy of the Measurement of Wisdom:

"Buddha means 'the wise one'. Sitting under the Bodhi tree, Sakyamuni became completely awakened to all kinds of Essential Universal Truths, including what is permanent and what is transient. Therefore, he was named Buddha."

About 565 years before Christ, in what is today Nepal, Kapilavastu's King Suddhodana had a son by the name of Gautama Siddhârtha. Seven days after the prince was born, his mother passed away. Prince Siddhârtha was a sentimental child who received a traditional Brâhman education. He often felt that things were transient and adopted the homeless style of a mendicant at the age of 29.

He first learned meditation from two Sramana gurus, Arada Kalama and Uddaka Ramaputra. Then he spent six years cultivating himself through self-mortification. Eventually, he became enlightened to the Path to Truths under a Bodhi tree.

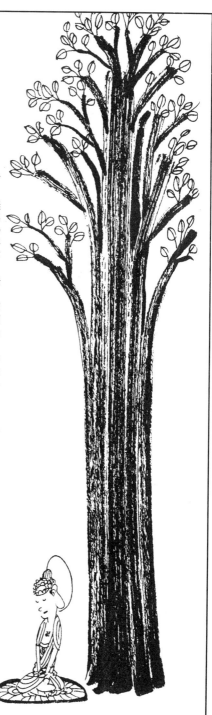

两千五百多年前，人类的智慧发生了全球性的大跃进，世界各地的很多思想家几乎都在这同一段时间里迸发出了智慧的火花。在中国，有老子、庄子等关于人与天地宇宙的哲学思想；有孔子、孟子关于人与社会群体关系应该遵守的人本原则的思想，还有如孙子、墨子、荀子、韩非子等百家的诸多辉煌的思想成果。

在古希腊，有哲学始祖泰利斯、赫拉克利特和德漠克里特（原子论学说），以及后来的苏格拉底、柏拉图、亚里士多德等智者，他们的学说影响了西方世界两千多年来哲学与科学的发展。

而在古印度，也出现了百家齐放的繁荣景象，当时的沙门思潮乃至后世形成的各种印度宗教——印度教、耆那教、瑜伽派等等……其中对东方世界影响最大的要数出生于尼泊尔的佛陀了！

佛陀被后世尊称为世界四大圣哲之一，是与孔子、苏格拉底、耶稣居同等地位的精神领袖。两千多年来他深远地影响了东方世界人们的思想，甚至到后来有很多信徒还把他尊奉为"神"。

More than twenty-five hundred years ago, the wisdom of humans took a great leap forward on a global level. Many philosophers all over the world erupted with sparks of wisdom at the same time.

In China, there were the philosophies about humans and the universe by Lao Zi, Zhuang Zi, etc.; the philosophies on the principles of humanity to guide inter-relations among humans and social groups by Confucius and Meng Zi; and, in addition, numerous and glorious fruits of thought by Sun zi, Mo Zi, Xun Zi, Han Fei Zi, and close to one hundred schools of thought.

In ancient Greece, there were the ancestors of philosophy, such as Telis, Heraclitus and Democritus (the Theory of Atoms), as well as subsequent wise ones, such as Socrates, Plato and Aristotle, whose theories have been influencing the development of philosophy and science in the Western World for more than two thousand years.

While in ancient India, there was also a flourishing of many schools of thought which bloomed at the same time, including the philosophy of Srmana, as well as the seeds for various religions which developed in India later-Hinduism, Jainism, Yoga, etc. Among these, the most influential for the Eastern World was definitely Sakyamuni Buddha born in Nepal.

Sakyamuni Buddha is regarded by people of later generations as one of the four greatest saintly philosophers of the world. He was a spiritual leader of the same status as Confucius, Socrates and Jesus. For more than two thousand years, he deeply influenced the thinking of people in the Eastern World. Later on, followers of the Buddha even worshipped him as a deity.

佛教

BUDDHISM

佛之教法也

The Teaching of the Essential Universal Truths by the Buddha Sakyamuni

佛陀教化众生
远离感官的贪瞋痴
远离染着一切诱人的事物
明心断念地去修行
以达寂静之境
得智慧大解脱

The Buddha taught all living beings to cultivate themselves:
By distancing themselves from greed, resentment and delusion;
By distancing themselves from all seductive objects and events that pollute the minds;
By centring their minds and severing their thoughts of the material world.
This is how they will reach the state of tranquillity;
This is how they will achieve superb wisdom and ultimate relief.

请大家跟随我走向彼岸的方法，遵照它去实践。这方法便是三法印、四圣谛、八正道、十二缘起法……
Would you all please follow me in practising the proper methods to move onto the path to the "Other Shore". These methods are the Three Imprints of Essential Universal Truths, the Four Phases of Cultivation, the Eightfold Proper Path, and the Twelve Laws of Causal Preconditioning.

佛教是佛陀的教导，是他所说的法。当然，你也可以称它为以佛陀为首的一种教团、教派，或一种宗教。

一百多年来，以弗洛伊德、荣格为首的学者掀起了一股心理学的研究思潮……但早在两千五百年前，东方世界的思想家们对人性心理学的专研便已取得很大成果，只是隐藏在哲学、兵法或宗教教义里罢了。

而佛陀正是对心理学研究得最透彻的一位智者，他还是一位实用心理学的导师。依照他的方法，经过生活中的实践修行，我们可以从错误的认知走向正确的观念；从痛苦烦恼中止息改变为永恒的喜悦安详。

Buddhism is the teaching of Sakyamuni Buddha on Essential Universal Truths. Of course, you may refer to it as a religious group or sect or denomination led by the Buddha.

In the past one hundred years, scholars such as Sigmund Freud and Carl Gustav Jung popularized research into human psychology...

But more than 2500 years ago, the thinkers of the Eastern World had already gained great accomplishments in studying the psychology of human nature. These accomplishments were not recognized because they were hidden in philosophy, strategies of war, or precepts of religions.

The Buddha happened to be the wise one who most thoroughly researched psychology. He was also a teacher in applied psychology. By following his methods of practice and cultivation in everyday life, we will be able to walk towards proper concepts and avoid erroneous identification. This is how we can put an end to our suffering as we transcend to eternal joy and peace.

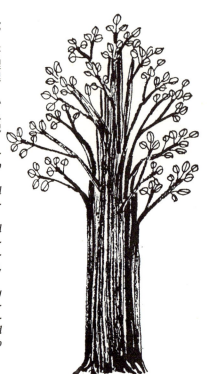

本来我是这样说的……
BUDDHA'S TEACHING
ON SPIRITUAL CULTIVTION

From the beginning, this was the way I taught...

三法印
THE THREE IMPRINTS OF TRUTH

三法印是佛陀印证无误的真理。
佛陀一生追求人生真谛，到最后终于悟出宇宙中的三个真理……
The Three Imprints of Truth are the universal laws that the Buddha personally verified. The Buddha spent his whole life seeking the essence of living. Eventually, he was enlightened to the Essential Universal Truths...

诸行无常
All acts are transient.

诸法无我
Essential Universal Truths contain no ego-self.

涅槃寂静
The state of Nirvâna** is perfect tranquillity.

* *"Essential Universal Truths" is often translated as Dharma in Buddhism.*
***Nirvâna, "the other shore", is a state of enlightenment attainable in this life by extinguishing all desires and hereby achieving liberation from the cycle of birth and death. One who has attained Nirvâna is called an Arhat.*

当初佛陀在郁卢吠罗村尼连禅那河畔的菩提树下开悟，成为一个全然觉知的智者，他悟出了什么真理？接着，佛陀游行四十五年传法，他说的又是什么法？佛陀在树下觉悟的人与世界的三个真理就是：
"诸行无常，诸法无我，涅槃寂静。"

At the time Buddha attained supreme enlightenment, under the Bodhi tree on the bank of the Neranjarâ River at Bodh Gayâ, he became the ultimate wise one with complete awareness. What kind of truth was he enlightened to?

Subsequently, the Buddha travelled for 45 years to spread his teaching. What kind of basic universal wisdom was he teaching?

The three absolute Truths about human beings and the world around us that came to the Buddha through enlightenment were:

"All acts are transient.
Essential Universal Truths contain no ego-self.
Nirvâna is perfect tranquillity."

诸行无常
ALL ACTS ARETRANSIENT

世间万象，没有任何是常恒永驻不变的。
一切都是由一个起因和后来的条件互相配合变化而成的。
而这种因缘条件组合构成的无常变迁，就是我们宇宙的实性。

Out of tens of thousands of phenomena in the world, nothing is eternally permanent and everlasting.
All manifestations originate from particular causes which, in turn, interact with subsequent conditions to mould and change each other.
Such unenduring variability, formed by the preconditioned synchronicity of time and space, is the true nature of our universe.

有生命就会有死亡，美好的事物也会变坏，变化不已是宇宙的真理。人因企求永远美好、不死而生出了痛苦，就是不懂得这个道理。
So long as there is life, there is death. All good things must end someday. Constant change is the Truth of the universe. Human beings suffer because they insist on seeking permanent beauty and life, and don't understand this basic Truth.

宇宙的实相是永远变化不已、没有一刻停息的实体。

而人由于自我短期利益的考虑，从自我的立场希望好的事物能常存，不好的事物不要降临在自己身上。

但这种一厢情愿的想法并不能使事事都遂自己的意，因而生出了苦。

人会痛苦大多是因为人有"自我"的观念，而又不真正明白身、心，内在外在的一切都不可能永远不变，即"诸行无常"这个宇宙的真理。

所以，佛陀在入灭之前对阿难说："阿难啊！凡是我们所爱的，终将离去；凡是有生命的，终将死亡。所以不必为美好的事物不能常存、变质败坏而痛苦悲伤啊。"

The true nature of the universe is that its essence is forever changing, without stopping, without resting for one moment.

Humans base their judgements on short-term benefits for the ego-self. From the self's point of view, humans often wish that good things would last forever and that bad things would never happen.

Nevertheless, this kind of single-minded thinking does not make everything go the ego-self's way. That is how suffering originates.

Humans suffer mostly because they have the concept of "self". In addition, they do not really understand that all things, whether physical or mental, internal or external, cannot possibly remain constant forever. In other words, they do not understand the Essential Universal Truth that "all acts are transient".

For this reason, before he passed away, Buddha said to Ananda: "My dear Ananda, all that we love will eventually leave us. All that lives will eventually die. Therefore, do not suffer because pretty and lovely things do not last forever."

万物皆无常，有生必有灭；不执著于生灭，心便能寂静不起念，而得到永恒的喜乐。
All things are transient. So long as there is birth, there will be death. If we are not attached to birth and death, our mind will be able to acquire quietness without thoughts. This is how we may achieve eternal joy.

是的，老师。
Yes, teacher.

我为无师者
I Am the One without Any Guide

我是个无师者。
I am a selflearner without any master.

是我自己成全了自己，是唯一的存在。
I alone achieved self-knowing and became one with existence.

在此俗界无一人与我相同，自为尊者，自为最高师。
In this worldly place, nobody is like me. I am the honoured one; I am the ultimate master.

只有我是佛陀，是认识真理的觉悟者。
In this world, I am the only Buddha, the supremely enlightened one who knows all Essential Universal Truths.

我将在无知的黑暗世界为真理敲出木铎指南！
I will beat the "teaching bell" to guide people to the true path in this ignorant and dark world.

佛陀在树下沉思，终于悟出原本存在的宇宙法则。他知道人由于不认识、不明白这个法则而抱持着错误的观念活在颠倒梦想之中。于是，他用余生将这个真理传播给生活于苦难中的人们，也自创出佛学理论。

After meditation, Buddha came to supreme enlightenment on the Universal Laws that were always there. He knew that people live in upside-down delusions while holding onto erroneous attitudes. This is all because people do not recognize and understand Universal Truths. Therefore, he used the rest of his life to communicate these Truths to people living in suffering and thereby developed the philosophies of Buddhism.

一切行皆无常
Every Act Is
Transient

我是这样听说的：
This is how I have heard it:

*2 那时候，佛陀在舍卫国祇树给孤独园里……

*1 杂阿含经

你们应当观察到世间的一切东西都不是永恒不变的，这样的观察即是正确的观察。
You should have observed by now that nothing in this world stays the same forever. This observation is true.

那时，释尊对比丘们说：
The Honourable Sakyamuni said to the monks:

*1 The Sutra of Agama:
*2 At the time, Sakyamuni Buddha was at the Jetavana Monastery in Srâvasti, a city in Northern India...

15

正确观察就能产生离厌心，而不会有喜爱贪图之心，心灵就获得解脱了。
Proper observation enables us to generate a detached mind instead of a mind full of desires and longing. This is how the mind becomes carefree.

对外部世界的形形色色应该这样观察；对自己内在的感受、思辨、冲动、意识也都要这样观察，看出它们的无常来。
We should observe the colourful external world with a detached mind. We should also observe our internal feelings, thoughts, impulses and consciousness in this same proper way. This is how we can see through their ever-changing nature.

这就是正确的观察。正确的观察就能产生离厌心……
This is indeed the proper kind of observation. Once we have this proper ability to observe, we will be able to generate a mind of detachment which is free from longing...

有离厌心，喜爱贪图之念就会消失，心灵也就解脱了。
With a detached mind, thoughts of desiring and wanting will automatically disappear, and our mind will therefore be set free.

比丘们啊！这样的心灵解脱者，如果他想亲自证实，就能够亲自证实。
My fellow monks! Only for those with such carefree minds is personal verification of the Truth as achievable as one wishes.

我自己已证得这个道理，从生死爱欲的束缚中解脱出来……
I myself have personally confirmed this Truth and released myself from the bondage of life and death, attachment and desires...

心灵获得真正的自由，过着清净纯正的生活，将来也不会再受缚于爱欲中流转。
Once our spirit attains true freedom and starts living a life of purity and righteousness, we will never be trapped by the churning cycles of attachment.

那时候，比丘们听完佛陀所说的法，都高高兴兴地去奉行。
After the monks heard Essential Universal Truths preached by Buddha, they all went on to practise it happily.

比丘们啊！还要注意一点，对无常，对苦、空与非我，也应该要这样观察啊！
My fellow monks, pay attention to one more thing. Always observe in this same proper manner the transient nature of everything, the suffering in life, the kong* essence of the universe, and the non-existence of the ego-self!

世间万事万物都是变化不已的，自己的内心对外界的感受也因时、地、心境的不同而异。
看清世间的一切及内心的感受意识并非绝对，便能从爱欲的执著中解脱出来，获得心灵的自由。
All people, places and things in this world are constantly changing: our inner sensations towards the external world also vary due to differences of time, space and our attitudes.
If we can see that all worldly existence and our inner consciousness are not absolute, then we will be able to release ourselves from the attachment of longing and obtain freedom of the spirit.

*Kong is the essence of which everything the universe is composed. According to the Heart Sutra, all events and objects, regardless of their current transient manifestation, are kong. For more on kong, see Tsai Chih Chung's The Illustrated Heart Sutra, Asiapac, 1997.

存在就有变化
Wherever There Is Existence, There Is Change

世界是一个随时间流转变迁的过渡现象，我们只属于一段时间内的世界。
The world is a transient manifestation that is constantly in motion and changing with time. We belong only to the unique world of a particular time.

每一个写下来的字、每一件石刻、每一幅画、文明的结构、每一代人，终将如同落叶一样消失。
Every written word, every stone carving, every painting, the structure of civilization, and every generation of people will all eventually disappear like fallen leaves.

有存在就有变化，没有变化的，就不存在。
Wherever there is existence, there is change. Whatever is without change does not exist at all.

生就是生生不息、变化不停，不变的即是死亡。
所有的存在都是生住异灭变化中的一个短暂现象而已，这就是宇宙的法则。
人冀求现世的永恒不变违背了宇宙规律，当然不可能实现。
Life is ceaselessly growing, constantly changing. Only death is without change. Any existence is but a temporary manifestation of the ever-changing cycle of life. This is the Law of the Universe. When human beings search for eternal stability in their material world, they violate the universal rhythm of change and naturally can never find what they seek.

不昧于因缘
Do not Igno-
re the Pre-
conditioned
Nature of
Events and
Objects

一切事物都有变迁，凡是存在的就有变化消失的过程和结果。
Everything is always changing and disappearing. As long as there is existence, there is the process and the results of change.

你的心，只有不被这种生灭变化所束缚，才会有恬静、安适的状态。
Only when your mind is not bound by such natural cycles of birth and death, can you be in a mental state of calmness and serenity.

世间的一切都是变化不停的，人期望美好的事物不要变质，不要离去；希望坏的事物不要到来。但这是一种不切实际的想妄，也正是这种想妄困住了人的感受。
Everything in this world is constantly changing and eventually disappears. People often expect that beautiful experiences will stay the same and not pass away; they hope that unpleasant experiences will never happen. But such wishful thinking is an impractical fantasy that keeps people trapped in their own feelings so they cannot move forward.

19

诸行
无常
All Acts
Are Tran-
sient

阿难啊！凡是我们所爱的，终将别离。有生的一切，不能无坏。
Ananda, my disciple, all of the people, places and things that we love will eventually part from us. Everything that is alive cannot defy the fate of decay.

所以不必为美好事物的不能永存、变质变坏而悲伤啊！
Therefore, do not be hurt by the sadness that all good things must end someday!

"世间的一切事物都是流变不定的。"抱持这样正确的心去看待世上的一切变化，那么这些变化就再也不能影响我们的心了。
Everything in this world is everchanging and never stays the same. If we adopt this proper attitude to observe all worldly changes, then these changes will no longer be able to affect our mind.

诸法无我
ESSENTIAL UNIVERSAL
TRUTHS CONTAIN NO EGO-SELF

宇宙中的一切现象都是因缘条件相加而形成变化不已的现象……
因此，没有一个永恒不变的宇宙，人也是一样，从出生到死亡每一刻都在变化之中，没有一个实质不变的我存在。

very phenomenon in the universe is an ever-changing manifestation due to the cumulative effect of pre-conditioned meaningful coincidences...

Therefore, there is no enduring universe. By the same reasoning, human beings are constantly changing during every moment from birth to death. There is no permanent ego-self that manifests the same qualities throughout time and space.

人会自以为有个"我"，不知这只是存在的假象。因为这个我是随时空不同而变化不停的，并没有一个永恒不变的实质的我存在。由出生到死亡，每一分每一秒的我，条件都不一样。我们由刚出生没有什么行为能力，到长大后叱咤风云，乃至老死之前又回复到没有行为能力，都是随着自己的能力、条件而变迁的。

而我们的身心感受也是因时空条件而异，生出快乐、悲伤、愤怒、恐惧等诸多不同的情绪，随着时空的不同起伏不定。

佛陀印证出最重要的第二个真理便是："诸法无我。"

没有一个永恒不变的客观宇宙，也没有一个永恒不变、可以流转三世的我存在。一切都在变化之中……

Many people perceive "I" to be an independent entity, without knowing that it is a false illusion of synchronous manifestations. Because this "I" is constantly changing with variations of space and time, there is no "I" entity that endures through eternity. From birth to death, different conditions are associated with the "I" of each particular moment. There is the time of the newborn who is not really capable of independent activities, the time of the adult who moves and shakes the world, and then the later years in life when independent actions are again not possible. Throughout this life cycle, everyone changes according to the capabilities and conditions of a particular stage in the cycle.

Our physical and mental sensations also vary according to time and space. Various emotions, such as happiness, sadness, anger and fear, all fluctuate with variations of time and space.

One of the major Truths personally verified by the Buddha is that "Essential Universal Truths contain no ego-self".

There is no objective universe that is enduring and everlasting. There is also no ego-self that is enduring and everlasting and subject to reincarnation over and over again.

Everything is in the process of changing...

人无我，法无我……
The essence of a human being contains no ego-self. The Essential Truths of the Universe also contain no ego-self...

法无我
No Universal Truth Contains the Ego-Self

那时候，释尊对比丘们说：
At that time, the Honourable Sakyamuni said to his fellow monks:

比丘们啊！不论过去或未来的万事万物，都没有绝对不变的，何况是现在的呢！
Listen, my fellow monks! There are no events and objects of the past or the future that are absolutely constant, not to mention anything of the present moment.

聪明的弟子若照这个真实的状况去看：不背负过去、不企盼将来，也不沉醉于现在的欲望……
If the intelligent disciple looks at everything from this perspective, he will not carry the burden of the past, not indulge in the fantasies of the future, and not intoxicate himself with the desires of the present...

他走对了方向，就能消除欲望，得到自在解脱。
He would be moving in the right direction. This is how he will be able to rid himself of his desires and free himself from bondage.

同样，过去与未来的内心感受与观念意识也不是绝对的，何况是现在的呢？
Our internal feelings and consciousness of the past as well as of the future are not absolute. By the same reasoning, how could our perceptions of the present be any different?

聪明的弟子若按照这个真实的状况去看：不背负过去的经验，不活在想象中的将来……
If the intelligent disciple looks at everything in life from this perspective, he will not carry the burden of the past, not fantasize about the future...

坦然面对接受现在，而不是心存欲望地期待，他便走对了方向，将欲望灭尽得到了自在。
He faces and accepts the present moment with an open mind, instead of waiting anxiously for all desires to be fulfilled. He would then have moved in the right direction, extinguished desires, and acquired freedom.

它们所带来的苦、空与没有永恒的我，也是如此。
Such is also the case for all resulting suffering, the kong nature of the universe, and the unenduring ego-self.

外在的万事万物与内在的感受意识的无常性是如此，
Such is the transient nature of all external events and objects as well as internal sensations and consciousness,

那时候，比丘们听了佛陀所说的法，都欢欢喜喜地奉行。
The monks took Buddha's teaching of Essential Universal Truths to heart, and they all went about joyfully practising what they had learned.

人因为有"自我"，于是痛苦就产生了！由自我的观点产生了过去、现在、未来，产生了好、坏、顺、逆，于是一直活在企盼与欲望之中。
Because human beings have the separate identity of an ego-self, all types of suffering start taking place. From the perspective of self, there is the past versus the present versus the future. There is also good versus bad, and things that go my way versus things that don't go my way. Therefore, we end up living in anticipation and desire.

每一滴水都是海，只是它自己不知道！当"小我"消失变成"无我"时，那滴海水即融入了海洋而得到自在。
Every drop of water is the ocean, but each individual drop does not know this truth! When the egoself becomes selfless, that drop of water then becomes an integral part of the ocean and, at the same time, becomes carefree.

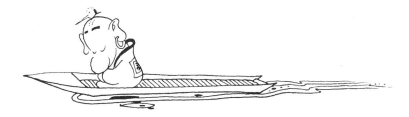

人无我
The Human Essence
Contains No Ego-Self

我是这样听说的：那时候，佛陀在舍卫国祇树给孤独园里对比丘们说……
This is the way I heard it: At the time. Buddha was teaching his monk disciples at the Jetavana Monastery in Srâvasti...

世间外在的万事万物都是无常的，因为无常所以人会感到痛苦……
All external events and objects are transient. This ever-changing nature of things often makes people feel pain...

这个感到痛苦的我其实不是真正的我，所以不应该停留在这个痛苦的我之中。
In fact, this self that feels the pain is not the true essence of the self. This is why we should not stay in the consciousness of the ego-self that suffers from pain.

用这种观念来看待，才是真实正确的！
This is indeed the proper attitude for looking at everything in life!

世间的一切都是变化无常的，没有永恒不灭的时、事、物。
能明白这无常，便会明白没有永恒不灭的我，也没有任何东西是我可永远拥有的。
因此人要无我地超脱于外在的变幻，融于这层外在的时空，无论生、老、病、死都坦然而受，于是再不受"小我"生死之念的困扰了。

All phenomena in the world are ever-changing and transient. No times, events, or objects are eternally everlasting.

Once we understand the impermanent nature of things, we will understand that there is neither an "I" that is eternally permanent, nor anything that "I" can possess forever.

Therefore, humans need to transcend external changes by living without an ego-self and by dissolving into the external layer of time and space. It doesn't matter that there is birth, ageing, illness and death.

We will be able to accept them peacefully. This is how we can no longer be bothered by the thought of the life or death of the "ego-self".

五下分结
Identifying and Ending
Five Types of Troubles

没有叫做我的，也没有叫做我的物。
There is no real entity that can be called "I"; there is also no entity that can be called "mine".

既然知道没有我，又凭什么有我的物？
Given that there is no "I", how can there be any basis for any entity called "mine"?

如果人能够这样去了解，他便能切断将我们与欲界联结在一起的五种烦恼。
If a human being can approach an understanding of life through this perspective, he will be able to cut himself loose from five kinds of worries that connect him with the consciousness of desires.

人因为身、心的观、念，引起了有我、我所有的一己之私的观念。于是便产生了贪欲，瞋忿，自以为是、无能为力、狐疑无知五种苦恼。要斩断这些烦恼，唯有从无我、无我所有着手。
Because human beings think they have a body and mind separate from the rest of the universe, we generate the perceptions of selfcentredness, such as "I" and "mine". This is the origin of five types of troubles: greed, resentment, righteousness, negligence and doubtfulness. The only way to end these worries is to start by developing the perspectives of selflessness and of not owning anything.

不可因为符合先入为主的观念，就信以为真。
Do not believe anything to be true because it fits your preconceived notions.

不可因为权威人士所言，就信以为真。
Do not believe anything to be true because authority figures say so.

纵使是你的老师如来所说，也不可马上信以为真。
Even though your teacher, "Ultimate Essence Arriving",*says so, do not immediately believe it to be true.

* *"Ultimate Essence Arriving", or Tachâgata in Sanskrit, is sometimes translated as "Thus Come One". It also means "one who follows the ways of previous Buddhas" and is a title Sakyamuni Buddha used for himself and his disciples.*

没经过自己亲自证实，而听到就相信的叫做"迷信"。
Any beliefs that we accept as true without personal verification are called "superstition".

经过自己证实才相信的，叫做"正信"。
Only when we hold supposed truth to the light of personal verification, can we achieve proper beliefs.

要消除我们的无明，得从一切的"如实知"开始，如实知一切不是只听别人所言，而是经过自己证实才去相信，故佛陀说的"正法眼"，就是像亲自见到一样。
To rid ourselves of our delusions, we have to start from learning to know every belief as it truly is. This knowing of what is true is not obtained by just listening to what others have to say, but only after personal verification. Therefore, the Buddha says, "acquire the proper eyesight for Universal Truths"—this is just like one has personally witnessed what is true.

实践是抵达真理的唯一途径
Practice Is the Only Path to Reach Truth

比丘们啊！不要因为你们尊敬我，而接受我的教训。

My monk disciples! Do not accept my lessons because you respect me!

你们应该要像以火试真金一样，通过实践来考验我所说的法。

You should use practice to personally test the Essential Universal Truths that I teach, just like using fire to test real gold.

真理
TRUTHS

真理不能借由别人嘴里说而得到；真理必须自己去体会实践，才能成为自己的真理。人借着自己一生的实践就可以揭示一切的秘密，而你自己就是你自己最好的裁判。

Truths cannot be acquired from words out of other people's mouths. Before Truths can be internalized, they must come from one's own realizations and practices. Through a lifetime of personal practice, human beings are capable of revealing all of the secrets of the cosmic essence. You are your own best judge.

从它们所结出的果子，你可以去认识它们。

You can learn to recognize the Essential Universal Truths from the fruits of their manifestations.

法
ESSENTIAL
UNIVERSAL
TRUTH

观察
Observation

智者不依凭学说……
The wise ones do not depend on philosophical theories...

智者不捆缚自己……
The wise ones do not bind themselves...

他们只是仔细地看、仔细地听。
They only observe carefully and listen intently.

智慧的觉悟者们证悟出人生的道理与平和身心的方法。他们通过观察和体验，把自己的身心当作一个观察的对象，去了解痛苦等情绪的产生与消退，最后得到了降服它的方法。
每个人也可以把自己的情绪作为观察对象，从中证悟出身心统一的方法。

The enlightened wise ones have personally verified the truths in life as well as the means of balancing the body and the mind. Through personal observations and experiences, they treat their own body and mind as objects under observation. Therefore they learn to understand the rise and fall of feelings, such as pain, and eventually acquire the methods of conquering the body and the mind. Every one of us can also treat our emotions as objects of observation and through the experience personally verify effective means of unifying the body and the mind.

邪思与正思
Deviant Thinking and Proper Thinking

将虚假的误为真实，将真实的误为虚假……
To mistake the false for the true, to mistake the true for the false...

抱持着错误的观念，他就抵达不了真实。
If one holds onto the wrong concepts, one will never arrive at the destination of Truth.

将真实的看成真实，虚假的知道是虚假……
To recognize the true as true, to recognize the false as untrue...

洞察自己的心正确地看待世间的一切，他便能抵达真实。
Only when one can see through one's own mind and look at everything in this world with the proper perspective, can one arrive at the destination of Truth.

由于无知，我们都用不正确的观念看这个世界，于是才活在欲望、敌意、愚蠢的痛苦之海。我们应该用正确的头脑去思考，以正确的心去看这个世界，才能活在幸福之海。

Due to ignorance, many of us look at this world from an incorrect point of view. That is why people live in the painful sea of desires, hostility and delusion. To live in the sea of joy, we should think with a proper mind and look at this world with a proper heart.

33

可以验证的才是真理
Only Truths that Can Be Tested Are Real

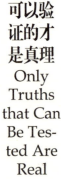

最好的功德莫过于大悲心，最甜蜜的快乐莫过于心的宁静。
There is no better virtue than a heart of grand compassion; there is no sweeter joy than a mind of quiet serenity.

最清净的真理莫过于无常的存在，最高的宗教莫过于道德智慧的开展。
There is no purer Truth than the existence of impermanence; there is no higher religion than the development of moral wisdom.

最伟大的哲理莫过于能教导我们当下就能验证的真理。
There is no greater philosophy than the teaching of Truth that can be tested by all of us right here and now.

真理是可以实践与验证的。如果是正确的真理，我们必能在实践中立即获得甜蜜的果实。如果只是虚无地允诺来世的报酬，这可能是对无知者施展的不负责任的骗术。
Truth is subject to practice and testing. If it is proper Truth, we definitely should be able to acquire sweet fruits through practice right away. If it only abstractly promises a reward in the next life, this may be an irresponsible trick to delude the ignorant.

涅槃寂静
NIRVÂNA IS PERFECT TRAN-QUILLITY

人由于自我的利益考量而生出了贪欲、不满、愚痴、忧伤、悲痛、苦闷等烦恼……因此，人应该通过正确的修行了解到诸行无常的真理，了解到宇宙中没有一个永恒不变的实体，也没有一个永恒不变的我存在。用这种态度去看待内在、外在，不因为时空的不如己意而产生痛苦，慢慢地，就能让自我的情绪不再产生而达至轻安、喜悦的永恒祥和境地……

Human beings, because of the interests of the ego-self, generate worries, such as desires, dissatisfaction, delusion, depression, grief and boredom...

Therefore, human beings should learn through proper cultivation to understand the Truth that all acts are transient. We need to understand that there is not a single entity in the universe that is eternally everlasting. There is also not an ego-self that is eternally everlasting. With this kind of viewpoint towards the internal and external worlds, we will no longer generate pain because manifestations of time and space do not follow our wishes. Gradually, we will be able to curtail our personal emotions and reach a place of eternal tranquillity with peace and joy.

每个人都可以正确的人生观念、正确的生活方式、正确的修行方法达到令苦不再生起的安详喜悦境界。

这个永恒的喜悦境界就是智慧的彼岸。

我们的痛苦是来自于我们的无知——去强求违反世间宇宙真理的事物，也就因为世事不能如人意、不符合内心自我的期望而产生了烦恼。

我们每个人都可以通过对宇宙真理的正确认知，通过正确修行的实践慢慢向契合于宇宙真理的方向迈进，而达至没有痛苦与烦恼的境界。

这种境界就是智慧的彼岸——涅槃寂静。

Every person has the capacity to reach a place of serene tranquillity through a proper viewpoint towards life, a proper lifestyle, and proper methods of cultivation.

This state of eternal joy is the "other shore" of wisdom.

Our sufferings arise from our ignorance—trying to force worldly issues that violate Essential Universal Truths.

Because worldly matters cannot always follow our wishful thinking and self-expectations, worries naturally arise.

Every one of us has the choice of reaching a state without suffering and worries. Through an understanding of the Truths of the universe and through practice of proper cultivation, we can slowly march in a direction compatible with Essential Universal Truths.

This state of mind is "the other shore" of wisdom—perfect tranquillity is Nirvâna.

通往世间的利益是一条路，通往涅槃之道的又是另一条路。

One road leads to worldly profits, while a separate road leads the way to Nirvâna.

寂静之道
The Path to Tran-
quillity

佛陀在舍卫国祇树给孤独园时，有一位其他教派的比丘来请教佛陀……
Once, when Buddha was at the Jetavana Monastery in Srâvasti, a monk from another sect came to him for advice...

释尊，请将您所传佛法的精要说给我听好吗？
Oh, Honourable Sakyamuni, would you please tell me the essence of your teaching of Buddhist truth?

听完以后，我会独自找个安静的地方修行，将心澄清凝聚而后再行思维，直达到最终豁然开朗的境地。
After I hear it, I will find a quiet place to cultivate myself alone. I will purify and concentrate my mind and then meditate until I eventually reach a state of absolute clarity.

好吧！我仔细地为你说，你要好好体会思考我所说的话啊！
All right. I will explain to you in detail. Do take the effort to comprehend and contemplate carefully what I say!

是。
Yes, Your Honour.

谢谢释尊的开导，现在我可以一个人去修行释尊所说的法了。
Thank you for your guidance, Honourable Sakyamuni. Now I can cultivate the Truth Your Honour has taught me by myself.

太好了，你领悟得真快。比丘啊！在色的方面如果不被欲望驱使，就不会被它带至死地，就可以解脱贪欲之心。同样，在受、想、行、识方面，如果不听凭欲望驱使，便不会被它们带至死境，就能解脱贪欲之心。
That is wonderful! You comprehend very quickly. My dear monk, in regard to the physical world, if you do not let yourself to be driven by desires, you will not be carried to the point of no return. You will have the opportunity to release yourself from the mind of greed. In the same way, that is also true for your inner sensations, perceptions, decisions and consciousness. If you do not allow yourself to be driven by desires, you will not be carried to the point of no return and you will be able to achieve freedom from a greedy mind.

于是，他找了一个安静的地方精勤修行……
Later, he went to a quiet place to cultivate himself diligently...

不久之后，他的心灵终于得到解脱，一个比丘便成为一个得道的罗汉了！
Before long, his mind gained final release. This is how one monk became an Arhat, one who has attained Nirvâna.

人，追逐外在的一切事物，内在的感受思维随着外在的事物起伏，于是他的心也被外在的一切所控制、所掳获而得不到解脱啊！
Because human beings pursue all external events and objects, their internal feelings and thoughts fluctuate with these external conditions. As a result, their minds are kept captive by all sorts of external factors and cannot be released.

苦
Suffering

这世间充满着各式各样的苦。
This world is filled with various kinds of suffering.

生是苦，老是苦，病是苦，死也是苦。
Birth is suffering, ageing is suffering, illness is suffering, death is also suffering.

与心里所喜欢的人事物分离是苦，想拥有而不能如自己之意也是苦……
To be separated from people, places and things we like is suffering, to want ownership and not be able to do whatever one likes is suffering...

不能远离执著的人啊，他的人生一皆都是苦啊！
Alas, those unfortunate people who cannot abandon attachment! For them, everything in life is suffering!

这就是苦的真理。
This is the Truth of suffering.

人都是站在一己的立场上，以自己的想法、自己的利益去评估一切，而世事并非都能尽如人意，因此，苦就产生了！
一切的苦受都来自内心中自以为的那个我，有了这个我，苦也就紧紧相随了。
Human beings often use an ego-self perspective to judge everything based on personal perceptions and benefits. Since worldly events cannot always go as we wish, suffering is inevitable. All kinds of sensations of suffering come from the self-perceived existence of the ego-self "I" in our mind. As long as we perceive the "I" to be separate from the rest of the world, suffering will surely follow.

集
Causes
of Suffe-
ring

这些人生之苦是如何产生的呢？苦产生于心中的烦恼。
How do these sufferings in life originate? Sufferings spring from the worries of the mind.

而烦恼又从何而生呢？烦恼是来自于人们与生俱来的那股强烈的欲望。
Where do worries come from? Worries come from the strong desires inborn in humans.

这就是形成苦的原因。
This, indeed, is the reason for the formation of suffering.

这种欲望就是生命中对生存本能的强烈执著——凡是遇上好的、有利于自己的就有渴望拥有、想成为之念。
Such desires are our intense attachments to survival instincts — whenever there is something beneficial to us, we formulate thoughts of greed for ownership of the objects or the characteristics of others.

生命的本能就是自利，以便让自己和自己的后代维续下来。因此凡是有利于己的便想拥有、想成为……但外在的客观环境并不顺人心意，于是由渴望的不能及时满足而生出烦恼，由烦恼便形成了苦。
The survival instinct is totally self-serving to ensure that the ego-self and the offspring of the ego-self will continue to thrive. Therefore, whenever there is anything of benefit to the ego-self, we want to have it for ourselves. However, the objective environment outside our ego-self does not usually go as we wish. Because our wishes are not immediately gratified, we start having worries, which in turn lead to suffering.

灭
Ending Suffering

如果我们能将这令我们烦恼的根本原因切除灭尽，舍离一切对自己、对外在的执著……
If we are capable of cutting the roots of worries by letting go of all attachments to the ego-self and the external world...

那时，因为没有形成苦的种子，苦也就消除而不生了……
Then because there are no seeds for the formation of suffering, suffering naturally disappears...

这就是灭苦的真理啊！
Such is the Truth of eliminating suffering.

要消除苦，必须将其根源拔除，没有苦的因也没有苦的果。
什么是形成苦的种子呢？就是自我，由自我形成的渴望、由渴望所造成的烦恼……
To be free of suffering, we must uproot its source. Without the cause of suffering, there will be no fruit of suffering. What are the seeds for the formation of suffering? They are the ego-self, the desires formed by the ego-self, and, in turn, the worries formed by desires...

道
The Path of Cultivation to End Suffering

要达到苦的灭除这终极目标，不能只闻法而不行，而是要通过生活中的修行渐渐使自己的身心达到没有我执、没有渴望欲爱、没有烦恼的境地。只有真正做到这些，苦才会从根本上消除。

In order to reach the final goal of freeing oneself of suffering, it is not enough to just understand the Essential Universal Truths if we don't apply them in our daily lives. We must use daily cultivation to slowly modify our body and mind. Eventually we will reach the state of no attachment to self, no desires and wants, and therefore no worries. Only when we have actually practised these principles in daily living will our suffering be uprooted.

43

不染
Rise above
Pollution

莲花生于水长于水，却高出水面，纯洁而不受污染。
The lotus grows in muddy water, but is rises above the water level, stays pure, and is not polluted by its environment.

人也能像莲花一样，生于俗世，长于俗世……
We human beings are also capable of being like the lotus—born in this worldly environment, grow up in this worldly environment...

但借由心灵的升华而高出俗世，不受俗世的污染。
But by means of elevating our consciousness, we are able to rise above the worldly environment and not be polluted by it.

人生于时空，活于时空，应该与时空融合为一。冥想所面临的时、事、物为自己，是苦、是乐、是净、是秽，这些都是你自己的本体。于是这苦、乐、净、秽都不再会染著于你。
We humans are born into a certain time and space and live in our unique time and space. As a result, we should become one with our specific time and space. Meditate on the fact that the particular time and space we face is merely a manifestation of ourselves. Whether it is pain or joy, purity or filth, these are all part of our true essence. Therefore, attachment to pain, joy, purity and filth will no longer pollute you any more.

世界如心所呈现
The World Is a Reflection of Your Mind

一阵和煦的微风，一株盛开的花朵，点出春天来临的讯息……

A gentle breeze, a blossoming flower, messages signalling the arrival of spring...

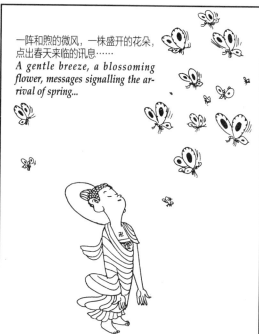

一个人一旦觉悟，眼前的草木国土山河大地都变成天堂般的美丽……

Once a person reaches supreme enlightenment, all grasses, trees, mountains, rivers and landscapes in front of the eyes appear as beautiful as scenery from heaven...

为何会这样呢？因为我们的心如果清净，其所及之处也都是清净。

Why is this the case? It is because, if our mind is pure, any place it contacts will be as pure.

我们觉得世界如何，完全是因我们的心怎么想！

如果我们的心认为世间肮脏丑陋，我们便看到肮脏丑陋的部分。

如果我们的心觉得世间美妙，我们便看到美妙。

How we feel about the world depends completely on how our mind thinks.

If our mind believes that the world is dirty and ugly, then we will focus on the part that is dirty and ugly.

If our mind believes that the world is wonderful, we will see the wonder.

修心
Cultivating the Mind

了知身体有如易碎的瓶子，防护心如固守城堡一样。
We should understand that the body is like an easily broken bottle. We should also guard our mind with the ferocious fortifications of a castle.

用智慧做武器与心生出的邪魔作战,保卫胜利,不可失守放弃。
We can fight the evils coming from our own mind by using wisdom as our best weapon. We should always fight for victory in this internal war of protecting our own mind and never back off or give up.

我们的身体十分脆弱，很容易受欲望控制，唯有依靠坚定的心识去抵抗身心的诱惑，就像战士守护城池一样，下决心去抵抗任何邪魔。

Our physical bodies are very vulnerable and easily controlled by desires. We can only depend on a strong and steady mind to defend against the temptations of the body as well as those of the mind. We need to make the decision to defend ourselves from any evil just as vigorously as any knight would protect his castle.

心地清净
Keep the Mind Pure

我们的心如果混浊不清澈，行为即污秽。
If we start with a muddy and unclear mind, then our outward behaviour will be polluted for sure.

行为有了染污，就会带来苦恼不断……
Once our behaviour are polluted, we will encounter endless worries...

所以心地清净、行为谨慎，这是学道的基本要件。
Therefore a pure mind and cautious behaviour are the basic foundationfor learning the path to enlightenment.

行为是心地的反映，心有了负面的想法，就有负面的行为。
而错误的行为就会引来后续的烦恼与痛苦的后果，情绪因而激动不安，
心自然就不清净了。
Our behaviour are the reflections of our minds. Once the mind has negative thoughts, they are bound to be reflected in negative behaviour. In turn, improper behaviour will bring about the fruits of worries and suffering. As a result, our emotions will be disturbed, thus polluting the mind and invariably perpetuating the vicious cycle.

控制心意
Controlling the Mind

我们的心如果充满着贪念、瞋怒、愚痴三毒，就不可以信任它。

If our mind is filled with the three types of poison—greed, resentment and delusion—then it is not to be trusted.

心像猿猴无时无刻不往外张望，没有止息的时候，心像野马，随时随地地四处奔驰，没有静止的时候。禅定是学习控制心识的方法，将心止于一境不使散动。我们人在哪里，心就在哪里，我们正在做什么，心也观照所做的事。

The mind is like a monkey that it constantly looking outside every moment and never stops. The mind is also like a wild horse that is continuously galloping all over the place and never rests. Centring the mind through meditation means learning the method of being mindful. This is how our mind can be trained to stay in tranquillity and not scatter its thoughts around. Wherever we are physically, our mind is at exactly the same place. Whatever we are doing physically, our mind is observing and reflecting on the same thing.

我们的心不能让它随意予取予求，必须努力抑制心意，以免它放纵地追逐欲望。

Our mind cannot be allowed to have everything it desires at will. We must make every effort to restrain the mind, so that it will not indulge in pursuing desires.

一夜贤者偈
The Poem of the Virtuous One Who Has One More Night to Live

不要追悔过去，不要企求将来，过去的已经过去了，而未来的还没有到来。唯有掌握现在，仔细观察眼前的存在，既不动荡也不摇摆。

Do not regret the past, do not fantasize about the future, the past is already gone, while the future has not arrived. We can only grab onto the present moment, carefully observing what is in front of our eyes, without rocking and rolling from side to side.

必须如实地观察实践，努力做今天该做的事，谁也不知道明天会不会死……

We must realistically observe ourselves and the world around us and practise pragmatically what we should do today. Nobody knows whether death will come tomorrow...

凡是能这样观照的人，他便会聚精会神、不分昼夜地去实践，这就叫做一夜贤者，也叫做心止于一境的人。

Anybody who can reflect on life this way will focus on practising day and night. This is referred to as "the virtuous one who behaves as if he has one more night to live". This is the state of the centred mind.

每个人要珍惜手上拥有的，不要想要没有的，或追悔已经失去不再来的。
渴望目前还没有的就是"贪念"，而珍惜目前拥有的就是惜福。

Everyone should cherish what is held in the hands. Do not desire what we do not have or fret over what has past and will not come back.
To desire what we do not yet have is a greedy thought. On the contrary, to cherish what we currently have is to treasure our blessings.

忍辱的方法
The Method of Patient Tolerance

当别人伤害了我们时，我们应该这样想……
When other people hurt us, we should be thinking this way...

"这是因为他不能自主的缘故。"
"这是因为我自己过去的错误行为才遭致如此。"
"这是因为我自己行为上的过失才变成这样。"
"这是因为我自己的心有过失的缘故。"
"This is because he could not help himself."
"This is just because of my own wrong actions in the past that have led to this result."
"This is only because of my mistakes in conduct that have led to such happenings."
"This is only because my own mind was at the wrong place."

"无论是谁都会有过失呀！"
"这种逆缘对我的修行很有帮助呀！"
"众生对我的修行有很大的恩德啊！"
"我这样忍辱能令诸佛欢喜啊！"
"这样做会获得广大的功德啊！"
"Nobody is without mistakes!"
"The preconditioning to adversity in life is indeed quite helpful for my own cultivation!"
"All living beings are messengers bringing me lessons in cultivation, and I surely owe them a great deal of gratitude!"
"My ability to tolerate adversity patiently is making all Buddhas happy for my progress in cultivation."
"This will help me accumulate a tremendous amount of merit and virtue."

什么是忍辱呢？就是要能做到：此心不激动、不愤怒、不伤害任何人，也不执著，这样的心境才叫做忍辱之心。
What is patient tolerance? It means to be able to keep our mind undisturbed, not angry, not wanting to hurt anyone, and not attached. This kind of mindset is called the patient and tolerant mind.

自主
Be One's Own Master

有必要的话才说，不必要的话不说。
Only say words that are necessary; do not say words that are unnecessary.

必须要断绝的，当下就要戒绝；必须修学的，要全力以赴去求取。
Things that need to be severed; get rid of them right away. Things that must be learned, pursue them with full force.

人必须面对几个问题：
什么是对自己最重要的事？
什么事是第一优先要做的？
Human beings must face several questions in life: What are the most important things in one's life? What kind of things are of first priority?

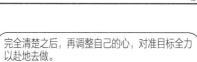

完全清楚之后，再调整自己的心，对准目标全力以赴地去做。
When there is complete clarity, one can adjust attitudes in the mind and focus on proper targets with full force.

我们是我们自己身心的主人，如果我们不能控制自己的心、不能控制自己的身，我们怎会是自己的主人呢？
We are the masters of our own body and mind. If we are incapable of managing our own mind and unable to control our own body, how can we possibly be our own masters?

実践是唯一的道路
Practice Is the Only Way

依教实行
Practise What
Is Preached

如果你诵读的经典虽少，但能遵照着去实践……
Though you only read a few scriptures, you follow their teachings and practise what they preach in daily life...

用正确的方法除灭贪念、恚怒，愚痴的火焰而得到平静安详的心……
...and use the correct methods to eliminate the flames of greed, resentment and delusion. In this way you will be able to acquire a peaceful and serene mind...

放弃旧有的方式，抛弃欲望、敌意和愚蠢这三种增添我们身心不平和痛苦的根源，我们才能找到平和的心境。
Let go of old ways that no longer work for us. Get rid of desires, hostility and ignorance. These are the three roots of imbalance and pain for our body as well as our mind. This is how we will find the mental state of peace and tranquillity.

那么你于现在或将来便都能处在最上的幸福中了。
Now, and in the future, you will be in the midst of ultimate joy.

53

不见真如来
Not Seeing the Real "Ultimate Essence Arriving"

如果有个人手拉着我的衣摆，紧紧地跟随着我，但他还抱着强烈的欲望、激情、怨念之心，行为放荡又无知的话……

If a person has his hand holding onto the end of my clothes, he physically can follow me closely step by step;
But if he still possesses a mind of strong desires, passions and resentments and behaves loosely and ignorantly...

那么他跟我离得很远，而我也距离他很遥远。我为什么说他距离我很远呢？

Then he is quite distant from me, and I am quite distant from him. Why do I say that he is quite distant from me?

因为他没有看到我所说的法，没有看到法的人也不能看到我。

Because he does not see the Essential Universal Truths that I am teaching. Whoever does not see the universal truth also cannot see the true me.

"佛"是智慧的觉悟之义，"佛教"是智慧之教。信仰佛陀就是遵循他所说的言教，用自己的力量去实践而达到平静安详的心、以正确态度看待世界的境地。

"Buddha" means wise enlightenment. "Buddhism" is a teaching of wisdom. To believe in the Buddha is to follow his teachings. We can choose to use our own efforts to practise and thereby reach the state of a tranquil mind and proper attitude in dealing with the world.

如见真如来
As If You Met the "Ultimate Essence Arriving" in Person

如果有个人他距离我很遥远，但他不抱着激烈的欲望，不抱激情、不抱忿怒之心，不被错误的观念所驱使，能不放纵自己又有正确的知解……

If a person is physically very far from me but he does not have desperate desires, does not get infatuated easily, does not have a resentful mind, is not driven by wrong attitudes, does not indulge himself, and also has a proper understanding of Truth...

那么他就像跟随在我身边一样，而我也在他的身边。

Then it is as if he is accompanying me by my side, and I am likewise by his side.

因为他看到我所说的法，看到法的人也看到我。

This is because he can see the Essential Universal Truths I teach. Anyone who sees these Truths also sees me.

佛陀虽然距离我们两千五百多年，但要见如来还是很简单。因为他说：
看到法的人，
就是看到我；
看到我的人，
就是看到法。

Although the Buddha is 2,500 years removed from us, it is still quite simple to see "Ultimate Essence Arriving" himself because he said: "Anyone who sees Essential Universal Truth, sees me in person; anyone who sees me in person sees Essential Universal Truth."

涅槃寂静
Nirvâna Is Tranquillity

有一位其他教派的比丘来到佛陀住的地方……
A monk from another sect came to where Buddha lived...

我是这样听说的，那时候佛陀在舍卫国祇树给孤独园中……
This is the way I heard it: At the time, Sakyamuni Buddha was in the Jetavana monastery in Srâvasti...

释尊，您曾提到法师，什么是您认为的法师？
Honourable Sakyamuni, you mentioned the term "a teacher of the truth". What do you think are the criteria for "a teacher of the truth"?

问得好！你用心听，我仔细地为你说。
Very good question! Listen closely and I will explain to you carefully.

他应该主张世间外在的一切价值欲望都应该远离，应将之消灭以达至涅槃寂静之境……
He should hold the belief that we need to distance ourselves from all values and desires based in the external world. He should extinguish all desires outside of himself in order to reach the state of perfect tranquillity in Nirvâna.

人应该厌离"色"，想办法灭尽"色"这个观念，而达到涅槃寂静的彼岸。
Human beings should detach from the "material world" and try to completely abolish the notion of "material world". This is how we may reach "the other shore" of Nirvâna in perfect tranquillity.

…

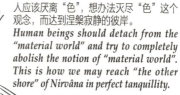

同样，对于内心世界的感受冲动也要远离……
In the same way, he needs to detach from all feelings and impulses of the inner world...

一步一步地把内在欲望灭尽，这就是直达彼岸的步骤与方向。
One step at a time, abolish all inner desires. These are the steps and the direction to go straight to "the other shore".

明白。
I understand.

比丘应该如何才能抵达涅槃寂静的彼岸？
How should monks cultivate themselves to reach "the other shore" of tranquil Nirvâna?

问得好，你用心听，好好思量，我就为你说。
That is a good question. Listen carefully and contemplate deeply, and I will explain to you.

对于"色"，产生离厌之心，将欲望灭尽，慢慢就不再有欲望与烦恼了，心灵得到正确的解脱，于是就到达了涅槃之境。
Develop a detached mind towards the "material world" and extinguish all desires completely. Gradually, there will be no more desires and worries and the mind will accomplish proper release — that will be Nirvâna.

同样，要对受、想、行、识产生厌离，将欲望灭尽，不再有欲望与烦恼，心灵得到真正的解脱，这就抵达涅槃之境了。
In the same way, we need to develop detachment towards sensations, perceptions, decisions and consciousness and to extinguish all desires. When we no longer have desires and worries, our mind will achieve real release. We will have arrived at the state of Nirvâna.

涅槃寂静
Tranquillity is Nirvâna

释尊您曾提到"说法师"……
Honourable Sakyamuni, you have just mentioned "a teacher of Truth".

什么才是释尊所认为的"说法师"？
What qualifications are necessary for you to regard someone as a "teacher of Truth"?

对于外在的"色"，比丘如果演说厌离"色"的道理，演说灭尽"色"的方法，就叫做说法师。
If a monk meditates on the principles of detaching from the material world and on the methods of extinguishing attachment to the material world, he would qualify as a "teacher of Truth".

色
Material World

耳
Ears

眼
Eyes

身
Body

鼻
Nose

舌
Tongue

意
Mind

59

同样，对于内在的受、想、行、识，如果演说厌离它们的道理，灭尽它们的方法，就叫做说法师。

In the same way, one who explains the reasoning for detaching from internal sensations, perceptions, decisions and consciousness, and the methods for terminating them is called "a teacher of Truth".

受 *Sensations*
想 *Perceptions*
行 *Decisions*
识 *Consciousness*

比丘听完佛所说，欢欣地作礼而去。

After the monk finished listening to what Buddha said, he joyfully bowed to show his respect and left.

谢谢释尊，我真正懂得直达彼岸的方法了。

Thanks, Honourable Sakyamuni. Now I really understand the direct path to reach "the other shore".

多闻善说法，向法及涅槃，三密离提问，云何说法师。

Be knowledgeable and effective at teaching Essential Universal Truths. Always position the Truth as a guide to point towards Nirvâna.

In response to the question of a monk from another sect, this is what "a teacher of Truth" is.

彼岸 *The Other Shore*

"三皈依"才能称得上是真正的佛教弟子：
皈依佛，
皈依法，
皈依僧。
而什么才是佛陀真正所说的"法"？佛陀一生说法四十余年，所说的无非是——直抵涅槃寂静之法！
一个佛弟子应该执佛所交付给我们的地图，依佛所指示的路去实践才能抵达彼岸啊！

Only after one "vows to return home to" ("Vows to return home to" is often translated as "finds refuge in".) the awareness of the Buddha, to the proper Truths(Dharma), and to the purity of monks(Sangha) can one truly qualify as a disciple of Buddhism. So, what are the Essential Universal "Truths" that Buddha really meant? What he meant is nothing other than the Essential Universal Truths which lead directly to the state of tranquillity in Nirvâna.

A Buddhist disciple should hold onto the road map Buddha handed over to us and walk on the path Buddha directed us to follow. This is indeed the path to reach "the other shore"!

一切因缘生
ALL IS BORN OUT OF CAUSAL PRECON-DITIONING

一切因缘生，
一切因缘灭。
世间一切现象的产生，都是由于有个起因，再加上条件的助缘而形成的。
如果我们追根究底，
追究到它的源头，会发现根本没有一个不变的实体存在，
一切
都只是因缘形成的而已。

Everything is born out of a causal preconditioning of time and space. Everything also disappears out of causal preconditioning. Every phenomenon in this world is due to an original cause, with preconditioning of correlated factors adding to the completion of the whole picture puzzle.

If we pursue anything to the end, once we reach its source of origin, we will find that there is no existence of an absolute essence that is unchangeable. All things—all in all—all nothing but aggregates of preconditioned factors.

一颗种子是可以成长的因，加上土壤、雨水的助缘就成长为一棵大树了。为何会有这棵大树呢？一切都是因缘而生的啊！
One seed may be the cause of growth. With the proper preconditioning of soil and rain added to the same time and space, it will grow into a big tree. Why is there this big tree? It is because all is born out of causal preconditioning.

"此有故彼有，此起故彼起；
此无故彼无，此灭故彼灭。"
宇宙的本质是变化无常、流转不居，变化是宇宙的实相。而宇宙中的一切现象都是出自于因缘条件相合的作用。
这些都是佛陀所证悟出的宇宙真理，人会痛苦是因为不明白诸行无常，一切皆因缘起的道理，而强求不可能的事物，
生就不想死，美好的希望不变质。而这无知的妄想当然不会实现，因为它违反了宇宙原理。
佛陀说：
诸比丘啊！缘起是什么呢？诸比丘啊！因为有生，才会有老死。不论智者出不出世，智者有没有发现……这个事实
定律早就存在于宇宙的运行之中了。我所觉悟的，我所说的，就是缘起法的这个相依性，就是这个宇宙的法则。

This one exists,therefore that one exists.
This one rises,therefore that one rises.
This one no longer exists,therefore that one no longer exists.
This one is extinguished,therefore that one is extinguished.
The nature of the universe is ever-changing and constantly flowing. Change is the true essence of the universe.
Therefore,all phenomena of the universe originate from the interaction and synchronicity of precoditioned factors
occurring at the same time and space.

These are all Truths of the universe to which Buddha be-
came enlightened and personally testified. Human beings
only suffer because we do not understand that all acts are
impermanent and that all manifestations arise from causal
preconditioning. Therefore we insist on pursuing the impos-
sible—when we are living we just don't want to die; whate-
ver we find pretty and lovely,we wish it would always stay
the same. Of course,these unrealistic fantasies will never be
realized because they totally violate the principles of the
universe.

Buddha says: "My fellow monks! What is meant by pre-
conditioned origination? My fellow monks,because there
is birth,that's why there is ageing and death. No matter
whether wise ones are born or not,whether wise ones have
discovered the Truth or not,this basic principle of reality
has always governed the motion of the universe. What I was
enlightened to—what I have been teaching—is this principle
of mutual dependency for the Truth of preconditioned origi-
nation. Such is the ruling law of the unviesre."

只要有生，就会有灭。世间的一切现
象，都会有生、住、异、灭，成、住、
坏、空，生、老、病、死。这种相依
变化的法则，谁都不可能停止。
So long as there is birth, there is
bound to be death.
All phenomena in the world are
either birth, existence, deviance and
disappearance of all living creatures;
formation, existence, decay and
emptiness of material objects;
or birth, ageing, illness and death of hu-
mans. Such principles of interdependent
change cannot be stopped by anyone.

因
Cause

缘
Effect

苦的缘起
The Preconditioned Origin of Suffering

我是这样听说的：那时候佛陀在舍卫国祇树给孤独园里对比丘们说……
This is how I have heard it: At the time, Buddha was lecturing to the monks at the Jetavana Monastery in Srâvasti...

一个人如果不明白一切外在有形事物的真正实相，就不能断除对这些事物的喜爱贪求，就不能断除痛苦。
If one person does not understand the true nature of all physical events and objects of the outside world, he will not be able to sever his longings and desires towards them and will not be able to free himself from suffering.

对自己内心的感受、思辨、冲动、意识这些心智状态，如果不明白其不定性……
Relative to our inner mental state—sensations, perceptions, motivations and consciousness—if we do not understand their nature is uncertainty...

就不能断除欲望，也就因而不能断除痛苦。
...we will not be able to cut ourselves loose from desires and therefore not be able to free ourselves from suffering.

63

比丘们啊！对于世间外在的形形色色，如若能明了它们的真实状态……
My fellow monks! Relative to the external manifestations of colours and forms in the world—if we are capable of understanding their true nature...

就能断除对这些形形色色的喜爱贪求，就能断除痛苦。
...we will be able to extinguish our longings and desires towards these manifestations of colours and forms and then be free from suffering.

人往往随着身外的一切有形事物而产生内心起伏不定的情绪感受，于是就产生了痛苦。
看清外在形形色色的价值并非绝对，内心也不随外在事物激荡，心灵就不会受爱欲的束缚了。
Human beings often allow themselves to generate fluctuating emotions internally in response to all events and objects outside of themselves. This is how suffering originates. Once we can see through the truth that the values of all external manifestations of colours and forms are not absolutes, our mind will no longer be stirred up easily by external events and objects. Thus, our mind will no longer be chained to longings and desires.

同样，对自己内心的感受，如果能明白其真实样子，就能远离欲望，断除痛苦。
In the same way, relative to our own internal sensations—if we are able to understand their true nature, we will be able to distance ourselves from desires and free ourselves from suffering.

那时候，比丘们听完佛陀所说的话，都高高兴兴地去遵行。
After the monks had finished listening to what the Buddha had to say, they all joyfully went about practising what had been preached.

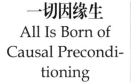

一切因缘生
All Is Born of Causal Preconditioning

知识、技能和才干有助于成功和利益。
Knowledge, skills and capabilities are helpful to attain success and profits.

正确美好的吉祥之兆是依循人的能力与行为，而无关于宇宙星体的移动。
The proper and promising sign of good luck is people's own abilities and conduct. It does not have anything to do with the movement of stars in the universe.

是它们带来收获和幸福的保证……
They are the factors that bring the guarantee of good harvest and good fortune...

一切皆是因缘，我们的结果如何？完全取决于我们自己的能力、条件、意念和行为所呈现的后果，而无关于命运、星相。每个人都是自己命运的主宰，我们如何，完全取决于我们自己，把命运委罪于神秘力量是弱者的托词。
All is based on causal preconditioning. What kind of fruit will we harvest? It completely depends upon manifestations of the cumulative results of our own abilities, qualities, consciousness and conduct, and does not have anything to do with fate and astrology. Every person is the master of his own fate. How well we do is completely up to each of us individually. To blame our fate on mysterious forces is the excuse of the weak.

65

恶的果报
The Fruits that Result from Evil

你们不是害怕苦吗？你们不是不喜欢苦吗？
Aren't you afraid of pain? Don't you dislike pain?

如果你们害怕苦，不喜欢苦，就不应该在别人看不到的地方作恶。
If you are afriad of pain and dislike pain, you should not do evil deeds in secret.

如果你们做了恶的行为，无论你们飞逃到任何地方，苦一定会跟上你们。
If you have done evil deeds, no matter where you flee to escape, pain will surely catch up with you.

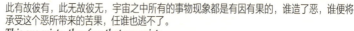

此有故彼有，此无故彼无，宇宙之中所有的事物现象都是有因有果的，谁造了恶，谁便将承受这个恶所带来的苦果，任谁也逃不了。
This one exists, therefore that one exists.
This one no longer exists, therefore the one no longer exists.
Everything in the universe has its original cause and resulting fruit. Whoever commits evil acts will eventually receive the bitter fruit brought about by this evil. No one can ever escape this reality.

无烦恼系缚者 得大安乐
Those Not Bound by Worries Gain Great Peace and Joy

没有被烦恼绑住的人，一定活得很安详快乐。
Those who are not bound by worries certainly live in peace and joy.

常听闻真理的人，很容易看透烦恼的人为何苦恼。
Those who often hear about Truth can easily see through the reasons why people with worries suffer.

追逐世间一切价值，随世间的节奏起舞的人必有苦恼。
Those who pursue all worldly values and march to the beat of the worldly drum will definitely suffer.

人追逐什么，必因所追逐的事物而烦恼。如果希望获得安详快乐的生活，得先改变追逐的对象：不追求外在的一切价值，而追求内在身心的净化，则必得大安乐。

Whatever people pursue, they will definitely worry about the things that they pursue. If we wish to have a life of peace and joy, we first need to change what we are after. Do not pursue any external values. Seek instead the internal purification of the body and mind. This is how we will gain great peace and joy.

67

触因五蕴而生
Feelings Are Born Out of the Five Aspects of Existence*

比丘们啊！你们在村庄或森林里感受到苦或乐时，绝不要把那个苦乐变成自己的苦乐，也别把它变成别人的苦乐。

My fellow monks! When you are touched by feelings of sadness or happiness in the village or in the forest, never allow those feelings to become your own. Also, do not pass this sadness and happiness on to others.

主观感受是由于人以一己的标准去分析判断，才有了好与不好之分，如果我们不去分别它，那么外在的苦乐就不会变成我们的苦乐感受了。

Subjective feelings are based on the analysis and judgement of one's own standards. This is how the difference between good and bad is created. If we do not judge and differentiate between these experiences — and just accept them as they are — then external sadness and happiness will not become internalized as our own feelings.

我们觉得如何，是因为我们以后天形成的标准去评判外在的一切……不被这评分标准左右，排除思想框框，便能返璞归真，外在的苦乐也就影响不了我们的心了。

We "feel" because we judge all external experiences based on arbitrary standards...If we are not led by such judgmental attitudes and discard the restraints of our intellectual mind, then we will be able to fine the essence of our true being. This is how our mind can transcend external experiences of sadness and joy.

*The five aspects of existence are(1) the external material world, and the(2) sensations, (3) perceptions, (4) decisions and(5) consciousness of our inner world.

不刑害众生
Do Not Hurt Other Living Beings

如果我们为了自己的快乐而伤害了也在追求快乐的别的生命，将来必不得安乐。

If for own happiness, we hurt others who are also pursuing happiness, we will not be able to gain serenity in the future.

如果我们追求自己的快乐，而不去伤害同样也在追求快乐的别的生命……

If we pursue our own happiness and do not hurt others who are also pursuing happiness...

将来一定能得到所追求的快乐。

...in the future, we will definitely receive the happiness that we have been seeking.

人不应踩着别人的身躯去达成自己的目的。
人在追求快乐时，不能把这追求踏在别人的痛苦上。
人在追求获得时，不能把这获得建立在别人的损失上。

People should not step on the bodies of others to accomplish their own goals. In pursuit of happiness, people should not walk on top of the pain of other. In pursuit of abundance, people should not build their gain on the loss of others.

一切皆苦
ALL IS SUFFERING

人由自我的利益观点去考量一切事物，凡是对我有利的就乐；凡是对我不利的就苦。
但现前有利的乐，也是形成将来苦的原因，为什么呢？因为一切都遵循着生、住、异、灭的运行法则，现前美好的事物定有变异、变坏、变灭，而导致与心所喜欢的事物别离之苦，今天的美丽、年轻、强壮，就全是将来不再美丽年轻时的苦的原因了。
所以佛陀说：一切皆苦。

Generally, human beings evaluate everything based on their own perspective of benefit. Anything that is beneficial to me is happiness, while anything that is not beneficial to me is pain.
However, even happiness that is of benefit at the moment if also the cause of future pain. Why is that? Because all living things follow the evolving rule of birth, existence, deviation and disappearance. All things that are pretty and lovely in the present will definitely become different, become worse, and become ruined—thus causing us the pain of separation from all events and objects that we long for. Today's beauty, youth and strength will be the cause of pain when we are no longer beautiful, young and strong.
Therefore, Buddha says, "All is suffering."

现前对我不利的产生即刻的苦；
现前对我有利的虽然是乐，但它也是将来苦的种子。
All that is not beneficial to me produces immediate pain. All things that are beneficial for me, of course, produce happiness for the present moment; but in them are also the seeds of future suffering.

佛陀说：

比丘们！现在和从前一样，我只教导苦和苦的止息方法。

佛陀一生传法不谈无关于苦的止息的形而上哲学，他说这些形而上的理论无法用吾人的经验去证实，也无益于痛苦的止息。

而佛陀所要的，是确确实实帮助弟子们于现世中以正确的认知与修行终止痛苦烦恼的产生。

佛陀说，一个人的苦，苦的起因，苦的灭除，以及达成苦的灭尽的修行之道，都存在于结合"心"、"想"的这个活生生的六尺之躯中。

每个人可以依循佛陀的教导，终止苦而达至永恒的喜乐。

Buddha says: "My fellow monks, now and as usual, I only teach about suffering and the means to be free of suffering."

Buddha's lifetime teaching did not discuss metaphysical philosophy which has nothing to do with eliminating suffering. He said that these metaphysical theories can neither be tested with our own personal experience, nor help in eliminating pain.

What Buddha wanted was to help his disciples in pragmatic ways to properly recognize Essential Universal Truths and cultivate themselves. This is how they could put an end to the generation of worries in their present life.

Buddha says: "A person's suffering, the origin of suffering, the ending of suffering, and the methods of cultivation to achieve the elimination of suffering... They all exist in this several-foot-tall physical body that is fully alive, and that combines 'mind' and 'perceptions'."

Everyone can follow Buddha's guidance to eliminate suffering and reach eternal joy.

我所说的法，就是终止苦的方法。每个人若遵照我指引的道路去实行，就可以成为另一个佛陀。

The Essential Universal Truths that I talk about is the method to terminate suffering. If everyone follows and practises along the road I point to, each one can become a Buddha.

苦和苦的止息
Suffering and Eliminating Suffering

比丘们啊！现在和从前一样，我只教导什么是苦和终止苦的方法。

My fellow monks, now and as usual, I only teach about suffering and the means to end suffering.

凡是跟终止苦无关的，就不是我所说的。

Anything that is not relevant to eliminating suffering is not what I have said.

佛陀一生说法的目的，就是要令弟子们切断因缘法而达至永恒寂静安详的涅槃之境。我们每一个佛弟子都可以遵奉佛陀所传的方法去终止苦，令苦永不再生。

The purpose of Buddha's lifetime lecturing on Essential Universal Truths is to enable his disciples to cut themselves free of the cyclical law of cause and effect and, in turn, reach the state of Nirvâna with eternal tranquillity and peace. As a student of Buddhism, every one of us is capable of following the methods Buddha has passed down to end suffering and to keep suffering from ever being born again.

离欲则苦解脱
Eliminate Desires and
Then Suffering Is Relieved

那时候，佛陀在舍卫国祇树给孤独园对比丘们说……
At the time, Buddha Sakyamuni was lecturing to the monks of Jetavana Monastery in Srâvasti...

受制于外在一切有形事物的爱欲，就受制于苦，就不能得解脱。
If we are controlled by longing and desires for all physical events and objects in the external world, then we are controlled by suffering. We will not be able to gain relief and freedom.

受制于自身内心的感受，就受制于苦，也不能解脱苦。
If we are controlled by the feelings of our inner world, we are also controlled by suffering. We will also not be able to gain relief from suffering.

比丘们啊！不受制于一切事物就不受制于苦而可解脱苦。
My fellow monks! If all events and objects do not control us, then we are not controlled by suffering. This is how we transcend suffering.

比丘们听完之后，都高兴地照佛陀的指示去做。
After the monks heard the lecture, they all happily went to practise what Buddha had preached.

同样，不受制于自身内心的感受就不受制于苦，而能解脱苦了。
In the same way, if we are not controlled by our inner feelings, then we are not controlled by suffering. This is how we will gain relief from suffering.

知道事物的无常及它所带来的苦与空，知道没有永恒的"我"这才是正确的观念。
Know the transient nature of everything and the resulting suffering and emptiness. Know there is not an external "I". These are the proper concepts.

对事物本相的无知、不明、不断、不离欲贪，乃是迷恋于有形事物的原因啊！
Ignorance, delusion, attachment and longing are the reasons for our infatuation with the physical world.

人会痛苦乃是因为有自我——自我内心的感受。而这些感受乃来自于自己对外在世界的价值标准。
人要断除痛苦，先得要明白外在世界事物的价值与内心世界的感受都是自我这颗心所造成的啊！
Human beings suffer because of the ego-self—the inner feelings of the ego. These feelings come from our values and expectations in regard to the external world.
For human beings to terminate suffering, we first need to understand that the values of everything in the external world, as well as the feelings of our inner world, are both formed by our own mind.

74

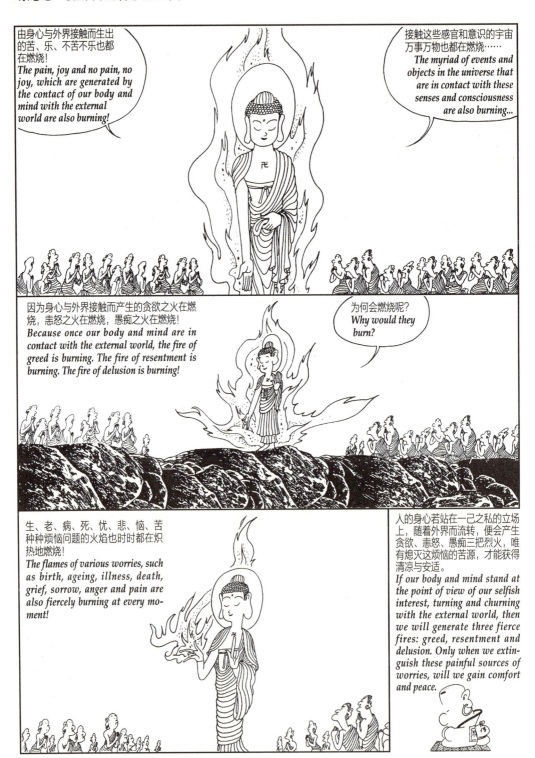

由身心与外界接触而生出的苦、乐、不苦不乐也都在燃烧!
The pain, joy and no pain, no joy, which are generated by the contact of our body and mind with the external world are also burning!

接触这些感官和意识的宇宙万事万物也都在燃烧……
The myriad of events and objects in the universe that are in contact with these senses and consciousness are also burning...

因为身心与外界接触而产生的贪欲之火在燃烧；恚怒之火在燃烧，愚痴之火在燃烧!
Because once our body and mind are in contact with the external world, the fire of greed is burning. The fire of resentment is burning. The fire of delusion is burning!

为何会燃烧呢?
Why would they burn?

生、老、病、死、忧、悲、恼、苦种种烦恼问题的火焰也时时都在炽热地燃烧!
The flames of various worries, such as birth, ageing, illness, death, grief, sorrow, anger and pain are also fiercely burning at every moment!

人的身心若站在一己之私的立场上，随着外界而流转，便会产生贪欲、恚怒、愚痴三把烈火，唯有熄灭这烦恼的苦源，才能获得清凉与安适。
If our body and mind stand at the point of view of our selfish interest, turning and churning with the external world, then we will generate three fierce fires: greed, resentment and delusion. Only when we extinguish these painful sources of worries, will we gain comfort and peace.

76

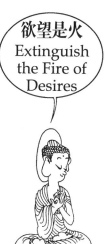

欲望是火
Extinguish the Fire of Desires

想要求得最高觉悟的人，必须熄灭欲望之火。
Those who wish to achieve the highest level of enlightenment must extinguish the fire of desires.

就像背负干草的人见到野火必须走避一样……
Obviously, those who carry dried hay on their backs must run away from the first sign of a wild fire...

期求解脱之道的人，亦必须远离欲望之火。
In the same manner, those who aspire to the path of salvation must stay far away from the fire of desires.

自我是引起痛苦的根源，我们痛苦都因为与我有关；所发生的事物对我的触动愈小，痛苦也就愈少。而欲望是人最难以克服的火，有的欲望是生理性的，有的则是心理性的，人要克服欲望当然心要清净，自我克制不去想，而身也要远离产生欲望的处所，以免一触即发不可收拾。

The ego-self is the root that causes pain. Our pains are all because of something that has to do with "I". The less any happenings affect me, the less intense the pain. Desire is the most difficult fire for human beings to control. Some desires are physiological, while others are psychological. To control desires we must have a pure mind. We need to keep certain thoughts out of the mind, as well as keep far away from places that generate desires, so that we will not erupt into flames without any chance for salvation.

欲望是一种陷阱
Desires Are Traps

眼所见物、耳所听声、鼻所嗅香、舌所尝味、身所接触，这五种由外在而来的感受最容易引发欲望。

The objects seen by the eyes, the voices heard by the ears, the fragrances smelled by the nose, the flavours tasted by the tongue, the materials touched by the body,—these five internal sensations of the external world are the easiest to provoke desires.

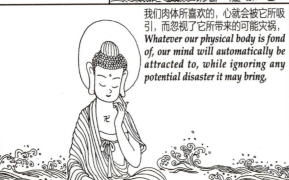

我们肉体所喜欢的，心就会被它所吸引，而忽视了它所带来的可能灾祸，

Whatever our physical body is fond of, our mind will automatically be attracted to, while ignoring any potential disaster it may bring,

就像森林里的鹿陷入猎人所设的圈套而被捕获。

It is like the deer in the forest which falls into the trap set by hunters and gets captured.

无疑的，五欲就是圈套，我们如果陷入了圈套，烦恼马上就会兴起，痛苦也随之而来。因此见了这五欲之灾，就必须有避免中圈套的方寸，不要误入其中。

No doubt, the five desires I just mentioned are our traps. If we fall into these traps, worries will soon arise and suffering will automatically follow.
Therefore, after we have seen the troubles caused by these five desires, we must have the mind to avoid being trapped and not get captured by mistake.
Desires are generated by our own senses coming into contact with all external events and objects.

欲望是由我们自己的感官接触到外在的一切事物而发生的。
当我们遇到自己喜欢的一切，我们的心马上兴起一股希望拥有、希望成为的渴望。当我们得到心所喜欢或达成心里希望成为的事物时，又期望喜欢的事物不要变质，不要离去……

When we come across anything that we like, our mind immediately produces an urgent longing to own the object or possess the characteristic. When we acquire what our mind is fond of, or accomplish something that our mind wishes to achieve, we in turn expect that whatever we like will not change its quality or leave us...

**不能忍辱
不能享诸乐
Without Endu-
rance There Is
No Enjo-
yment**

一个人如果不能忍辱，则瞋怒之心常积聚心中，也因而内心失去了平静，
If a person cannot endure adversity, resentment will accumulate time and again in the mind. The mind will therefore lose its calmness,

就像毒箭射在心中一样苦痛难当，身心煎熬……
It will be unbearably painful and torturous, like having a poisoned arrow shot into your mind...

因此内心不能享受宁静安详及任何快乐，甚至连睡觉也睡不着。
Under these circumstances, the mind cannot enjoy peace, quiet or any joy. It is even hard to sleep through the night.

瞋怒煎熬心，失宁静和平，不能享诸乐，睡亦不安宁。
Resentment fries the mind, which loses quietness and peace. Nothing is a joy to find. And there is not even a good night's sleep.

79

瞋怒能消毁百千劫内之善根
Anger Can Destroy Kindness Back to Its Very Roots — Zillions of Years Ago

一个人如果真做到了布施、持戒，但是不能忍辱，他就仍会发怒……一旦发怒，他过去布施、持戒所积聚的一切成就，在刹那间便破坏无余了。

If a person can indeed give unconditionally and abide by proper precepts, but is not able to tolerate adversity, then he will still get angry...Once he blows up in anger, then all of his accumulated virtues of giving and abiding by precepts will be completely destroyed instantaneously, with nothing left!

这就是瞋怒能摧毁万善，瞋怒能消毁百千劫内所积聚之善根啊！

This is how anger can break down thousands of kind deeds. Indeed, anger is capable of putting an end to the roots of kindness accumulated over zillions of years.*

千劫所积聚，布施供养德，及种种善行，一念瞋心起，皆摧毁无余。

Zillions of years in time* offering virtuous gifts all together combined with every deed of kindness. One single angry thought of mind destroys all—with nothing left.

*The duration of time given here is a kalpa, one hundred thousand eons. An eon is calculated as 1,344,000,000 human years. It represents the period from the begining of a universe until its destruction and another begins in its place.

80

我们的身心是自己的地狱
Our Own Body and Mind Are Our Hell

有一个平凡人下了一个断言：
"海洋底下有一个地狱。"
An ordinary person concluded that, "There is a hell under the ocean."

这样的说法是错误而毫无根据的……
This theory is erroneous and has no basis in fact whatsoever...

地狱是个形容词，它是指我们自己身心的痛苦感受。
Hell is an adjective. It describes the feelings of excruciating pain in our body or mind.

地狱在哪里？地狱不在那边，也不在这边，地狱在我们的身心里：我们由于欲望难以达成，渴望、贪念难以满足，而产生贪欲之渴与瞋恨不满之火，焚烧我们的身心。
Where is hell? Hell is neither here nor there. Hell is inside our own body and mind. Due to our desires that cannot be fulfilled and due to longings and greed that cannot be satisfied, we generate the fires of greedy desire and resentful anger which burn our own body and mind.

吾身即是道场
Our Body Is Indeed a Hall of Worship

一个人的身躯虽然只是六尺之长，虽然有生死……
Although a person's body is only a few feet tall and although this body inevitably goes through cycles of life and death...

但我却要告诉你们，苦的起源……
...still, I want to explain to you that the origin of suffering...

苦的终止与导向终止的道路都在其中。
...the elimination of suffering, as well as the road leading to the elimination of suffering, are all contained within this physical body.

你自己的天堂与你的地狱都在这六尺之躯里。
Your own heaven and your own hell are both contained within this physical body of a few feet in height.

不要担心于过去与未来，也不要沉思世界的始与终之类的难题，要把关怀与努力放在这"一躯之体中痛苦的起与灭"。若能觉醒、获得解脱，每个人就可成为他自己的上帝。
Do not worry about the past or future, and do not ponder challenging questions, such as the beginning and the end of this world. Focus all of your attention and effort on "the origin and elimination of pain in this body". If a person can achieve spiritual awakening and relief, then he is becoming one with his own divinity.

我执
ATTACHMENT TO THE EGO-SELF OF "I"

大多数的痛苦是由人的自我观念产生的。
人执著于"我",执著于"我所有"……因此,凡是不利于"我"和"我所有"的就为之痛苦。
Most pains are produced by people's perception of the ego-self.
Human beings are attached to "I", attached to "mine"... Therefore, anything that is adverse to "I" and "mine" becomes pain.

人执迷于有关"自我"的一切……我的欲望、我的利益、我的所有、我的光荣、我的骄傲，和我自己本身
凡是跟我有关的，就会因而产生喜乐与哀伤之情，也因此一生都受缚于这个我和我所有。
我执是最大的痛苦来源，所以佛陀说：
没有我这个人，也没有属于我的物，如果已经知道没有"我"，又凭什么有"我的物"？假如能这样理解，也就能斩断所有的烦恼。

People are attached and infatuated with everything concerning "self"... My desires, my profits, my belongings, my honours, my pride, and my own self...

As a result, anything that has to do with me will produce feelings of happiness and sadness; also, because of this self, the whole of life is bounded by "I" and "mine".

Attachment to the ego-self of "I" is the biggest source of pain. Therefore, Buddha says: "There is really no existence of 'I' as a person; there is nothing that belongs to 'me'. If we already know that there is no 'I', on what basis do we believe that there are 'my belongings'? If we can understand everything from this point of view, then we will be empowered to sever all worries."

我们连自己的生命都不能有效地掌握，何来属于我的物呢？
We cannot even effectively handle our own lives. How could there possibly be anything that belongs to me?

舍弃妄我
Abandon the
False Ego-Self
of "I"

人追随着内心世界与外在世界，受欲望与烦恼的驱使，陡增加命运的遭遇……
Driven by desires and worries, human beings chase after their inner world as well as the outer world. They only add in vain to the vicissitudes in life...

欲
Desires

由色、受、想、行、识假合成的我，既非我也非非我……
The "I" that is the transitional collective manifestation of the material world, sensations, perceptions, decisions and consciousness, is neither the real essence of "I" nor of "non-I"...

色
Material World

色
Material World

色
Material World

色
Material World

色
Material World

受
Sensations

想
Perceptions

行
Decisions

识
Consciousness

色
Material World

85

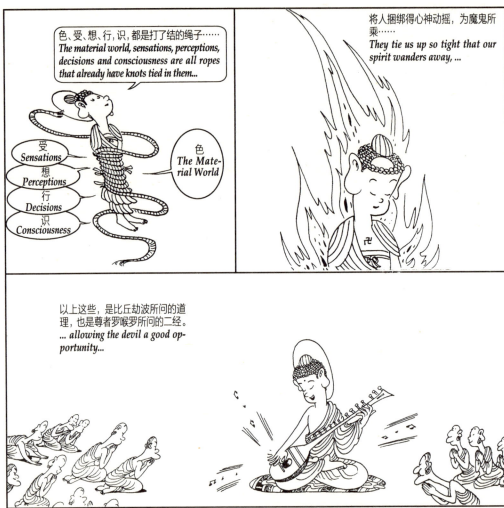

色、受、想、行、识，都是打了结的绳子……
The material world, sensations, perceptions, decisions and consciousness are all ropes that already have knots tied in them...

受
Sensations
想
Perceptions
行
Decisions
识
Consciousness

色
The Material World

将人捆绑得心神动摇，为魔鬼所乘……
They tie us up so tight that our spirit wanders away, ...

以上这些，是比丘劫波所问的道理，也是尊者罗睺罗所问的二经。
... allowing the devil a good opportunity...

色
The Material World

受
Sensations
想
Perceptions
行
Decisions
识
Consciousness

人由外在世界的色与内心世界的受想行识构成了一个假我、妄我，一生都被这个假我、妄我所驱役。
人应该舍弃这个妄我，而无我地融入所处的时空中。当妄我消失，你就得到了全世界。

Human beings put together a false ego-self of "I", a fantasy of "I" due to the material world externally and the sensations, perceptions, decisions and consciousness internally. All their lives they are driven as slaves by this false self, this fantasy of self. Humans should give up this fantasy of self and dissolve into the space and time they happen to find themselves in the present moment selflessly. When the fantasy of "I" disappears, you will gain the whole world.

融入
Dissolving into...

如果我站着不动……
If I stand motionless...

我就沉下去。
I will definitely sink.

如果我挣扎，我就被卷走。
If I struggle, I will be swept away by the current.

我既不站着不动，也不挣扎……
I neither stand motionless nor struggle...

因此，我渡过了河。
This is how I was able to pass across the river.

人，有我。于是他面对时空，想改变时空，与时空对立。
人，若能无我地随时随地融入时空，他便成了时空的本体。
A human being has the concept of a separate "I". Therefore, when he faces a certain time and space, he thinks about changing that particular time and space and positioning himself against that time and space. If a human at any time and place can dissolve into that particular time and space, then he will become one with the essence of that time and space.

舍弃小我
Letting Go of the Small Ego-Self of "I"

我们每个人都是由很多的我所构成的。这里我有：小我、中我、大我……
凡夫都只为自我的短期利益考量，斤斤计较于微小而短暂的利益，为之而乐而忧。
智者则舍弃小我，而朝向长远的整体目标。

Each one of us is made up of layers of self. Among these are: the small ego-self of "I", the "I" at a medium level, and the highest sense of self... Ordinary people often only consider the short-term benefit of the ego-self of "I". They calculate those menial and short-lived benefits inch by inch, becoming ecstatic over them and worried sick over them. The wise ones choose to let go of one small ego-self and orient themselves towards the long term goal of wholeness.

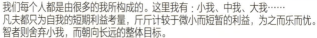

心是身的主导
The Mind Is the Guide of the Body

见到美色，唯恐心受到诱惑，连忙把眼睛挖出来是愚蠢的行为。
Upon encountering beauty and lust, digging out your eyes for fear of being tempted is stupid behaviour.

因为心才是受诱惑的主角，邪恶之心如能斩断，作为配角的眼睛就不会输入邪念了。
The mind is the major actor in being tempted. If the evil mind could be cut off instead of the eyes which are only supporting actors, there would be no evil thoughts.

心是身的主导，心里怎么想，身就怎么行。人要降服自己的身心，使自己成为自己的主人，首先必先要降服自己的心。能够降服自己的心，身自然就听话了。
The mind is the guide of the body. The mind thinks, and the body follows in action. Humans need to conquer their body and mind and be their own master. The first important thing is to discipline your mind. Once your own mind submits to control, the body will naturally obey.

心随意转
The Mind
Follows
the Will

人的心，往往都倾向于他所企求的方向。
A person's mind leans towards the direction that his will pursues.

想到贪，贪心即生起：想到瞋，不满就特别强烈，想到损害人，损害心就增长。
Thinking of greed, his greedy mind immediately arises; thinking of resentment, his discontentment becomes especially strong; thinking of hurting people, his thoughts about injuring others grow right away.

平常人的心并不常随着他的身处在一境，而是随着他的意奔驰。因此，人应该清净自我的意识，不令贪欲、瞋恚和害人之心存留在自我意识里，心自然就会清净了。
The mind of an ordinary person does not usually stay with his body at one place, rather it follows his will and gallops around. Therefore, humans should cleanse the consciousness of the ego-self. Do not allow greed, resentment and a vicious mind to remain in the existence of self-consciousness. This is how the mind automatically becomes pure.

自作自受
The Self Acts and the Self Receives

任何敌人对我们的伤害就算再大……
No matter how great the harm that any enemy can inflict upon us...

也比不上我们自己的贪欲、不满、嫉妒对我们自己的伤害来得大。
They can never hurt us as much as our own greed, discontentment and jealousy.

我们最大的敌人就是我们自己，我们遭遇的不好后果通常都是自己的错误造成的。"胜人者有力，自胜者强。"能战胜自己身心的是最勇敢的斗士。
Our biggest enemy is ourselves. Poor results in our encounters are usually caused by our own mistakes. "Those who win over others are merely forceful, those who win over their own selves are really strong." To be able to conquer one's own body and mind is the act of the bravest warrior.

欲望是火
Desires Are Fires that Burn

追逐欲望而不知道满足的人，如同抓着火炬迎风向前奔走一样……
Those who run after desire and do not know satisfaction are like a person who grabs a torch and runs into the wind...

最后被火把灼伤手臂，被火焚身是理所当然的结果。
Eventually, they will, by all reasoning, end up burning their arms with the torch and even engulfing their whole body in flames.

欲望像大海一样，永远也无法填满。
人追逐欲望，满足了一个之后会再形成另一个更大的欲望，乃至最后被欲望所毁灭。
Desires are like the ocean—they can never be filled up. When people run after their desires, they will definitely form another greater desire after the last one has been fulfilled. In the end, they are going to be utterly destroyed by their own desires.

93

一切都不要执取
Do Not Become Atta-
ched to Anything

如果人不执著于世间的一切物质名利，就不会被物质名利所控制；正由于人追求这些，才被它们所缠困不得解脱。
If humans are not attached to material fortune and fame in this world, they will not be controlled by fortune and fame. Because people pursue these entities, they are bound and are not able to live freely.

如果人能无我地不在意自己内心的感觉、感受、思维、观念，也就不会被自己的感动所控制。
If humans can selflessly detach from their own internal sensations, feelings, thoughts and ideas, they will not be controlled by their own impulses.

但人太在乎自己的感觉、感受，因而才被它们所缠困不得解脱。
But people care too much about their sensations and feelings and are therefore bound by these sentiments without relief.

比丘们啊！如果外在的物与内在的欲对人无害，那么人就不应该厌弃它们……
My fellow monks! If external materials and internal desires are benign to people, then people do not need to detach from them...

正因为这些外在的物质名利与内在的欲望对人有害，所以人才要厌弃它们啊！
The fame and fortune of the external world as well as internal desires are quite harmful to people. This is why people must abandon them with disgust!

比丘们啊！对外在的物与内心的欲如果不能看清它们，而迷恋、追逐、沉溺其中……
My fellow monks, if one cannot see through the external materials and internal desires while infatuated with pursuing and indulging in them...

那么他将永远停留在是非颠倒的错误中，无法得到正确的智慧和自在解脱。
Then he will always stay in his mistaken upside-down thinking and will have no way of obtaining correct wisdom and achieving freedom and relief.

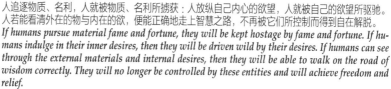

人追逐物质、名利，人就被物质、名利所掳获；人放纵自己内心的欲望，人就被自己的欲望所驱驰。人若能看清外在的物与内在的欲，便能正确地走上智慧之路，不再被它们所控制而得到自在解脱。
If humans pursue material fame and fortune, they will be kept hostage by fame and fortune. If humans indulge in their inner desires, then they will be driven wild by their desires. If humans can see through the external materials and internal desires, then they will be able to walk on the road of wisdom correctly. They will no longer be controlled by these entities and will achieve freedom and relief.

空
KONG

世间的所有现象皆生于因缘……

如果我们对任何现象、事物的发展结果，追究到它们发生的源头，会发现除了因缘际会条件相生之外，并没有一个实实在在的东西使得它产生。

因缘所生之法，究竟而无实体，曰"空"。

All manifestations in the world are born out of preconditioned meaningful coincidences...

If we search for the very origin of occurrences in regard to the resulting development of any events and objects, we will find that there is no real entity which produced it. There is only the interaction of related characteristics brought about by preconditioned synchronous coincidences.

All phenomena appear because of cause and effect. They have no real essence and are distorted by each ego-self's mindset. This is what is meant by "kong".

一切因缘生，一切因缘灭。除此，并无原本不变不异的实体存在……这个真理就叫做"空"。

All is born out of preconditioned meaningful coincidences. All disappears due to preconditioned meaningful coincidences. Except for these principles, there is no real entity that is truly everlasting and eternally enduring... This Universal Truth is defined as "kong".

空不是空无所有，
空更不是无所谓。
空是宇宙的本质、宇宙的实相。
宇宙万象都是由条件的变化与互动才产生的，宇宙的本质并没有一个实质而永恒不变的东西，宇宙的这种本质属性，佛陀称之为空性。
空，是一种状态，是一种观念，是一种生活态度。
一个人了解宇宙中的空的真理，他在生活的实践中就不会妄想执取任何不变、永恒的事物，也不会因事物的成、住、坏、空和生、住、异、灭的变化而痛苦了。
因为他知道，变化不已是宇宙的韵律。

Kong is not emptiness without anything.

Kong is definitely not being uncaring.

Kong is the essence of the universe, the real nature of the universe.

All sorts of phenomena in the universe originate from the change and interaction of various characteristics. The intrinsic nature of the universe does not consist of any substantial and eternally enduring entity. The essential quality of the universe of referred to by Buddha as the nature of kong.

Kong:

Is a state;

Is a concept;

Is an attitude of living.

When a person understands the truth about the kong of the universe, his practice in life will not be to fantasize about holding onto any unchanging and eternal things. He will no longer suffer pain because of the natural cycles of change — such as the formation, existence, destruction and emptiness of material objects and the birth, existence, deviation and disappearance of lives.

This is because he knows by now that constant change is the rhythm of the universe.

世间一切皆空性，没有永恒不变的东西。美好的事物希望永远保有，这种想法违背宇宙的真理。

Everything in this world is kong by nature. There is nothing that is externally enduring. The wish to hold onto pretty and lovely things forever is totally in violation of universal law.

不偏不倚之道
Not Steering
to Either Side
of the Road

一根木材在大河中顺流而下……它既不靠岸，也不沉没，不漂向陆地，也不被人捞取，不被卷入漩涡，也不从内部腐烂，最后，它一定会流入大海。

One log flows down a big river—It does not run aground, neither does it sink. It does not drift ashore, nor is it caught by people. It is not drawn into a whirlpool, nor does it rot from inside. Eventually, it is guaranteed to flow into the vast ocean.

一个修行者也要像这根木头一样：既不执内，也不执外；既不执有，也不执无；既不执正，也不执邪。

A person who cultivates himself should be like this log—neither attached to the inside, nor attached to the inside, nor attached to the outside, neither attached to being, nor attached to not being, neither attached to righteousness nor attached to evil.

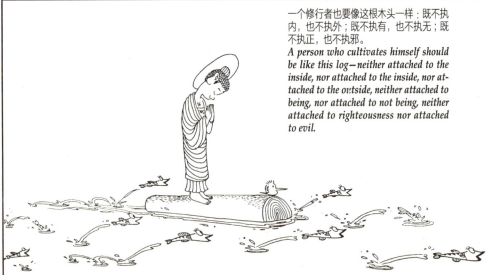

他虽远离迷惘，但也不拘泥于觉悟，任其一身在道的河流中浮游，最后终将流入智慧的大海。这种态度就是修道者应有的中道见解与中道生活。

Although he distances himself from confusion, he is not obsessed with enlightenment. He just allows himself to drift in the stream on the path to the vast ocean of wisdom. This kind of "middle of the road" attitude is what all people who cultivate themselves spiritually should hold in mind and practise in their daily living.

执著是个陷阱，人执著于什么，就被什么所困：执著于觉悟，就被觉悟所困。

Attachment is a trap. Whatever people are attached to will entrap them. Even those attached to the notion of enlightenment will be trapped by it.

所有的外在对象不论过去、未来、现在、内在、外在、大的、小的、美的、丑的、远的、近的，都是非我，但又不异于我。

All external objects—no matter whether past, future or present, whether big or small, pretty or ugly, far or near—they are all not me, but also are not separated from me.

人处在任何时空之中，就与那时间、空间同体地完全融合，你属于那时间空间，而那时间空间也属于你。

When you happen to be in any particular space and time, you need to completely dissolve into one essence with that space and time—you belong to that space and time, while that space and time also belongs to you.

用这种态度去看待我与外在的世界，才是"无我融入的最高智慧"。

To use this attitude to look upon "I" and the external world is indeed "selflessly dissolving into the ultimate wisdom".

人与时空不应有我与对象之分。我即外在世界的时空，时空即我。

You and your space and time should not be separated from each other. You are the space and time of the external world, and the space and time are you.

100

对于自己内在的感受、思维也是同样，不论是过去、未来、现在、内在、外在、大的、小的、美的、丑的、远的、近的，这一切都不是我，但也不异于我，不应该有我与这些对象的对立二元看法。

With regard to our internal feelings and thoughgts, it is the same. Not matter whether past, future or present, whether big or small, pretty or ugly, far or near—they are all not me, but also are not separated from me. We should not hold the point of view that I and any objects around me are two opposite parties.

于是就能无我，也无内心的世界，受、想、行、识也就消失了。

That is how it is possible for there to be no "I" and no internal world. The sensations, perceptions, decisions and consciousness will therefore disappear by themselves.

内心的世界即是我，我即是内心的世界……

The internal world is me, and I am the internal mental world...

无我地把自己融入内心的世界……

Dissolve oneself into the internal mental world selflessly...

以这种无我地融入的智慧去看待我与内心的世界，即是最正确、至高无上的智慧。

To use this kind of selfless wisdom to look upon "I" and the inner world is the most proper and ultimate wisdom.

罗睺罗啊！
比丘们若能用这种观点看待外在的世界和内心世界，能够“无我”、“无对象”、“无自我的骄傲”，就能断除贪爱与欲望。
My dear Rahula, if monks can use this point of view to look at the external as well as the inner world, achieving "no I", "no object", and "no pride of the ego-self of I", then they will be able to sever longings and desires.

他就可以脱离种种捆绑束缚，远离种种极端的痛苦了。
They will be able to release themselves from all sorts of bondage and distance themselves from a variety of extreme pains.

这时，罗睺罗听到佛陀所说的法，很高兴地去遵循奉行。
Rahula understood the Buddha's teachings and gladly went on to follow and practise them.

人活在时空中，无哪一部分是我、哪一部分是对象。应该把自己化为亿万个微粒分子，融入所处的任何时空，时时是我，片片是我，无分好、坏、顺、逆，都珍视地去品尝。
Humans live in space and time. There is really not a separate part of the universal essence that is "I" and another part of the separate essence that is the opposing objects. We should dissolve into any space and time in which we find ourselves. Every moment is "I", and every piece is also "I". There is not judgement of good or bad, my way or not my way. Let us just treasure the taste of all experiences.

中道
The Middle of the Road

比丘们! 世间有两个极端, 出家人不应该接近。
My fellow monks, there are two extremes in the world that the ordained ones should not come close to:

一个是极端放纵自己欲望的享乐主义; 一个是极端的苦行……
One is the principle of hedonistic pleasure that promotes the extreme indulgence of one's desires. The other is extreme austerity...

比丘们啊! 如来舍两边, 走的是中道! 那就是睁开双眼发出智慧, 才能抵达寂静, 证智、等觉和涅槃啊!
My fellow monks! "Ultimate Essence Arriving" gives up both extremes and walks in the middle of the road. Keep your eyes open wide and draw on your wisdom. This is how we can reach tranquillity, wisdom, awareness and eventually Nirvâna!

只知道满足欲望和一味的苦行, 都不是求道者应走的道路。
佛陀年轻的时候过的是极为养尊处优的生活, 后来他一心想证得真理而苦行六年, 却没有获得真正的觉悟。
于是他离弃两端, 领悟到中道才是证悟所应走的道路。

Neither those who only care about satisfying desires nor those who simple-mindedly practise religious self-mortification are following the right path for seekers of truth. When Buddha was young, he lived and extremely luxurious and pampered life. Afterwards, he practised self-mortification for six years, thinking that he would obtain enlightenment to Truth this way, but in vain. Therefore, he abandoned both extremes and came to enlightenment through the middle way that is the right path for reaching enlightenment.

求道如弹琴
Seeking the Road to Truth Is Like Playing a Stringed Instrument

琴弦绷得太紧或太松，都弹奏不出和谐的声音，唯有适当的松紧才能奏出美妙的乐曲。
When the string of a musical instrument is too taut or too loose, harmonious sounds cannot be played. Only the proper degree of tension will produce beautiful music.

修行寻求觉悟之道也如同弹琴一样，怠惰松懈不能得道，太过专注紧张也同样不得成就。
Cultivation to seek the path to enlightenment is also like playing a stringed instrument. Laziness and complacency will not get you there; neither will too much eagerness and obsession to accomplish it.

因此，我们努力向道必须慎重地掌握适当的尺度，不令太紧也不令太松。
Therefore, our effort towards the road to truth must be cautiously handled at the right level and not allowed to be too taut or too loose.

修行者应摆脱两种极端的生活，启开心眼，进修智慧，行走于导向觉悟的生活。
什么是中道生活呢？正见、正思、正语、正业、正命、正精进、正念、正定，这"八正道"即是中道生活。
Someone who cultivates spirituality should get away from both extremes of lifestyle. This is how the heart is opened up, wisdom is cultivalted, and one gets to walk in the lifestyle leading to enlightenment. What is the middle-of-the-road lifestyle? A proper point of view, proper thoughts, a proper way of speaking to others, proper behaviour, a proper lifestyle, proper efforts, proper mindfulness, and a proper centring of the mind through meditation. These eight components are the middle-of-the-road lifestyle.

非有非无
Not
Being and
Not Not
Being

宇宙中的一切万象，都是依缘而有生灭，没有所谓的有、无……
Every phenomenon in the universe follows preconditioned synchronicity in creation and disappearance. There is being or not being...

愚痴的人会抱持着有，或抱持着无的观念……
Those people in delusion either hold onto the concept of being or not being...

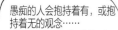

但真正有智慧的人，他们知道宇宙的实相是超越有无的，这就是中道的正确见解。
But the really wise ones know that the true nature of the universal essence is beyond being or not being.

如果我们觉得对方比较大、比较强，那是站在外在的立场看事物，是因为我们自己比较小、比较弱。如果我们抱持着这样的想法，那也是站在自我的立场上看事物了。真理超越两边，既不站这边也不站那边……
If we feel the opposite party is bigger and stronger, that means we are using the external point of view to observe things. If we feel that we are smaller and weaker, then we are using the point of view of the ego-self to observe everything. Truth is beyond both sides, neither on this side nor on that side...

105

受只是受，不理是福是祸
Acceptance Is Acceptance, Whether of Fortune or Disaster

有生就有死，有福就有祸，有好事就有坏事，人必须知道这个道理。

So long as there is birth, there is death.
So long as there is good fortune, there is disaster.
So long as there are lucky events, there are unlucky events.
Humans must acknowledge this principle.

而愚痴之人只会企求幸福而厌恶灾祸。

People in delusion only anticipate happiness and hate disasters.

学道修行之人超越这两种，不执著于任何一边。

A person who is cultivating spirituality will transcend both and not attach himself to either side.

聪明的人知道凡事要看两边，有好的一面也有坏的一面，愚痴的人则是企求好的那一面，抱怨坏的那一面。智者超越两边，他融入善恶福祸，因为他能无我，故也无好、坏、福、祸。

Intelligent people know that everything needs to be looked at from both sides there is always a positive side and a negative side. People in delusion always anticipate the positive side and complain about the negative side. The wise ones transcend both sides and dissolve into good and bad, good fortune and disaster. Because they are capable of being without the ego-self, they can also be in a space of no good and bad, no good fortune and disaster.

一切不可
执著
Do Not
Attach to
Anything

人，当他兴起执著之心时，
迷惘就开始产生了。
When the mind of attach-
ment arises, humans start
to get confused.

因此，步向觉悟之道的修行者应该要做到：
不坚持、不执取、不停滞、不自我拘束地生活。
Therefore, a person practising cultivation
and walking along the path of enlightenment should be walking the path of no
insistence, possessiveness, stubbornness,
or excessive restraint.

如果我们执著，便不可能融入⋯⋯
生命的意义在于无论处于任何时间、任何地点，都无我地融入自己所处的境地，这时
看起来虽一无所得⋯⋯但其实我们得到了"全部"。
If we are attached to anything, then it is impossible to dissolve into the present...
The meaning of life is that no matter when and where we happen to be we should
always dissolve selflessly into it. Then, although it may look like one has gained
nothing... indeed, we have acquired "everything".

毁誉不能改变事实
Neither Slander Nor Praise Changes the Truth

如果有人毁谤我，毁谤我的教义或是我的弟子……不要因而沮丧或烦乱。
If somebody slanders me, or the meanings of my teaching, or my disciples... do not get depressed or irritated.

因为这样的反应只会造成更大的损害。
Because this way of reacting will only bring about more damage.

如果有人赞美我、我的教义或我的弟子……
If somebody praises me, or the meanings of my teaching, or my disciples...

不要因而过分欢喜得意，因为这样的反应会妨碍了正确的判断。
...do not become joyous and proud, because this way of reacting will interfere with the proper evaluation.

人要有自主的认知能力，我们如何，完全是因为我们本身，并不因为别人称我们好就变成好；也不因为别人说我们坏而变质变坏。
Humans must have the awareness and ability to be their own master. How we are is completely based on the quality of ourselves. It is not because others praise us that we become good all of a sudden, and it is not because others despise us that we change our qualities and become bad.

融入一切才是智者
A Wise Person Dissolves into All

我是这样听说的，那时候，佛陀住在舍卫国祇树给孤独园，他对比丘们说：
This is how I have heard it: At the time, Buddha was living at the Jetavana Monastery in Srâvasti and lecturing to the monks.

你们仔细听，我来为各位说什么是所知法、什么是智、什么是智者。
Listen carefully. I am going to explain to you what is the known Essential Truth of the universe, what is wisdom, and what makes a wise person.

色
the material world

能正确地看清世间外在的一切，能正确地认识自身内心世界的受、想、行、识，即是所知法。
To be able to see through all external phenomena in the world and to recognize correctly the sensations, perceptions, decisions and consciousness of the inner world of oneself, this is the known Essential Truth of the universe.

受
perceptions

想
sensations

行
consciousness

识
decisions

能调伏贪欲，断绝贪欲的诱惑，能超越贪欲，这才能叫做"智"！
To be able to tame desires, to cut off the temptations of desires, and to transcend desires... this is what wisdom is about.

什么是智者呢？阿罗汉就是智者。
*What makes a wise person? One who has attained nirvâna is a wise one.**

*One who has attained Nirvâna is an Arhat, someone who has used particular methods of spiritual cultivation, such as the Noble Eightfold Path, to gain release from desires and defilement, as well as the ever-repeating cycle of reincarnation

阿罗汉的层次达到……没有过去、现在、未来……没有无过去、无现在、无未来……也不是没有过去、现在、未来……也不是没有无过去、无现在、无未来……

The level of this Arhat is that there is no past, present, future... there is also no not having a past, present and future...
It is also not having a past, present and future...
It is also no not having a past, present and future...

过去
past

现在
present

未来
future

他无我地把自己融入所有的空间，融入所有的时间，他能达到这种境界，所以才叫做智者。

He dissolves himself without ego into all space, into all time. Because he can achieve this kind of state of mind, he is therefore referred to as a wise one.

我是山
我是水
我是云
我是鸟

I am the mountain.
I am the water.
I am the cloud.
I am the bird.

以上是我所说明的所知法、智及智者。

The foregoing teaching was my explanation of the Essential Truth of the universe, wisdom and being a wise one.

比丘们听完佛所说，都欢喜奉行。

After the monks heard the Buddha's words, they all joyfully went out to practise.

能正确地看清色、受、想、行、识五蕴皆空，即是明白生命的真理。
能调伏贪欲、断贪欲、越贪欲，是名为"智"。
能超越时空，融入时空，无我地融合于万象，就是"智者"。

To be able to correctly see through all five aggregates of activities in the universe is kong: including all the material world and all sensations, perceptions, decisions and consciousness. This means understanding the truth about life. To be able to tame desires, to detach from desires, and to transcend desires is the state of "wisdom". To transcend time and space, to dissolve into time and space, to melt without ego into unity with thousands of phenomena is being "a wise one".

自净其意
PURIFYING ONE'S OWN WILL

世界万物皆呈现它自己原本的样子，条件都各不相同。而人也是一样，每个人都有自己的条件、能力、性向、意愿和机会，也因而发展成了不一样的结果。但每个人自己觉得快乐、幸福或是痛苦、悲伤的人生观并不取决于他自己本身的条件与境遇，而是他自己心里怎么想……如果我们的心抱持着错误的负面观念，我们就活在痛苦之中；如果我们的心抱持着正确积极的观念，我们便活在快乐喜悦之中。

Thousands of things in the world all manifest their natural qualities with their own individual variations of conditions. This is also the case with humans since every person has his own conditions, abilities, personality, orientation and opportunities. Therefore, different results consequently develop. However, each person's outlook on life, whether happy and fortunate or painful and sad, is not determined by his own conditions and circumstances. Instead, his outlook is based on what kind of thoughts are in his mind... If our mind incorrectly holds negative concepts, then we will live in pain; if our mind correctly holds assertive concepts, then we will in turn live in joy.

111

佛陀说，天堂和地狱不在世界以外，天堂和地狱就在我们自己的这个六尺之躯里。

人会依过去的生活经验对任何事物的好、坏做出评断，对每天所遭遇的任何事物，他都会用心里的这个好坏标准去对照。

凡是对他有利的就心生欢喜，凡是不如己意的就心生不满。内心的情绪也因外在的境遇而生出贪、瞋、痴、喜、怒、哀、乐……身心因而受缚于外在时空环境的转变，不能做一个自主的人。他的身心不能由自己掌控，便成为客观条件变化的天堂与地狱的化现场所。

Buddha says: "Heaven and hell are not outside of this world. Heaven and hell are actually inside our own bodies that are several feet tall."

Each human often relies on his previous life experiences to judge everything as good versus bad. In regard to everyday encounters, he will always use this mental standard of good versus bad to make contrasts.

Anything that is beneficial to him brings his mind delight, and anything against his will brings dissatisfaction to his mind. The inner emotions also generate greed, resentment, delusion, pleasure, anger, sadness and happiness in response to external encounters... Both the body and the mind are therefore bonded to changes in time and space in the external environment and cannot be their own master. When he cannot control his own body and mind, he becomes the place of manifestation for heaven and hell according to changes in objective conditions.

我们觉知的世界真实只是集聚、存在、变化、消失的过程和心与物的再组合。

The world we know is actually in the constant process of creation, existence, destruction and emptiness, and is the cumulative manifestation of mental and material components.

世间的一切事物都是由原因和条件所产生的，原因和条件两者构成了因缘。
Everything in the world is the product of cause and conditions. These two factors, cause and conditions, make up preconditioned meaningful coincidences.

认清一切事物的实相，便能看清自己的执著妄念，因而对它们产生厌离的心。
If we can see through to the true nature of everything, we will then be able to see through our own attachments and delusions and in turn distance our mind from them.

能看清时空万物的实相，便能摆脱外在世界与内心世界的欲求而得到解脱。
能知晓一切事物的产生只是来自原因和条件的因缘聚合，便能看清自己的妄念执著，因而产生厌离欲望的心，摆脱外在世界与内心世界的束缚。

Once we are able to see through to the true nature of time, space and thousands of manifestations, we will be able to rid ourselves of attachment to the external world and our desires and thereby acquire relief. Recognize that the origins of everything are only the combined manifestations of causes and characteristics which make up preconditioned synchronicity. This will enable us to see through our own delusions and attachments, and subsequently be able to generate the mindset to distance ourselves from desires. This is how we can eventually get rid of our bondage to the external world and our egocentric impulses.

无常
impermanence

苦
suffering

空
kong

非我
no"I"

无明
Delusion

人由于愚痴和妄想而沉迷于梦幻之中。
Humans often indulge in fantasies due to delusion and daydreaming.

住
existence

异
deviation

误把灵魂想象成自己存在的实体，可以永续长存……
Mistaking the physical body in existence as ones's own spirit and permanently everlasting.

生
birth

灭
disappearance

他们的心仍攀缘于自我，他们渴望天堂的存在，
Their mind hangs onto the ego-self. They look forward to the existence of heaven...

而寻求死后的将来能进入天堂享受。
And expect to pursue an afterlife of enjoyment in heaven.

因此，他们无法发现正知、正见的无上幸福与不朽的真理。
Therefore, they will never be able to discover the ultimate joy and everlasting Truth of proper knowledge and a proper perspective.

人由于无知，一厢情愿地想获得不可能的结果。
人由于愚痴，只想相信自己愿意相信的事理，因此而更加不可能得到真知。
Due to ignorance humans single-mindedly wish to obtain impossible results. Due to delusion, they only believe in the theories and things that they themselves want to believe. Therefore, it becomes even more impossible to obtain true knowledge.

形式主义得不到成果

Doctrines Based on Formality Will Not Produce Fruits of Success

食肉、断食、裸体、光头、蓬头乱发、肮脏、粗糙皮肤、拜火、忏悔、唱诵赞美、奉献、祭祀、举行庆典……
Vegetarianism, fasting, going naked, going bald, not combing or cutting your hair, living in filth, letting the skin become dry and rough, worshipping fire, confessions, chanting to praise, making offerings, honouring with a rite, conducting celebration rituals...

这些行为都不能令人克服疑难，也不能净化人的身心。
None of these acts can help people solve their problems, nor purify their bodies and minds.

自我净化除了要知道净化的次第方法，最重要的是要自己亲自去实践。
佛陀指出通向彼岸的道路，修行者只有亲自去体验实践才有可能抵达最终的目标。路要亲自去走，形式主义的祭祀、唱诵、赞美并不能令我们抵达终点。
In order to purify the self, in addition to knowing the sequential methods for purification, the most important thing is to personally practise in one's own daily life. Although Buddha had pointed out the path to "the other shore" of enlightenment, those who cultivate can only possibly reach the final destination by personal experience and practice. The road has to be walked by one's own feet. All rituals, chanting and worshipping cannot enable us to arrive at the ultimate goal.

持戒、禅定、智慧
Abiding by Precepts, Centring the Mind, and Developing Wisdom

寻求觉悟之道首先必须修学三件事情，这就是：戒律的遵、心念的集中行和智慧的开发。

Pursuing the path to enlightenment requires that we first concentrate on the following three goals: abiding by precepts, centring the mind through meditation, and developing wisdom.

戒律是什么呢？遵守戒律以控制身心，把守五种感官的大门，再小的罪过也不去做，而对于善行则务必奋力去做。

What are precepts? We abide by the precepts to control our own bodies and minds: It is like watching the gate of the five senses. Do not act out the smallest sin; strive diligently to do good deeds.

心念的集中是什么呢？就是远离欲望和摆脱所有令我们引起情绪的事物，将心导入安定不动的境界。

What is meant by centring the mind through meditation? It means to distance oneself from desires, to rid oneself of all things that make one emotional, and to guide the mind into a state of tranquillity and stability by meditation.

智慧的发展是什么呢？就是要了解什么是苦、形成苦恼的原因、消灭苦恼的方法和如何达至无苦的境界。

What is meant by developing wisdom? That means to understand what suffering is, the reasons for suffering, the ways to be free of suffering, and how to reach the state of no suffering.

能做到戒、定、慧这三项，才可称为走上觉悟的正确道路。

After we are able to achieve these three goals—of commandments, stability and wisdom—then we can say we have walked onto the correct path for enlightenment.

是。
Yes.

要达到智慧的彼岸，心境得永恒的安详喜悦的修行次第是持戒、禅定、智慧。
持戒过简单的生活、不作恶，能令情绪不生；禅定将心止于一境，不妄想，会让欲望、贪念远离。
仔细观察自己的心，可以真正地了解苦的形式与苦的消失——苦集灭道的智慧。

To reach the other shore of wisdom as well as eternal peace and joy, the sequence of learning is abiding by precepts, centring the mind through meditation, and developing wisdom. Abiding by the precepts and living a simple lifestyle, as well as staying away from evil deeds, will minimize any emotions. Centring the mind through meditation—without any daydreaming—will keep desires and greed far away. By observing our own mind carfully, we will come to the true understanding of the formation of suffering, as well as the disappearance of suffering—the ultimate wisdom.

身语意的净化
Purification of
Body, Speech
and Mind

学道之人必须净化身、语、意三种行为。
Those who are learning the path to ultimate wisdom must purify all three types of conduct—that of the body, of speech, and of the mind.

不杀生、不偷盗、不犯邪恶的爱欲，就是净化身的行为。
No killing of any living beings, no taking of any materials without approval; no adultery. Such is the conduct for purifying the body.

不说谎、不恶口、不挑拨离间，就是净化语的行为。
No lying, no slander, no gossip to stir up conflicts. Such is the conduct for purifying speech.

不贪婪、不瞋恨、没有邪恶的见地，就是净化意的行为。
No greed, no resentment, no evil views. These are the conducts for purifying the mind.

持戒、禅定、智慧是抵达彼岸的修行次第。
持戒要先做到有关于个人的身、语、意三种行为的自我控制与净化，也就是行十善——不杀生、不偷盗、不邪淫、不妄言、不两舌、不恶口、不绮语、不贪欲、不瞋恚、不邪见。
Abiding by precepts, centring the mind through meditation, and the development of wisdom—this is the sequence for cultivation to reach the other shore of Nirvâna. Abiding by precepts requires that one first achieve self-control and purification concerning three areas of personal conduct: the body, personal speech, and the mind. This also means to carry on the ten types of kind deeds—no killing, no stealing, no adultery, no lying, no gossip, no slander, no flattery, no greed, no resentment, and no delusion.

语行
Proper Speech

一切语言分五种相对的形态：合乎时机与不合乎时机的言语；合乎事实与不合乎事实的言语；温和与粗野的言语；有益与无益的言语；慈祥与憎忿的言语。

All speech may be categorized into five opposing forms: timely versus untimely speech accurate versus inaccurate speech, gentle versus rough speech, useful versus useless speech, kind versus hateful speech.

我们日常言谈时要时时勉励自己：我的心不为外物所影响，粗野的话不应从我的口中溜出去，同情和慈悲要永远留存在心中，不让忿怒和憎恶的心生起。

During our daily conversations, we want to encourage ourselves all the time: My mind is not affected by external things; rough words should never slip out of my mouth; empathy and compassion will stay in my mind forever; anger and hatred will not be allowed to emerge in my mind.

人的行为引起了外在的反应，而这些反应又引起了人内心的感受。修行者要自我控制身、语、意的行为，因为错误、过度的行为会引来烦恼与痛苦。

而身、语、意三行中最易引起外来的纷争乃至影响我们情绪的就是语行了。

The behaviour of humans bring about external reactions and, in turn, these reactions bring about further inner feelings in people. A person who works on cultivation needs self-control to conduct the body, speech and the mind. Incorrect or compulsive behaviour will attract worries and pain. Among the three types of conduct—the body, speech and the mind—the easiest one to attract external conflicts and therefore affect our own mood is speech.

善不因为
别人而改变
Kindness Does
Not Change
Because of
Others

如果有人愚昧地对我做了错事，我将回报他无限的爱。
If somebody does me a wrong due to ignorance, I will return endless love to him.

他愈是作恶，
The more he does evil deeds...

我愈作善。
... the more I will do kind deeds.

我永远放出净善的芳香，如同一朵花一样。
I will always radiate the fragrance of purity and loving kindness, just like a flower.

每个人要做真正的自己，而不是随着时空境遇的不同而改变这个真正的我。一朵芳香的花朵不会因为别人认为它美或丑而改变它的芳香美丽。一个人也一样，如果我们是善的，就不应为别人的恶而使之变为恶啊！

Every person needs to be his true nature, instead of changing this true nature according to variations in time, space and encounters. A fragrant flower will not change its own aroma and beauty because others think it pretty or ugly. This should also be the case for a person. If we are kind, then we should not become evil ourselves because of other people's evil!

121

多闻
Be Knowled-
geable

我是这样听说的：那时佛陀住在舍卫国祇树给孤独园时，有一位其他教派的比丘来见佛陀……

This was the way I heard it: At the time, Buddha was living in the Jetavana Monastery in Srâvasti. A monk from another sect came to see Buddha...

释尊您常强调人应该多闻，请问什么才叫做多闻？

Honourable Sakyamuni, you often emphasize that we should be knowledgeable. May I ask what are the qualifications of being knowledgeable?

你用心听着，我来为你说。

Listen carefully, I will explain to you.

比丘们应该知道，如果他听闻领会到以下这样的道理，他就是多闻：

Monks should know. If one hears and appreciates the following kinds of principles, then one would qualify as being knowledgeable:

世间外在的一切形形色色是逼恼身心的东西，人应厌离它，并以正确的修行之法灭却它，而达到真空寂灭之境。

All shapes and colours in the external world are things that forcefully stimulate our body and mind. We should detach ourselves from them and use proper methods of cultivation to extinguish their impact on us. This is how we will reach the state of tranquillity in kong.

还有自身内心世界的受、想、行、识是逼恼身心的，人应厌离它，以正确的修行之法灭却它，以达到真空寂灭之境。

In addition, the sensations, perceptions, decisions and consciousness of our own inner world also forcefully stimulate our body and mind. We should detach from them and use proper methods of cultivation to extinguish their impact upon us. This is how we will reach the state of tranquillity in kong.

受
sensations

想
perceptions

行
decisions

识
consciousness

比丘啊！如果你听得这些并能贯通领会，你就可以称为多闻了。
My dear monk! If you can hear what I said and can integrate it into you own understanding, you will be qualified as being knowledgeable.

谢谢释尊。
Thank you, Honourable Sakyamuni.

哈哈哈，我懂得什么叫多闻了！
Ha, ha, ha! Now I understand what being knowledgeable is!

那位比丘听完佛所说，行了礼，高兴地告别而去。
After that monk listened to what Buddha said, he bowed and happily said goodbye.

佛陀一生说法数十载，重点只在强调一件事，即如何找出苦因并将之灭却而达到真空寂灭之境！
"多闻"即是听得佛陀所说的这个法并能体会实践，而不是听得很多不正确或无用的空洞言词。

Buddha lectured about Universal Truths for decades in his life. His emphasis was on one subject—how to find the causes of suffering and how to exterminate it in order to reach the state of tranquillity in kong! "Being knowledgeable" is knowing about this Truth explained by Buddha and being able to integrate and practise it in daily life. It does not mean to know about a great deal of incorrect or useless information that is irrelevant.

不修戒、定、慧者不是求道之人
Those Who Do Not Cultivate Precepts, Centre the Mind, and Develop Wisdom Are Not Seeking the True Path

求道修行的人最重要的是实践智者所指引的道路，朝向目标迈进。
学佛即是戒、定、慧的实行，如果不实际去实践，光是空口而谈，怎能抵达目标？

For those seeking the path to enlightenment, the most important part is to practise what is preached. This means to take the road directed by the wise ones who came before and forge ahead towards the goal. Learning Buddhism means to practise the precepts, centre the mind and develop wisdom. If we do not actually practise what we preach, how could empty talk get us to our goal?

苦解脱
Relief from Suffering

修行的目的是为了消除自我的痛苦烦恼而达至永恒的喜悦。
修行不是为了获得成就、知名度，也不是为了高人一等、成为别人的老师。
如果不能解除自己的痛苦，就是偏离了修行之路，不是真修行。
The purpose of spiritual cultivation is to rid ourselves of our own suffering and worries to reach eternal joy. Cultivation is not for achieving accomplishments or fame, nor is it for the sense of being "holier than thou", or for becoming a guru to others. If one is not capable of relieving one's own suffering, then one is deviating from the road of cultivation and not really cultivating spirituality.

掌握实际
Hold to Practising What Is Preached

兄弟们!
不要热衷于世俗的思想，把时间浪费在对于终止苦无益的事物上。
Brothers! Do not be infatuated with worldly thoughts and waste time on things that do not help you end suffering.

例如想确定这世界是永恒的还是无常的? 世界是有限的还是无限? ……
For example, like thinking about how to make sure that we know whether this world is eternal or transitional, or whether the universe has limits or has no boundary...

你们要把心致力于苦、集、灭、道四圣谛上，去了解并实践灭苦的方法。
You must focus your mind on the Four Noble Truths of suffering, the causes of suffering, the state of no ego-self and no suffering, and the path of cultivation to end suffering. Come to realize and practise the methods to exterminate suffering.

形而上的理论、超越吾人感官经验的玄学只会增加人的困惑，无益于消除痛苦的修行。实践是抵达真理的唯一方式，抵达而得智慧之后，很多事自然就知道了。
Supernatural theories and metaphysics that go beyond our sensory experiences only add to human confusion. They do not benefit the spiritual cultivation which extinguishes suffering. Practising the principles is the only means of reaching Truth. Once we have arrived there and have acquired wisdom, we will naturally understand many things without effort.

126

自灯明，法灯明

When One's Inner Light Is On, the Light of Truth Is On

阿难啊！你们要以自己为明灯，以自己为依处，没有别人能作为你们的依处。

Ananda, you should use your inner guidance as your beacon. Nobody else can always be depended upon.

以法为明灯，以法为依处，没有其他的能作为你的依据。

Use Essential Universal Truths as your beacon; use Essential Universal Truths as what you can depend upon. You can depend upon nothing else.

能够以自己为灯、以法为灯指引自己的道路的……

Those who are able to use the inner self as their beacon—Essential Universal Truths as the beacon— to guide their path...

这种人才是我们修行的比丘中境界最高的。

They are the ones who have reached the highest level among the monks who cultivate spirituality.

我们要依靠自己指引自己的道路；
我们要依据正确的方法，走向正确的方向。
我们每个人得要自救，别人是救不了我们的。

We must depend upon our inner guidance to direct us to the right path; we must depend upon the proper method to march in the right direction. Each of us has to help ourselves to salvation; nobody else is capable of our salvation.

路要自己走
Walk the Road
with Your
Own Feet

人，生而孤独……
A human is born alone...

死而孤独……
... and dies alone...

他要孤独地走向通往涅槃之路……
A human must walk alone towards the path to Nirvâna...

我只能指示你们的道路，但你们必须自己去走。
I can only direct your path, but you must walk it with your own feet.

佛陀不是一个神，不是救世主，而是一个老师，一个正确生活的典范。他生而为人，死而为人，每一个人都可以去学习他，每一个人都可以变成佛陀，变成一个觉悟的人。
Buddha is not a deity, not the saviour god of the world. Rather Buddha is a teacher, a role model for proper living. He was born a human and died as a human. Every person can learn from him. Every person can become Buddha, become an enlightened one.

结语
DO NOT BE DRIVEN BY MATERIAL DESIRES

佛法就是佛陀的教导。两千五百多年前，佛陀便悟出人生的道理，他说：
无限地扩展物质的欲望而忽略精神的净化是不智的，也是行不通的。不拓展丰富的心灵，让身心保持内在的和谐、喜悦，而盲目、一厢情愿地追逐名利、财富、纵情恣欲，贪图物质方面的享受，永远无法获得内在的健康与快乐。
我们应该自觉地去探讨心灵的奥秘，充实自己的内涵，朝向精神素质的内在进化发展。
最后终将发现，调御身心、开发精神宝藏所带来的喜悦竟然是如此的甜美与永恒啊……

Essential Universal Truths(Dharma) in Buddhism is the teaching of the Buddha.
More than twenty-five hundred years ago, the Buddha was already enlightened to the truth in life. He said:
"To endlessly expand our material desires while ignoring the purification of the spirit is unwise, as well as unsatisfying. If we do not expand the abundance of the spirit and enable the body and mind to keep their inner peace and joy, we will never be able to obtain internal health and happiness. Blindly and single-mindedly chasing after fame, fortune, wealth, indulgence in lust, and greed over material enjoyment, will never get us where we want to go."
With awareness, we should seek the secrets of our own spirits and enrich our inner content. We should march towards inner evolution and development in mental quality.
Eventually, we will find that the joy brought about by modifying our body and mind, and developing mental treasures in so surprisingly sweet and permanent...

BE THE REAL MASTER OF ONE'S OWN BODY AND MIND

每个人都有内在自我进化的能力，只要依正确的方式努力去实行，就必能得到成果。只要有心，就能分别善恶。只要有身体四肢，就能实践佛陀所说的道理。从一个深受时空环境变化的影响而痛苦烦恼的凡人，净化为一个自在自得、永远处于安详喜悦的觉悟者，成为自己身心的真正主人。

Every person has the inner ability to evolve. So long as one follows proper means to practise the principles diligently, one will definitely obtain the fruits of success. So long as one puts his mind to it, one will be able to distinguish goodness from evil. So long as one has a physical body with arms and legs, one will be able to implement the principles taught by the Buddha. An ordinary person is often deeply pained and troubled by changes in the time and space of his environment. The same person can be purified into an enlightened one who is carefree and always stays in peace and joy. This is how one becomes the real master of one's own body and mind.

附录·延伸阅读
APPENDIX Further reading

> 此部分为本书图画页的延伸阅读，
> 各段首所示的页码与图画页对应。

P14~P15　如是我闻（注）：

一时，佛住（注）舍卫国（注）祇树给孤独园（注）。

◎如是我闻：凡是佛经经首均加上这四个字，表示此经是结集者阿难尊者亲自听闻佛陀曾如此说。

◎住：居止、停留之意。

◎舍卫国：古印度拘萨罗国的首府，位于今日北印度近尼泊尔处。

◎祇树给孤独园：简称"祇园"。此园是给孤独长者向祇陀太子购买土地，建筑精舍供养佛陀之用，而园内的树林为祇陀太子所布施，因为是这两人所共同成就的功德，故合称"祇树给孤独园"。

P16　尔时，世尊告诸比丘（注）："当观色无常（注）。如是观者，则为正观，正观者，则生厌离；厌离者，喜贪尽；喜贪尽者，说心解脱。"

◎比丘：出家的修行人。

◎色无常：色者，指宇宙间所有一切存在的现象。无常，指事物多变化，色无常指眼所能见之各种形色、耳所能闻之各种声响，均有赖因缘而成，也将随缘而生灭，无法永住。

P17　"如是观受、想、行、识无常（注），如是观者，则为正观。正观者，则生厌离（注）；厌离者，喜贪尽；喜贪尽者，说心解脱。"

◎受、想、行、识无常：受、想、行、识四者和"色"合称五蕴；蕴是聚积。与现代心理学对比，受即感情、想即观念、行即意志、识即认识。

◎厌离：于事物生起讨厌之心，而思舍去、远离。

P18~P19　"如是，比丘！心解脱者，若欲自证，则能自证：我生已尽（注），梵行已立（注），所作已作（注），自知不受后有（注）。如观无常、苦、空、非我（注），亦复如是。"

时，诸比丘闻佛所说，欢喜奉行！

◎生已尽：即烦恼业缚已尽。从以往种种烦恼、生死的束缚中，得到解脱。

◎梵行已立：即脱离世间的爱欲，而过着正行、正精进的清净的生活。

◎所作已作：去除烦恼、得解脱的修行方法，都已经做到。

◎不受后有：现在已得解脱，不再随生死轮回流转，不再接受生死之身。

◎苦：与乐相对，泛指逼迫身心苦恼之状态。如人生之生、老、病、死诸苦。

◎空：指一切存在事物均虚幻不实，变化无常。

◉非我：指宇宙万物皆无独立实在的自体。

《杂阿含经卷第一——一》

P20　如是我闻：

一时，佛住舍卫国祇树给孤独园。

尔时，世尊告诸比丘："于色当正思惟，观色无常如实知。所以者何？比丘！于色正思惟，观色无常如实知者，于色欲贪断；欲贪断者，说心解脱。"

P23　"如是受、想、行、识当正思惟，观识无常如实知。所以者何？于识正思惟，观识无常者，则于识欲贪断；欲贪断者，说心解脱。"

P24　"如是心解脱者，若欲自证，则能自证：我生已尽，梵行已立，所作已作，自知不受后有。如是正思惟无常，若、空、非我，亦复如是。"

时，诸比丘闻佛所说，欢喜奉行！

《杂阿含经卷第一——二》

P25　如是我闻：

一时，佛住舍卫国祇树给孤独园。

尔时，世尊告诸比丘："于色不知、不明、不断、不离欲，则不能断苦；如是受、想、行、识，不知、不明、不断、不离欲，则不能断苦。"

P26　"诸比丘！于色若知、若明、若断、若离欲，则能断苦；如是受、想、行、识，若知、若明、若断、若离欲，则能堪任断苦。"

时，诸比丘闻佛所说，欢喜奉行！

《杂阿含经卷第一——三》

P27　如是我闻：

一时，佛住舍卫国祇树给孤独园。

尔时，世尊告诸比丘："于色不知、不明、不断、不离欲、心不解脱者，则不能越生、老、病、死怖；如是受、想、行、识、不知、不明、不断、不离欲贪、心不解脱者，则不能越生、老、病、死怖。"

P28　"比丘！于色若知、若明、若断、若离欲，则能越生、老、病、死怖。诸比丘！若知、若明、若离欲贪、心解脱者，则能越生、老、病、死怖；如是受、想、行、识，若知、若明、若断、若离欲贪、心解脱者，则能越生、老、病、死怖。"

时，诸比丘闻佛所说，欢喜奉行！

《杂阿含经卷第一——四》

P29　如是我闻：

一时，佛住舍卫国祇树给孤独园。

尔时，世尊告诸比丘："于色爱喜者，则于苦爱喜；于苦爱喜者，则于苦不得解脱、不明、不离欲。

如是受、想、行、识爱喜者，则爱喜苦；爱喜苦者，则于苦不得解脱。"

P30 "诸比丘！于色不爱喜者，则不喜于苦；不喜于苦者，则于苦得解脱。如是受、想、行、识不爱喜者，则不喜于苦；不喜于苦者，则于苦得解脱。"

"诸比丘！于色不知、不明、不离欲贪、心不解脱，贪心不解脱者，则不能断苦；如是受、想、行、识，不知、不明、不离欲贪、心不解脱者，则不能断苦。"

P31 "于色若知、若明、若离欲贪、心得解脱者，则能断苦；如是受、想、行、识，若知、若明、若离欲贪、心得解脱者，则能断苦。"

时，诸比丘闻佛所说，欢喜奉行！

《杂阿含经卷第一一五》

P32 如是我闻：

一时，佛住舍卫国祇树给孤独园。

尔时，世尊告诸比丘："于色不知、不明、不离欲贪、心不解脱者，则不能越生、老、病、死怖；如是受、想、行、识，不知、不明、不离欲贪、心不解脱者，则不能越生、老、病、死怖。"

P33 "诸比丘！于色若知、若明、若离欲贪、心解脱者，则能越生、老、病、死怖；如是受、想、行、识，若知、若明、若离欲贪、心解脱者，则能越生、老、病、死怖。"

时，诸比丘闻佛所说，欢喜奉行！

《杂阿含经卷第一一六》

P34 如是我闻：

一时，佛住舍卫国祇树给孤独园。

尔时，世尊告诸比丘："于色爱喜者，则于苦爱喜；于苦爱喜者，则于苦不得解脱。如是受、想、行、识爱喜者，则爱喜苦；爱喜苦者，则于苦不得解脱。"

P37 "诸比丘！于色不爱喜者，则不喜于苦；不喜于苦者，则于苦得解脱。如是受、想、行、识不爱喜者，则不喜于苦；不喜于苦者，则于苦得解脱。"

时，诸比丘闻佛所说，欢喜奉行！

P38 无常及苦·空，非我·正思惟，

无知等四种，及于色喜乐[注]。

◉无常及苦……及于色喜乐：此为古代集经之结颂，目的在使诵习者方便记忆、领悟经义。

《杂阿含经卷第一一七》

P39 如是我闻：

一时，佛住舍卫国祇树给孤独园。

尔时，世尊告诸比丘："过去、未来色无常，况现在色！圣弟子！如是观者，不愿过去色[注]，不欣未来色[注]，于现在色厌、离欲、正向灭尽。"

◉不愿过去色：不愿念过去的色境。

P40 "如是，过去、未来受、想、行、识无常，况现在识！圣弟子！如是观者，不愿过去识，不欣未来识，于现在识厌、离欲、正向灭尽。如无常，苦、空、非我^(注)亦复如是。"

时，诸比丘闻佛所说，欢喜奉行。

◉不欣未来色：不对未来的色境，升起欣喜、期待的心。

◉苦、空、非我：正确观察过去、现在、未来三世诸法本质之苦、空、非我。

《杂阿含经卷第一—八》

P41　如是我闻：

一时，佛住舍卫国祇树给孤独园。

尔时，世尊告诸比丘："色无常，无常即苦，苦即非我，非我者亦非我所^(注)。如是观者，名真实正观。如是受、想、行、识无常，无常即苦，苦即非我，非我者亦非我所。如是观者，名真实正观。^(注)"

◉我所：我之所有。

◉如是观者，名真实正观：能如实地以智慧观照色之无常，即能得真实智，所以称"真实正观"。

P42 "圣弟子！如是观者，厌于色，厌受、想、行、识，厌故不乐，不乐故得解脱。解脱者真实智生：我生已尽，梵行已立，所作已作，自知不受后有。"

时，诸比丘闻佛所说，欢喜奉行！

《杂阿含经卷第一—九》

P43　如是我闻：

一时，佛住舍卫国祇树给孤独园。

尔时，世尊告诸比丘："色无常，无常即苦，苦即非我，非我者即非我所。如是观者，名真实正观。如是受、想、行、识无常，无常即苦，苦即非我，非我者即非我所。如是观者，名真实正观。"

P44 "圣弟子！如是观者，于色解脱，于受、想、行、识解脱。我说是等解脱于生、老、病、死、忧、悲、苦恼。"

时，诸比丘闻佛所说，欢喜奉行！

《杂阿含经卷第一—十》

P45　如是我闻：

一时，佛住舍卫国祇树给孤独园。

尔时，世尊告诸比丘："色无常，若因、若缘^(注)生诸色者，彼亦无常。无常因、无常缘所生诸色，云何有常？如是受、想、行、识无常，若因、若缘生诸识者，彼亦无常。无常因、无常缘所生诸识，云何有常？如是，诸比丘！色无常，受、想、行、识无常。无常者则是苦，若者则非我，非我者则非我所。"

◉因、缘：因是指主要的原因，如种子；缘是指次要、间接的条件，如水分、土壤、阳光等；由此种种因缘和合，便能生出植物、稻谷来。

P46 "圣弟子！如是观者，厌于色，厌于受、想、行、识。厌者不乐，不乐则解脱，解脱知见：我生已尽，梵行已立，所作已作，自知不受后有。"

时，诸比丘闻佛所说，欢喜奉行！

《杂阿含经卷第一——十一》

P47 如是我闻：

一时，佛住舍卫国祇树给孤独园。

尔时，世尊告诸比丘："色无常，若因、若缘生诸色者，彼亦无常。无常因、无常缘所生诸色，云何有常？受、想、行、识无常，若因、若缘生诸识者，彼亦无常。无常因、无常缘所生诸识，云何有常？"

P48 "如是，比丘！色无常，受、想、行、识无常。无常者则是苦，若苦者则非我，非我者则非我所。如是观者，名真实正观。圣弟子！如是观者，于色解脱，于受、想、行、识解脱，我说是等为解脱生、老、病、死、忧、悲、苦恼。"

时，诸比丘闻佛所说，欢喜奉行！

《杂阿含经卷第一——十二》

P49 如是我闻：

一时，佛住舍卫国祇树给孤独园。

尔时，世尊告诸比丘："若众生于色不味者，则不染于色；以众生于色味故，则有染著。如是众生于受、想、行、识不味者，彼众生则不染于识；以众生味^(注)受、想、行、识故，彼众生染^(注)著于识。"

●味：又名味著，贪著而享乐。

●染：指烦恼。当动词时，称染著，就是执著。

P50 "诸比丘！若色于众生不为患^(注)者，彼诸众生不应厌色；以色为众生患故，彼诸众生则厌于色。如是受、想、行、识不为患者，彼诸众生不应厌识；以受、想、行、识为众生患故，彼诸众生则厌于识。"

●患：祸患。

P51 "诸比丘！若色于众生无出离^(注)者，彼诸众生不应出离于色；以色于众生有出离故，彼诸众生出离于色。如是受、想、行、识于众生无出离者，彼诸众生不应出离于识；以受、想、行、识于众生有出离故，彼诸众生出离于识。"

●出离：超出脱离。指超出生死轮回之苦而得解脱。

P52 "诸比丘！若我于此五受阴^(注)不如实知^(注)味是味、患是患、离是离者，我于诸天、若魔、若梵、沙门、婆罗门、天、人众中，不脱、不出、不离，永住颠倒，亦不能自证得阿耨多罗三藐三菩提^(注)。"

●于此五受阴：指于色、受、想、行、识等五取蕴。

●如实知：正确地了知真如实相。

●阿耨多罗三藐三菩提：译为无上正等正觉。即真正平等觉知宇宙一切真理的大智慧。

135

P53 "诸比丘！我以如实知此五受阴味是味、患是患、离是离故，我于诸天、若魔、若梵、沙门、婆罗门、天、人众中，自证得脱^(注)、得出、得离、得解脱结缚，永不住颠倒，亦能自证得阿耨多罗三藐三菩提。"

时，诸比丘闻佛所说，欢喜奉行！

◎得脱：得以出离、解脱。

《杂阿含经卷第一——十三》

P54 如是我闻：

一时，佛住舍卫国祇树给孤独园。

尔时，世尊告诸比丘："我昔于色味有求有行^(注)，若于色味随顺觉，则于色味以智慧如实见；如是于受、想、行、识味有求有行，若于受、想、行、识味随顺觉，则于识味以智慧如实见。"

◎于色味有求有行：对于色味进行追求；追求于色味。

P55 "诸比丘！我于色患有求有行，若于色患随顺觉，则于色患以智慧如实见；如是受、想、行、识患有求有行，若于识患随顺觉，则于识患以智慧如实见。"

"诸比丘！我于色离有求有行，若于色随顺觉，则于色离以智慧如实见；如是受、想、行、识离有求有行，若于受、想、行、识离随顺觉，则于受、想、行、识离以智慧如实见。"

P56 "诸比丘！我于五受阴不如实知味是味、患是患、离是离者，我于诸天、若魔、若梵、沙门、婆罗门、天、人众中，不脱、不离、不出，永住颠倒，不能自证得阿耨多罗三藐三菩提。"

"诸比丘！我以如实知五受阴味是味、患是患、离是离，我于诸天、若魔、若梵、沙门、婆罗门、天、人众中，已脱、已离、已出，永不住颠倒，能自证得阿耨多罗三藐三菩提。"

时，诸比丘闻佛所说，欢喜奉行！

P57 过去四种说，厌离及解脱；

二种说因缘，味亦复二种。

《杂阿含经卷第一——十四》

P58~P59 如是我闻：一时，佛住舍卫国祇树给孤独园。

尔时，有异比丘^(注)来诣佛所，稽首佛足，却住一面，白佛言："善哉！世尊！今当为我略说法要，我闻法已，当独一静处，修不放逸^(注)。修不放逸已，当复思惟：所以善男子^(注)出家，剃除须发，身着法服，信家、非家、出家^(注)，为究竟无上梵行，现法作证^(注)：我生已尽，梵行已立，所作已作，自知不受后有。"

◎异比丘：即"一比丘"之意。

◎不放逸：不怠情。

◎善男子：称呼信佛而未出家之男子。

◎信家、非家、出家：已正信佛教，而现在出家处于非家。

◎现法作证：在现实生活中实践梵行，而能以智慧了知（我生已尽……）。

P60 尔时，世尊告彼比丘："善哉！善哉！比丘快说此言：'云当为我略说法要，我闻法已，独一静处，修不放逸。……乃至自知不受后有。'如是说耶？"

比丘白佛："如是，世尊！"

P63 佛告比丘："谛听！谛听！善思念之，当为汝说，比丘！若随使使者，即随使死^(注)；若随死者，为取所缚。比丘！若不随使使，则不随使死；不随使死者，则于取解脱。"

比丘白佛："知已，世尊！知已，善逝！"

◉ 若随使使者，即随使死：正当执著于烦恼时，已被烦恼所缚。随使使，前一个"使"当名词，指执著等诸烦恼；后一个"使"作动词，有使促身心的意思。

P64 佛告比丘："汝云何于我略说法中，广解其义？"

比丘白佛言："世尊！色随使使、色随使死；随使使、随使死者，则为取所缚。如是受、想、行、识，随使使、随使死；随使使、随使死者，为取所缚。"

"世尊！若色不随使使、不随使死；不随使使、不随使死者，则于取解脱。如是受、想、行、识，不随使使、不随使死；不随使使、不随使死者，则于取解脱。如是，世尊！略说法中，广解其义。"

P65 佛告比丘："善哉！善哉！比丘于我略说法中，广解其义。所以者何？色随使使、随使死；随使使、随使死者，则为取所缚。如是受、想、行、识，随使使、随使死；随使使、随使死者，则为取所缚。"

"比丘！色不随使使、不随使死；不随使使、不随使死者，则于取解脱。如是受、想、行、识，不随使使、不随使死；不随使使、不随使死者，则于取解脱。"

P66 时，彼比丘闻佛所说，心大欢喜，礼佛而退。独在静处，精勤修习，住不放逸。精勤修习，住不放逸已，思惟：所以善男子出家，剃除须发，身着法服，信家、非家、出家……乃至自知不受后有。

时，彼比丘即成罗汉，心得解脱。

◉ 罗汉：声闻乘的最高果位。含有三义：一、杀贼，杀尽烦恼贼；二、无生，永入涅槃不受后有；三、应供，当受天上人间的供养。

《杂阿含经卷第一——十五》

P67~P68 如是我闻：

一时，佛住舍卫国祇树给孤独园。

尔时有异比丘来诣佛所。所问如上^(注)，差别者^(注)："随使使、随使死者，则增诸数^(注)；若不随使使、不随使死者，则不增诸数。"

佛告比丘："汝云何于我略说法中，广解其义？"

◉ 所问如上：该比丘所问佛的内容和前经中相同。以下各经亦同。

◉ 差别者：和前经不一样的地方。

◉ 则增诸数：就会增加于生死轮回中流转的次数。

P69 时，彼比丘白佛言："世尊！若色随使使、随使死；随使使、随使死者，则增诸数。如是受、想、行、识，随使使、随使死；随使使，随使死者，则增诸数。"

"世尊！若色不随使使、不随使死；不随使使、不随使死者，则不增诸数。如是受、想、行、识，不随使使、不随使死；不随使使，不随使死者，则不增诸数。如是，世尊！我于略说法中，广解其义。"如是……乃至得阿罗汉，心得解脱。

《杂阿含经卷第一—十六》

P72~73　如是我闻：

一时，佛住舍卫国祇树给孤独园。

有异比丘从座起，偏袒右肩^(注)，合掌^(注)白佛言："善哉！世尊！为我略说法要，我闻法已，当独一静处，专精思惟，住不放逸。所以善男子出家，剃除须发，身着法服，信家、非家、出家学道，为究竟无上梵行，现法身作证：我生已尽，梵行已立，所作已作，自知不受后有。"

◉偏袒右肩：将袈裟披在左肩上，袒露出右肩。如此穿着，一方面方便工作，再者随时准备听候长辈之命而服事之。

◉合掌：又称合十，即左右双掌及十指对合，表示极为恭敬，一心服从。

P74~P75　尔时，世尊告彼比丘："善哉！善哉！汝作是说：'世尊！为我略说法要，我于略说法中，广解其义，当独一静处，专精思惟，住不放逸。……乃至自知不受后有。'汝如是说耶？"

比丘白佛："如是，世尊！"

佛告比丘："谛听！谛听！善思念之，当为汝说。比丘！非汝所应之法^(注)，宜速断除。断彼法者，以义饶益^(注)，长夜安乐^(注)。"

◉非汝所应之法：此"法"指色、受、想、行、识，这些都不是我们所有的。

◉以义饶益：断除非法非义，而于正义增长。

◉长夜安乐：除去无明长夜之不安，而得到安乐。

P76　时，彼比丘白佛言："知已，世尊！知已，善逝！"

佛告比丘："云何于我略说法中，广解其义？"

比丘白佛言："世尊！色非我所应，宜速断除；受、想、行、识非我所应，宜速断除。以义饶益，长夜安乐。是故，世尊！我于世尊略说法中，广解其义。"

P77　佛言："善哉！善哉！比丘，汝于我略说法中，广解其义。所以者何？色者非汝所应，宜速断除；如是受、想、行、识非汝所应，宜速断除。断除已，以义饶益，长夜安乐。"

时，彼比丘闻佛所说，心大欢喜，礼佛而退。独一静处，精勤修习，住不放逸。精勤修习，住不放逸已，思惟：所以善男子出家，剃除须发，身着法服，正信、非家、出家……乃至自知不受后有。

时，彼比丘成阿罗汉，心得解脱。

《杂阿含经卷第一—十七》

P78　如是我闻：

一时，佛住舍卫国祇树给孤独园。

尔时，有异比丘从座起，偏袒右肩，为佛作礼，却住一面，而白佛言："善哉！世尊！为我略说法要，我闻法已，当独一静处，专精思惟，不放逸住。……乃至自知不受后有。"

P79　佛告比丘："善哉！善哉！汝作如是说：'世尊！为我略说法要，我闻法已，当独一静处，专精思惟，不放逸住。……乃至自知不受后有。'耶？"

时，彼比丘白佛言："如是，世尊！"

佛告比丘："谛听！谛听！善思念之，当为汝说。若非汝所应，亦非余人所应，此法宜速除断。断彼法已，以义饶益，长夜安乐。"

P80 时，彼比丘白佛言："知已，世尊！知已，善逝！"

佛告比丘："云何于我略说法中，广解其义？"

比丘白佛言："世尊！色非我、非我所应，亦非余人所应，是法宜速除断。断彼法已，以义饶益，长夜安乐。如是受、想、行、识，非我、非我所应，亦非余人所应，宜速除断。断彼法已，以义饶益，长夜安乐。是故，我于如来略说法中，广解其义。"

P81 佛告比丘："善哉！善哉！汝云何于我略说法中，广解其义？所以者何？比丘！色非我、非我所应，亦非余人所应，是法宜速除断。断彼法已，以义饶益，长夜安乐。如是受、想、行、识，非我、非我所应，亦非余人所应，是法宜速除断。断彼法已，以义饶益，长夜安乐。"

P82 时，彼此丘闻佛所说，心大欢喜，礼佛而退。独一静处，精勤修习，不放逸住……乃至自知不受后有。

时，彼比丘心得解脱，成阿罗汉。

《杂阿含经卷第一—十八》

P85 如是我闻：

一时，佛住舍卫国祇树给孤独园。

尔时，有异比丘从座起，为佛作礼，而白佛言："世尊！为我略说法要，我闻法已，当独一静处，专精思惟，不放逸住。不放逸住已，思惟：所以善男子正信家、非家、出家……乃至自知不受后有。"

P86 尔时，世尊告彼比丘："善哉！善哉！汝今作是说：'善哉！世尊！为我略说法要，我闻法已，当独一静处，专精思惟，不放逸住……乃至自知不受后有。'耶？"

比丘白佛言："如是，世尊！"

P87 佛告比丘："谛听！谛听！善思念之，当为汝说。比丘！结所系法宜速除断，断彼法已，以义饶益，长夜安乐。"

时，彼比丘白佛言："知已，世尊！知已，善逝！"

P88 佛告比丘："汝云何于我略说法中，广解其义？"

比丘白佛言："世尊！色是结所系^{（注）}，是结所系法宜速除断。断彼法已，以义饶益，长夜安乐。如是受、想、行、识结所系，是结所系法宜速除断。断彼法已，以义饶益，长夜安乐。是故我于世尊略说法中，广解其义。"

◉色是结所系法：色是烦恼诸结所依止。

P89 佛告比丘："善哉！善哉！汝于我略说法中，广解其义。所以者何？色是结所系法，此法宜速除断。断彼法已，以义饶益，长夜安乐。如是受、想、行、识是结所系法，此法宜速除断。断彼法已，以义饶益，长夜安乐。"

P90　时，彼比丘闻佛所说，心大欢喜，礼佛而退。独一静处，专精思惟，不放逸住……乃至心得解脱，成阿罗汉。

《杂阿含经卷第一—十九》

P91　如是我闻：

一时，佛住舍卫国祇树给孤独园。

尔时，有异比丘从座起，为佛作礼，而白佛言："世尊！为我略说法要，我闻法已，当独一静处，专精思惟，不放逸住。不放逸住已，思惟：所以善男子正信、非家、出家……乃至自知不受后有。"

P92　尔时，世尊告彼比丘："善哉！善哉！汝今作是说：'善哉！世尊！为我略说法要，我闻法已，当独一静处，专精思惟，不放逸住。……乃至自知不受后有。'耶？"

比丘白佛言："如是，世尊！"

P93　佛告比丘："谛听！谛听！善思念之，当为汝说。比丘！动摇时，则为魔所缚；若不动者，则解脱波旬(注)。"

比丘白佛言："知已，世尊！知，善逝！"

●动摇时，则为魔所缚；若不动者，则解脱波旬：一执取（五蕴）时，即为魔所缚；不执取（五蕴）时，魔将不能为缚，已从波旬得解脱。波旬，意为杀者，恶者，指扰乱修行的恶者。

P94　佛告比丘："汝云何于我略说法中，广解其义？"

比丘白佛言："世尊！色动摇时，则为魔所缚；若不动者，则解脱波旬。如是受、想、行、识动摇时，则为魔所缚；若不动者，则解脱波旬。是故我于世尊略说法中，广解其义。"

P95　佛告比丘："善哉！善哉！汝于我略说法中，广解其义。所以者何？若色动摇时，则为魔所缚；若不动者，则解脱波旬。如是受、想、行、识动摇时，则为魔所缚；若不动者，则解脱波旬。"……乃至自知不受后有，心得解脱，成阿罗汉。

《杂阿含经卷第一—二一》

P98　如是我闻：

一时，佛住舍卫国祇树给孤独园。

尔时，有比丘名劫波，来诣佛所，头面礼足(注)，却住一面，白佛言："如世尊说，比丘心得善解脱。世尊！云何比丘心得善解脱？"

●头面礼足：头面低垂，顶礼佛足，表非常恭敬之意。

P99　尔时，世尊告劫波曰："善哉！善哉！能问如来心善解脱。善哉！劫波！谛听！谛听！善思念之，当为汝说。劫波！当观知诸所有色，若过去、若未来、若现在，若内、若外、若麁、若细，若好、若丑，若远、若近，彼一切悉皆无常。正观无常已，色爱即除(注)。色爱除已，心善解脱。"

◉色爱即除：色爱是随物质产生的爱欲，一旦能觉知到色是无常，就能断除对它的执著而得解脱。

P100 "如是观受、想、行、识，若过去、若未来、若现在，若内、若外，若麁、若细，若好、若丑，若远、若近，彼一切悉皆无常。正观无常已，识爱^(注)即除。识爱除已，我说心善解脱。劫波！如是，比丘心善解脱者，如来说名心善解脱。所以者何？爱欲断故。爱欲断者，如来说名心善解脱。"

◉识爱：指人心中存有的我执、爱着。

P101 时，劫波比丘闻佛所说，心大欢喜，礼佛而退。

尔时，劫波比丘受佛教已，独一静处，专精思惟，不放逸住……乃至自知不受后有，心善解脱，成阿罗汉。

《杂阿含经卷第一——二二》

P102 如是我闻：

一时，佛住王舍城迦兰陀竹园。

尔时，尊者罗睺罗^(注)往诣佛所，头面礼足，却住一面，白佛言："世尊！云何知、云何见我此识身及外境界一切相，能令无有我、我所见、我慢使系着？"

◉罗睺罗：佛的嫡子，也是佛十大弟子之一，以密行第一著称。

P103 佛告罗睺罗："善哉！善哉！能问如来：'云何知、云何见我此识身及外境界一切相，令无有我、我所见、我慢使系着？'耶？"

罗睺罗白佛言："如是，世尊！"

P104 佛告罗睺罗："善哉！谛听！谛听！善思念之，当为汝说。罗睺罗！当观若所有诸色，若过去、若未来、若现在，若内、若外，若麁、若细，若好、若丑，若远、若近，彼一切悉皆非我、不异我、不相在^(注)，如是平等慧正观^(注)。"

◉非我、不异我、不相在：即无我、无我所，二者并不同在，五蕴与我不相属。

◉平等慧正观：如实地以正慧做观照。

P105 "如是受、想、行、识，若过去、若未来、若现在，若内、若外，若麁、若细，若好、若丑，若远、若近，彼一切非我、不异我、不相在，如是平等慧如实观。"

P106 "如是，罗睺罗！比丘如是知、如是见。如是知、如是见者，于此识身及外境界一切相，无有我、我所见、我慢使系着。"

P107 "罗睺罗！比丘若如是于此识身及外境界一切相，无有我、我所见、我慢使系着者，比丘是名断爱欲，转去诸结，正无间等^(注)，究竟苦边^(注)。"

时，罗睺罗闻佛所说，欢喜奉行！

◉正无间等：正断烦恼，不再为惑业所迷。

◉究竟苦边：苦边，指三恶道之生死苦境界。究竟苦边，即能完全解脱。

《杂阿含经卷第一——二三》

P108　如是我闻：

一时，佛住王舍城迦兰陀竹园。

尔时，世尊告罗睺罗："比丘！云何知、云何见我此识身及外境界一切相，无有我、我所见、我慢使系着？"

P109　罗睺罗白佛言："世尊为法主(注)、为导、为覆。善哉！世尊当为诸比丘演说此义，诸比丘从佛闻已，当受持奉行。"

◉法主：世尊说法第一，无人能比，故尊称为法主。

P110　佛告罗睺罗："谛听！谛听！善思念之，当为汝说。"

罗睺罗白佛："唯然，受教！"

P113　佛告罗睺罗："当观诸所有色，若过去、若未来、若现在，若内、若外，若麁、若细，若好、若丑，若远、若近，彼一切非我、不异我、不相在，如是平等慧如实观。如是受、想、行、识，若过去、若未来、若现在，若内、若外，若麁、若细，若好、若丑，若远、若近，彼一切非我、不异我、不相在，如是平等慧如实观。"

P114　"比丘！如是知、如是见我此识身及外境界一切相，无有我、我所见、我慢使系着。"

"罗睺罗！比丘如是识身及外境界一切相，无有我、我所见、我慢使系着者，超越疑心，远离诸相，寂静解脱，是名比丘断除爱欲，转去诸结，正无间等，究竟苦边。"

P115　时，罗睺罗闻佛所说，欢喜奉行！

使·增诸数，非我·非彼，结系·动摇，

劫波所问，亦罗睺罗，所问二经。

《杂阿含经卷第一—二四》

P116　如是我闻：

一时，佛住舍卫国祇树给孤独园。

时，有异比丘来诣佛所，为佛作礼，却住一面，白佛言："如世尊说多闻，云何为多闻？"

佛告比丘："善哉！善哉！汝今问我多闻义耶？"

比丘白佛："唯然，世尊！"

P117　佛告比丘："谛听！善思！当为汝说。比丘当知：若闻色是生厌、离欲、灭尽、寂静法，是名多闻(注)，如是闻受、想、行、识，是生厌、离欲、灭尽、寂静法，是名多闻比丘，是名如来所说多闻。"

时，彼比丘闻佛所说，踊跃欢喜，作礼而去。

◉多闻：一般指博学多闻，本经则以为由听闻受持经法而能厌离五蕴，方可称多闻。

《杂阿含经卷第一—二五》

P118　如是我闻：

一时，佛住舍卫国祇树给孤独园。

尔时，有异比丘来诣佛所，头面礼足，却住一面，白佛言："如世尊所说法师，云何名为法师？"

佛告比丘："善哉！善哉！汝今欲知如来所说法师义耶？"

P119 比丘白佛："唯然，世尊！"

佛告比丘："谛听！善思！当为汝说。"

佛告比丘："若于色说是生厌、离欲、灭尽、寂静法者，是名法师；若于受、想、行、识，说是生厌、离欲、灭尽、寂静法者，是名法师，是名如来所说法师。"

时，彼比丘闻佛所说，踊跃欢喜，作礼而去。

《杂阿含经卷第一—二六》

P120 如是我闻：

一时，佛住舍卫国祇树给孤独园。

尔时，有异比丘来诣佛所，头面作礼，却住一面，白佛言："如世尊说法次法向[注]，云何法次法向？"

◉法次法向：于色向厌、离欲、灭尽之谓。

P121 佛告比丘："善哉！善哉！汝今欲知法次法向耶？"

比丘白佛："唯然，世尊！"

P122 佛告比丘："谛听！善思！当为汝说。比丘！于色向厌、离欲、灭尽，是名法次法向；如是受、想、行、识，于识向厌、离欲、灭尽，是名法次法向。"

时，彼比丘闻佛所说，踊跃欢喜，作礼而去。

《杂阿含经卷第一—二七》

P123 如是我闻：

一时，佛住舍卫国祇树给孤独园。

尔时，有异比丘来诣佛所，头面礼足，却住一面，白佛言："世尊！如世尊所说，得见法涅槃，云何比丘得见法涅槃？"

P124 佛告比丘："善哉！善哉！汝今欲知见法涅槃耶？"

比丘白佛："唯然，世尊！"

佛告比丘："谛听！善思！当为汝说。"

P125 佛告比丘："于色生厌、离欲、灭尽，不起诸漏，心正解脱，是名比丘见法涅槃；如是受、想、行、识，于识生厌、离欲、灭尽，不起诸漏，心正解脱，是名比丘见法涅槃。"

时，彼比丘闻佛所说，踊跃欢喜，作礼而去。

《杂阿含经卷第一—二八》

P126 如是我闻：

　　一时，佛住舍卫国祇树给孤独园。

　　尔时，有异比丘名三蜜离提，来诣佛所，头面礼足，却住一面，白佛言："如世尊说说法师，云何名为说法师？"

P127　佛告比丘："汝今欲知说法师义耶？"
　　比丘白佛："唯然，世尊！"

P128　佛告比丘："谛听！善思！当为汝说。若比丘于色说厌、离欲、灭尽，是名说法师；如是于受、想、行、识，于识说厌、离欲、灭尽，是名说法师。"
　　时，彼比丘闻佛所说，踊跃欢喜，作礼而去。

《杂阿含经卷第一— 二九》

法句经

THE DHARMA SUTRA

法句
DHARMA SAYINGS

"法句"是法、教法、真理、法则之意，也是佛陀所印证过之后，用语言经句传给后人遵循而行的道迹。
所以法句有三种含义：
一、真理的章句，真理的言语。
二、佛陀教法的偈句。
三、依佛陀所言说的真理，可以遵循以达涅槃之境的道迹。
《法句经》的成书约在公元前 350 年，为佛弟子们在第二次结集后所摘录成册。
由于佛教流传的地区越来越广，部派的分裂也愈来愈多，因此《法句经》的编辑异本也愈来愈多。
目前留在世上通行的《法句经》有南传、北传两种，内容大致相同，但也有小部分稍异。
这本书所依据的原典为南传佛教所采用的南传《法句经》。

"Dharma Sayings" represents
Buddhist Dharma, Buddha's teaching methods, essential universal Truths, and laws of the universe.
They have been personally tested to be true by Buddha.
These are written scriptures that provide later generations with a trail to follow.
Therefore, Dharma Sayings contains three meanings:
1. written words of truth
2. quotes from Buddha's method of teaching
3. the true path to Nirvana as taught by Buddha
The Dharma Sutra, Dhammapada in the Pali language, and The Dharma Sayings Sutra in Chinese characters, origi-
nated about 350 BC. The scripture was edited into a volume after Buddhists gathered for a second council of disci-
ples, about 150 years after Sakyamuni Buddha passed away.
However, because Buddhism spread more widely in spatial terms and became diversified with numerous sects, more
and more different versions of the edited volume appeared.
At present, there are two popular versions, representing the southern-and northern-spread editions respectively.
Their contents are generally in agreement, but varied in minor details.
This book was besed on the version adopted by the Buddhism that spread south.

两千五百年前，世界各地的人类慢慢开启了人性的自觉，而由于自觉产生出智慧。

这时世界上各地各个民族都几乎同时出现了看清宇宙世界本质的智者，而其中有一位至今都影响深远的人物，那就是印度的佛陀。

《法句经》这本书摘录了两千五百年前的这位历史上的佛陀所说的话，是古代印度佛教的长老们摘录佛陀教法的偈句，是佛陀所说的真理言语，也是佛陀所指引真理的道迹。

当年《法句经》的编辑当然是为了作为佛弟子的修行指南，希望通过短短的经句能让佛弟子们遵照实行。

而今天"漫画《法句经》"的出版，也希望读者能通过这本书对当年这位历史上的佛陀有更活生生的认识，并能从他简短的言语之中获得正确的认知，乃至遵照着去实行而获得自己身心的净化，乃至直达寂静安详的最后彼岸。

Twenty-five hundred years ago, people around the world slowly opened up to an awareness of their human nature and innate wisdom.

During that time, wise ones, who saw through the truth of the universe, were appearing in many cultures around the world.

Among them was a person who has had far-reaching influence until today— Buddha Sakyamuni of India.

The Dharma Sutra is a compendium of words spoken by this historical Buddha around 2500 years ago.

They were the parts of the Buddha's teachings that were most often quoted, as recorded by Buddhist elders in ancient India.

They were the language of truth from Buddha, as well as the path to truth as directed by Buddha.

At the time of its consolidation, this Sutra was meant to serve as the guiding post for the cultivation of Buddhist disciples.

The short verses were meant for easy incorporation into daily practice.

Today,
the publication of this illustrated Sutra is meant to serve a similar purpose.

It is the author's wish that readers may come to know the historical Buddha better through this book, that they may gain "proper" knowledge from his concise verses, that they may follow his guidance to practise the principles, and that they may purify their own bodies and minds until they eventually arrive at "the Other Shore" of tranquillity and peace.

法句经
THE DHARMA SUTRA (DHAMMAPADA, THE DHARMA SAYINGS SUTRA)

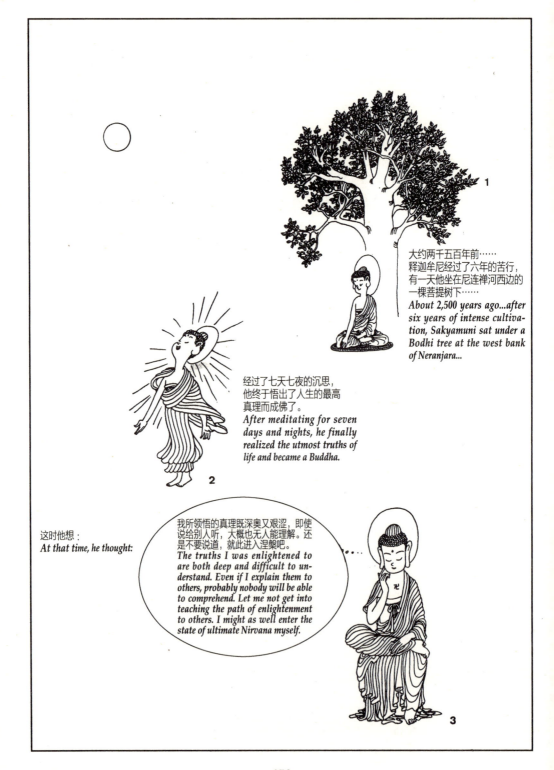

大约两千五百年前……
释迦牟尼经过了六年的苦行，
有一天他坐在尼连禅河西边的
一棵菩提树下……
*About 2,500 years ago...after
six years of intense cultivation, Sakyamuni sat under a
Bodhi tree at the west bank
of Neranjara...*

1

经过了七天七夜的沉思，
他终于悟出了人生的最高
真理而成佛了。
*After meditating for seven
days and nights, he finally
realized the utmost truths of
life and became a Buddha.*

2

这时他想：
At that time, he thought:

我所领悟的真理既深奥又艰涩，即使
说给别人听，大概也无人能理解。还
是不要说道，就此进入涅槃吧。
*The truths I was enlightened to
are both deep and difficult to understand. Even if I explain them to
others, probably nobody will be able
to comprehend. Let me not get into
teaching the path of enlightenment
to others. I might as well enter the
state of ultimate Nirvana myself.*

3

传说……
这时天上诸神的代表"梵天"出现在释迦牟尼的面前，劝告他说：
According to legend, a representative of gods from the Realm of the Heavens appeared in front of Sakyamuni at that time and pleaded with him:

"请看看这池里的莲花，有的花开在水面清香逸远，有的却埋于污泥……"
"Please take a look at the lotus blossoms in this pond. Some flowers bloom above water with far-reaching fragrance, while some buds remain buried in dirty mud forever...

4

"人也像这些莲花一样有千百种，无论真理多么难懂，总会有人了解的，请你对大家说明你的教义吧！"
Human beings come in hundreds and thousands of different kinds, just like these flowers. No matter how difficult it is to comprehend truths, there will always be some people who can understand them. Please explain the meaning of your Dharma to the public!"

5

"梵天"的话深深打动了释迦牟尼的心……
These words from Heavens' representative deeply moved Sakyamuni's heart...

于是他毅然起身，将此后的四十五年岁月都献给众生，为他们说法。
Therefore, he got up from his seat determined to educate. He then devoted more than 40 years of his earthly life to teaching The Dharma to all living beings.

6

本来我是这样说的……
THIS IS HOW I HAVE SAID IT...

无明
DELUSIONS

佛陀说：
一切痛苦都产生于无明，人由于无明而产生了偏见与固执，苦也就由此产生了。
什么是无明呢？
佛陀在《杂阿含经》里对无明有详尽的描述。
Buddha once said:
"All sufferings originate from delusions.
Prejudice and stubbornness arise from delusions.
Sufferings follow as a result."

蔡志忠 漫画中国传统文化经典

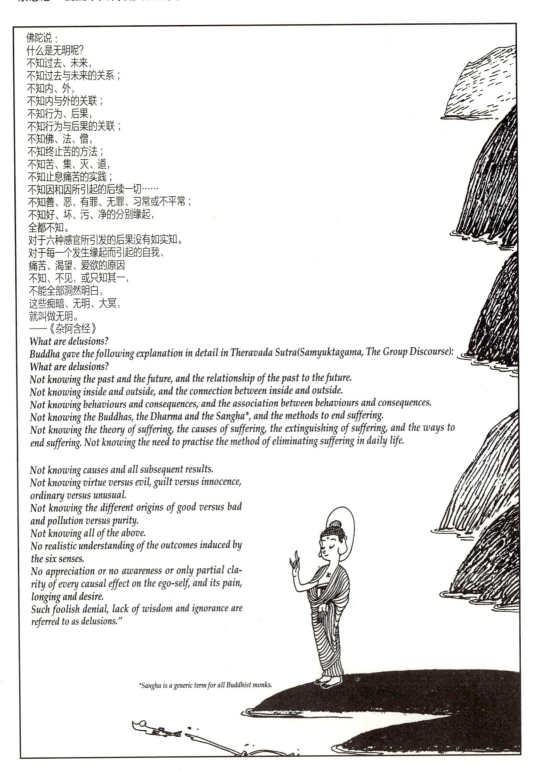

佛陀说：
什么是无明呢？
不知过去、未来，
不知过去与未来的关系；
不知内、外，
不知内与外的关联；
不知行为、后果，
不知行为与后果的关联；
不知佛、法、僧，
不知终止苦的方法；
不知苦、集、灭、道，
不知止息痛苦的实践；
不知因和因所引起的后续一切……
不知善、恶、有罪、无罪、习常或不平常；
不知好、坏、污、净的分别缘起，
全都不知。
对于六种感官所引发的后果没有如实知。
对于每一个发生缘起而引起的自我、
痛苦、渴望、爱欲的原因
不知、不见，或只知其一，
不能全部洞然明白，
这些痴暗、无明、大冥，
就叫做无明。
——《杂阿含经》

What are delusions?
Buddha gave the following explanation in detail in Theravada Sutra(Samyuktagama, The Group Discourse):
What are delusions?
Not knowing the past and the future, and the relationship of the past to the future.
Not knowing inside and outside, and the connection between inside and outside.
Not knowing behaviours and consequences, and the association between behaviours and consequences.
Not knowing the Buddhas, the Dharma and the Sangha*, and the methods to end suffering.
Not knowing the theory of suffering, the causes of suffering, the extinguishing of suffering, and the ways to end suffering. Not knowing the need to practise the method of eliminating suffering in daily life.

Not knowing causes and all subsequent results.
Not knowing virtue versus evil, guilt versus innocence, ordinary versus unusual.
Not knowing the different origins of good versus bad and pollution versus purity.
Not knowing all of the above.
No realistic understanding of the outcomes induced by the six senses.
No appreciation or no awareness or only partial clarity of every causal effect on the ego-self, and its pain, longing and desire.
Such foolish denial, lack of wisdom and ignorance are referred to as delusions."

*Sangha is a generic term for all Buddhist monks.

若以染污意
则苦随彼
Suffering
Follows Your
Polluted
Mind

我们就是我们所想的，我们是怎么样都是来自我们的思想。
We are what we think. How we are comes from our thoughts.

我们用我们的思想来创造这个世界……
We create this world with our own perception...

当我们用不正确的想法来说话或行动时……
When we speak or act with improper thoughts...

色
material world

受
sensations

想
perceptions

行
actions

识
consciousness

则烦恼和痛苦就会跟随着我们，就好像轮子跟随着拉车的牛。
...worries and pain will follow us just like wheels follow the oxen that pull the cart.

我们所感觉的世界是由我们的心所创造出来的，当我们自觉孤独时……一人独处时孤独，在人群中也孤独……
The world we perceive is created by our mind. When we feel lonely inside, we will feel the same loneliness whether we are alone or in a crowd...

157

若以清净意
则乐随彼
Joy Follows
Your Pure
Mind

我们就是我们所想的，我们是怎么样都来自我们的想法。
We are what we think. How we are comes from our own thoughts.

我们用我们的思想来创造这个世界。
We create this world with our own perception.

当我们用正确的思想来说话或行动时……
When we speak or act with proper thoughts ...

则快乐就会跟随着我们，就像影子跟随着人一样。
...joy will follow us just like shadows follow people.

我们的心反映出我们的世界！
当我们的心快乐时……
花在笑，云也在笑。
当我们悲伤时……风在哭，海在悲号。
Our mind shapes our world view!
When we are happy...
we see flowers smiling and clouds grinning joyfully.
When we are sad ...
we hear the wind sobbing, and the ocean weeping loudly.

怀念怨不息
Resentment Stays Alive In Relived Memories

"看他如何骂我、打我、破坏我、又侵夺我。"

"Look at how he curses me, beats me, destroys me, and even invades me."

如果你抱持着这样的想法，你就会活在怨恨之中。

If you hold on to this kind of thinking, you will be living in resentment.

我们的意识、心态决定了我们的世界，
当我们怀着怨恨时，我们就活在怨恨之中。
当我们怀着欢愉时，我们就得到欢愉的生活……
我们的世界，是我们的心的反映。

Our consciousness and mentality creates our world.
When we embrace resentment, we will live in resentment.
When we embrace joy, we will live in joy...
Our world is a reflection of our mind.

舍念怨自平
Resentment Dissolves When We Let Go

"看他如何骂我、打我、破坏我、又侵夺我。"
"Look at how he curses me, beats me, destroys me and even invades me."

如果你抛弃了这样的想法，你就会生活在爱之中。
If you abandon this kind of thinking, you will live in love.

我们的心可以改变我们对外在世界的看法，怀着怨恨得到的只会是怨恨，怀着爱将得到爱：怀着快乐的心得到的是快乐的生活。

Our mind alone can change how we perceive the external world. When we embrace resentment, we will get only more resentment. Embracing love will bring us more love. Embracing joy will spontaneously lead to a joyful life.

以忍止怨
Patience Stops Resentment

在这个世界里，从来就没有能用怨恨来解除怨恨……
In this world, resentment has never been resolved by resentment...

只有爱才能驱除怨恨，这是亘古不变的法则。
Only love can exterminate resentment. This is an ever-lasting law.

我们不能够以怨恨来平息怨恨。我们应该要用无怨的接受、承认、面对。把心融入对象，于是对象便消失了……
We cannot use resentments to cope with resentment. We should accept, acknowledge and face reality without resentment. When we place ourselves in our enemy's shoes, he will cease to be our enemy...

161

我且无有我
Even I DO
Not Own
Myself

愚昧的人总是认为："这是我的儿子，这是我的财富。"也经常苦恼于这些自认为自己所拥有的事物。
Ignorant people often believe: "These are my children, and those are my fortunes."

也经常为这些自认为自己所拥有的而苦恼。
They also worry quite often about these things that they supposedly own.

我们自己都不能算得上自己拥有自己，怎么能将儿子和财富自称为自己所拥有的呢？
We cannot even claim that we truly own ourselves. If so, how can we believe that we own children or wealth?

痛苦的产生和痛苦的强弱，是与自己的关系密切程度成正比。一个事件的发生如果与我们的关系很远，痛苦就不会产生。因此"无我"痛苦便无处可以升起。
The intensity of suffering is proportional to how closely we relate to a particular thing. If the occurrence of something is distantly related to us, then we do not suffer at all.
Therefore, suffering has no place in "self-lessness".

愚者自知愚
Ignorant People With Self-awareness

无知的人自知自己无知……
If ignorant people are aware of their own ignorance...

这样他便是有自知之明的聪明人。
...then they are actually the smart ones with self-knowledge.

无知的人若还自以为自己聪明，这才是真正愚笨的人。
Ignorant people who still consider themselves rather smart are the really foolish ones.

愚昧的人自知愚，他不自作聪明而误事，因此他可以说不是真愚昧；智者自知有所不能，因此他才是真智者，正如苏格拉底说："我知道自己有所不知道。"
Ignorant people with self-awareness will not act smart and get into trouble. Therefore, they are not truly foolish. Wise people know their own limitations; therefore, they are truly wise. This is why Socrates said he knew that he did not know everything.

163

十一种火
Eleven Kinds
Of Fire

凡夫被十一种能熊烈火灼身,这十一种火是:
Ordinary people are scorched by eleven kinds of violent fire. They are:

无知、固执
ignorance and stubbornness

贪欲
greed

怨恨不满
resentment and dissatisfaction

疾病
illness

老化、死亡
ageing and death

悲哀和身心上的种种病痛的苦恼。
...sadness and pains associated with various physical as well as mental illnesses.

忧愁、凄凉、郁闷……
grief, sorrow, depression ...

这些情绪与情感上的任何一种火,都能烧毁整个世界。
Any one of these emotional fires is capable of burning up the whole world.

瞋
resentment

痴
delusion

贪
greed

老
ageing

病
illness

死
death

我们的身心是自我的天堂与地狱,人生的痛苦大都是由自心所生,是内心中的贪欲、怨恨、不满、固执、忧愁令我们烈火灼身,是内心对身体的病痛、老化、死亡的不肯接受,令我们烈火灼身,活在如地狱般的痛苦之中。
Our body and mind can be both heaven and hell. Most sufferings in life are created by our own mind. It is our internal greed, resentment, dissatisfaction, stubbornness and sorrow that scorch us like a fierce blaze. It is our inner unwillingness to accept physical changes, such as illness, pain, ageing and death, that leads us to hellish misery.

无执著如瞋恚
No Atta-
chment Is
Worse Than
Resentment

没有什么火能比得上"贪欲"之火炽烈焚身。
No fire is comparable to the flame of "greed", which fiercely consumes the body.

没有什么执著能比得上"怨恨"更刻骨铭心，难以忘怀。
No attachment is comparable to "resentment", which permanently scars the mind.

没有什么网能比得上"愚昧"之网罗，系着人的固执。
No net is comparable to the web of "delusion", which stubbornly clings on to people.

没有什么河流能比得上"爱欲"的洪流更为凶猛，淹没人的一生。
No river is comparable to the current of "desire", which violently drowns one's whole life.

贪、瞋、痴和欲望是人的内心中最坏的素质，它们也是使人受苦的最大根由，守护自己的心最重要的是要将这四种祸害根除。
Greed, resentment, delusion and desire are the worst possible qualities of the human mind. They are also the biggest causes of hurt and suffering within humans. The most important task in protecting our minds is to eradicate these four scourges at the root.

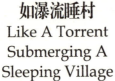

如瀑流睡村
Like A Torrent Submerging A Sleeping Village

"雨季时我住于此，非雨季时我也住于此。"

"I live here during the rainy season too, because I always live here during the dry season."

愚昧的人若存有这样的想法，他便一定遭洪流淹没。

If ignorant people have this type of thinking, they will invariably be drowned by torrential floods.

"这是我的子女，这是我的财富。愚昧的人心里存有着这样的想法，因此他的心便被欲望所迷惑。"

"These are my children, and those are my fortunes." Ignorant people have this type of thinking, therefore their minds are confused by desire.

因此，贪念、渴望、欲爱便占满了他的心，就像雨季的洪水淹没了低洼的村庄。

As a result, greed, longings and wants fill up their minds. It is just like the floods that submerge sleeping villages during the rainy season.

愚痴最大的恶，是不知道什么是恶，因此他做出了危害自己、危害别人的恶而不自知。

The worst sin of ignorance is not knowing what sin is. As a result, ignorant people are totally unaware of their own sins which hurt both themselves and others.

用心若镜
不将不迎
Hold The
Mind As
A Mirror,
Without
Bending
Forward
Or Back

渴望未来，追悔过去则是自寻烦恼，就像割下了的芦苇必将枯萎。
Longing for the future and regretting the past will only cause us troubles. Such behaviour is futile, just as cut reeds are destined to wilt.

我们若能做到不后悔过去、不渴望将来，则不自寻苦恼。
If we can refrain from longing for the future or regretting the past, then we will not bring troubles upon ourselves.

确实地把握现在，融入现前的一切，脚踏实地，则身心健康。
Grasp the present moment fully and immerse into everything ahead of us. When we keep our feet on the ground, we will naturally have physical and mental health.

智者无心，他只是仔细地观察和完全地融入，由于他融入自己所处的时空情境里，因此他没有自己，也没有情境所反映出来的好坏和自己的快乐、悲伤，于是他便能自在地浮沉于世而不自伤。
The wise have no ego-mind. They only carefully observe and completely immerse themselves. They immerse themselves in the space, time and circumstances where they happen to be in.
Therefore, they have no ego-self and no judgement of good versus bad. They do not project the joy or sadness of the ego-self onto any situation. Thus, they are able to bob along with the currents of society, carefree and unhurt.

智者不愁于未来
The Wise Ones Do Not Worry About The Future

智者不懊悔过去，不忧愁未来，他们生活于现在。所以生活得非常光彩！
The wise do not regret the past nor worry about the future. They live in the present; therefore, they shine radiantly!

愚人们懊悔过去……
Fools regret the past…

忧愁未来，乃至于无视现在。
..and worry about the future to the extent that they ignore the present.

他们干枯得如同折断了的青芦苇，曝晒于烈日之下。
These fools are as withered as the green reeds that have been broken off and dried up under the scorching sun.

无论我们拥有多少寿命，我们只能掌握当前。智者全力以赴地品尝当下毫无敷衍，因此他分分秒秒全神贯注，生活得非常光彩。
No matter how many years we may live, we can only grasp now. The wise ones savour the present wholeheartedly. Therefore, they are fully concentrated every second and live a radiant life.

不及思法者十六分之一
Less Than One-Sixteenth Of Dharma Joy

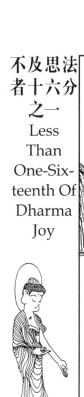

愚昧的人日复一日地追求世间的满足以填满欲望,自以为快乐幸福。
Fools pursue earthly delights to satisfy their desires day after day, and they believe themselves to be quite happy.

就有如满坑满谷的美味,他只取杂草的尖端而食。
It is as if they only eat the tips of weeds while leaving an entire valley of gourmet delights completely alone.

这样的满足比起净化自己去除贪欲的快乐,还不值十六分之一。
Such satisfaction is worth less than one-sixteenth of the joy of purifying oneself and extinguishing desires.

生命是美好的,活着就是最大的快乐。智者不需要到面临死亡之前就早已知道这个真理。凡夫老是用他的生命去换取外在不实的名利,而扭曲了生命的意义。智者不以生命与虚幻的短暂利益作交换,他享受着实质的生命的无尽美好。

Life is precious; to be able to live is the greatest delight. The wise already know this truth well without having to face death. Ordinary people often use up their lives in exchange for the external frills of fame and fortune. They end up twisting the meaning of life. The wise do not exchange life for short-term benefit.

星相的迷惘
Delusion Over Astrology

170

人要自救
People Need To Save Themselves

智慧的行持，才能获得真正的利益。
Only wise dispositions will attain real gains in life.

我们应该远离向天神祈求获得利益的愚蠢行为……
We should distance ourselves from those foolish behaviours that completely rely on deities for blessings.

就像天上的星星、月亮无法帮助我们。
This is as silly as asking the stars and the moon to help us.

我们要依靠觉智和自己的力量去发掘引发身心痛苦的原因，并用正确的方法去止息这些烦恼的生成。我们只能自己救自己，没有谁能救得了我们。
We must rely on our awareness, wisdom and power to dig out the real causes of pain in life. We also need to use the correct methods to put an end to such worried completely. We are the only ones who are capable of saving ourselves. Nobody else can bring salvation to our lives.

**实践是
唯一之路**
Practice Is
The Only
Way

真理是用来实践的，以达到觉悟的最终目的。
Truths are to be practised so as to attain the final goal of enlightenment.

而那些形而上的纯理论问题不能帮助我们……
Metaphysical and theoretical questions cannot help us.

无助于领导我们走向正确的修行之道，涤净执著、烦恼，而达至寂静的究竟涅槃。
They are useless in guiding us onto the correct way of cultivation, in eradicating attachment and worries, and in reaching the ultimate Nirvana of quiescence.

佛陀对于生前死后的问题，和世界的大小、时间的过去、未来等十四个形而上的问题不发表任何意见，因为他说："这些问题无助于对终止痛苦的修行，只会徒增一个人对未来的贪欲。"
Buddha had no comments on 14 metaphysical questions asked of him, concerning issuse of life before birth and death, the size of the world, past and future time, etc. He explained: "These questions are useless for cultivation aimed at eradicating sufferings. They only add to people's greedy desires for the future."

云何一切?
What Is All?

比丘们啊! 我们觉知的世界是什么构成的呢?
那就是眼、色、耳、声、鼻、香、舌、味、身、触、意、法。诸比丘啊! 就是这些构成了我们所觉知的世界的一切。

My fellow monks! What constitutes the world that we have come to know?

It includes the eyes and forms, the ears and sounds, the nose and smells, the tongue and tastes, the body and touch, the mind and consciousness.
Fellow monks! Such are the components that make up all of the world that we know.

比丘们啊! 如果有人说:"除了这一切之外, 我还要说有别的一切。"

My fellow monks! If someone says: "In addition to all that have been mentioned, I still need to say that there are other components."

说这种话的人是不负责任的, 因为他不能提出任何证明、不能验证的啊……

People who talk like this are not being responsible. They can neither come up with any proof nor test their ideas in real life.
People who talk like this are not being responsible. They can neither come up with any proof nor test their ideas in real life.

这种说法只会使人更陷入苦境, 为什么呢?
This kind of talk only pushes humans deeper into a state of suffering. Why is that so?

因为这是无益的说法, 无益于替人们解除痛苦烦恼。
Because this is useless talk and does not help release humans from their pains and worries.

佛陀不讨论经验以外不能证明的事物, 他有十四个形而上的问题拒绝评论。
因为他认为这些问题的探讨无助于净化自己的心, 无助于一个人痛苦的终止。
佛陀说:"努力寻求解脱苦, 而不要做无补于事的玄学推测。"
Buddha refuses to discuss all subjects beyond immediate human experience.
Once, he was known to have had no comment on 14 metaphysical questions.
This is because he considered such investigations useless for the purification of the mind and the termination of human suffering.
Therefore, Buddha said: "Work diligently at seeking a release from suffering.
Do not involve yourself in the useless guesswork of metaphysics."

诸行无常
All Acts Are Transient

宇宙间的一切有形无形都是变化不已的，这是宇宙的物理定律。人站在自己的利益观点冀求美好的事物永存，对于自己不利的不要临身，由于昧于宇宙定律强求不可能之事，因此痛苦于自己的无知昧于事实。
All visible and invisible phenomena in the universe are ever-changing. Such is the physical law of the universe. Standing at the vantage point of their personal interests, humans wish beautiful things will last forever and catastrophes will never happen to them. Because of their ignorance of the universal law, they insist on pursuing the impossible. Therefore, humans suffer from their own delusions about the universal truth.

痛苦
SUFFERING

佛陀说：
追寻外在感官的快乐是使人痛苦的原因。
生而为生命是非常珍贵的，
能生而为有觉知、意识的人更是特别难得的。
人生活于世上当然要快快乐乐地活着才懂得生命，
但人由于过度的自我觉知，
发展出了"有我"的自我意识。

Buddha once said:
"Pursuing external sensory pleasure is the reason for human suffering."
Being born into life is worth treasuring,
while being born as a human with consciousness is especially precious.
Humans in this world naturally seek happiness to give their lives meaning.
However, due to an over-development in self-consciousness, the "ego-self of I" emerges.

由于有我，从自我的出发点去看事物，
站在一己之私的偏差角度乃至产生了偏见，
不能看清一切事物的真实，
于是痛苦便产生了。
人为了追逐个人的快乐，而痛苦也因此产生了……
为什么会产生痛苦呢？
痛苦产自于人的无知，不能如实地看清一切事物。

Because of the "ego-self of I", we look at all external things from our own perspective.
We generate prejudice due to the biased angle of our selfish point of view.
We can no longer see through the truths in everything, and we end up creating our own sufferings.
It is ironic that sufferings result from our pursuit of happiness...
Why do we create our sufferings?
Sufferings originate from our delusions which keep us from seeing through all things as they truly are.

佛陀说：
凡是与终止苦无关的，就不是我所说的。
佛陀由观人的生老病死而发愿修行，
他通过六年的苦行乃至在菩提树下悟出真理，
并于遗生的四十年间传法说道，
所证所言所传所教的无非是苦的真理。
苦的本质、苦的聚集原因、消灭苦的方法、抵达无苦之境的次第修行。
人的一生如果一直都很快乐，那也就不必要什么修行。
但人在追求快乐的过程中遭受到极大的痛苦、压力，
这些苦的产生乃来自于人的无知和心灵的不纯净。
佛陀说：
天堂与地狱不在世界之外，天堂与地狱就在我们这个六尺之躯里。
一个人觉得自己苦或乐不在于外在获得的多少，
而在于心灵的满足与否。
当我们的心充满着欲望，在乎外在对我们的评价之时，
我们就受制于外在的名、色、物质。
而心灵的净与不净是依自己，没有一个人能从外面净化另一个人。
净化心灵得完全要靠自己，
当心灵里的全部自我欲念都消逝之后，我们就会重生而获得永恒的安详寂静，
进入一种无苦之境。

Buddha once said:
"Any saying that does not relate to extinguishing suffering is not taught by me".
Buddha vowed to cultivate himself as a result of his observations of birth, ageing, illness and death in life.
Through six years of intense cultivation, he attained enlightenment to truths under a Bodhi tree.
He spent more than 40 years spreading the Dharma.
All things he tested, spoke, promoted and taught were nothing but the truths about suffering.
He thereby developed sequential steps for cultivation, including the nature of suffering, its causes, the methods to end suffering, and the arrival at the state of "no suffering".
If human lives were extremely happy all the time, then there would be no need for cultivation.
But humans always experience tremendous pain and pressure in the process of pursuing happiness.
Such suffering arises from the ignorance and impurity of humans.
Buddha therefore said:
"Heaven and hell are not outside of this world. They both exist in our body which is several feet tall."
Whether we feel pain or joy is not dependent on the magnitude of external gain.
Rather, it depends on whether our heart is satisfied.
When our heart is full of desires, and concerned about the external judgement of ourselves, then we will be controlled by external fame,
fortuned and material goods.
In contrast, purity or impurity of the heart depends only on ourselves.
No one can purify another person from the outside.

It is entirely up to us to purify our own heart.
When all desires of the ego-self have
dissipated in our heart, we will be reborn
again to attain eternal peace and
tranquillity — a state of "no suffering".

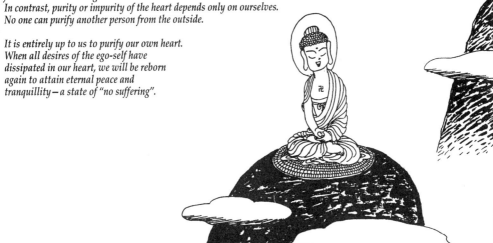

寻求造屋者
Looking For
The House
Builder

人的一生当中经历了多少次一次又一次的痛苦轮转，来了又消失，消失了又来，一次一次永不停息……

In a human lifetime, we all experience many cycles of suffering over and over again. Suffering comes and goes, the comes again. Time after time, it never ends...

是谁造的痛苦呢？这痛苦是哪里产生出来的呢？

Who created such sufferings? Where did sufferings come from?

又想、又思、又寻、又觅，找不到造苦之人……而痛苦却又一次一次地循回轮转缠绕着我们不肯远离。

We think and wonder, seek and search. We still cannot find the creator of suffering...
while suffering circles us again and again and never leaves us alone.

人常感受到痛苦。但除了委罪他人与命运之外，有多少人能躬身自省这些痛苦产生的真正原因来自何处？苦来自何处？造苦的人又是谁？大多数的苦是产自于错误的心！

Humans often experience suffering.
But most of us blame others or fate for our misfortune. How many people are capable of humbly reflecting upon such questions as:"Where do the real causes of such suffering come from? Where do the sufferings themselves come from? Who created sufferings after all?"
The truth is that most sufferings are generated by having our hearts in the wrong place!

心若不安定
If The Heart Is Unsettled

如果我们的心不安定，又不了解观照静心的方法……
If our heart is unsettled, and we do not know how to calm down and reflect...

信心不足，又无毅力……
...plus our faith is weak, and our endurance is poor...

这样就不可能达到智慧的境地。
...then we will not be able to attain the state of wisdom.

如果我们的心不落入贪欲，净心而无疑惑……
If our heart is far away from greedy desires, is pure and without doubt...

舍弃自我的偏见，超越善恶两端，这样地觉悟心中便不再有恐怖。
...plus we can let go of our prejudice and transcend beyond the extremes of good and evil, then our new realization will free us from all fear.

心是一切行为的主人，修行就是修炼这颗处处做主的心。排除心那部分会引发痛苦烦恼的素质，发扬内心那部分会引发有益行为的素质。这样净化自己的心，使它有能力当正确的主。

Our heart is the master of all behaviours and guides us wherever we go consciously or subconsciously. Cultivation can put our heart in the right place. Get rid of those character defects that induce worries, bring out those character assets that induce positive behaviours. Purifying the heart this way will enable it to be a proper master.

179

仇敌害仇敌
An Enemy Mentality Is The Worst Enemy

仇敌就以仇敌的方式对待；
Treat an enemy with the mentality of an enemy;

怨家就以怨家的态度应付。
and treat a rival with the attitude of a rival.

心走向错误的道路，为自己所造的恶最大。
When our heart is in the wrong place, it is the worst evil we could ever create.

最善待自己的不是父母，
Those who treat us best are not our parents,

也不是亲属。
or our relatives.

让自己的心走向正确的道路……
Directing our heart onto the correct path...

这就是善待自己最好的方式。
...is the best possible way to treat ourselves.

我们的心引发的错误行为，为害自己最大；我们的心引发的正确行为，自己受益最大。善恶由自己的心生出，受益受害也是生心的这个人。
Wrongdoings induced by our own heart hurt us the most. Righteous acts induced by our heart also benefit us the most. Both good and evil manifestations originate from our heart. We ourselves reap the benefit or the harm from the manifestations of our heart.

180

181

心无所住
The Heart Does Not Judge

我们不要以一己的立场生出分别心，去分好与不好而执著其中。

We should not create a dualism in our own point of view. It is not helpful to be obsessed with the difference between good and bad.

因为有了好与不好的分别，便有了喜爱与憎恶的偏见……

The separation of good versus bad will bring about the prejudice of likes versus dislikes...

于是便有了贪念、憎恨、忧愁、不满，而生恐怖，生束缚。

Furthermore, greed, resentment, grief and dissatisfaction will be generated. Fear and bondage for ourselves will invariably result from them.

行为原本没有所谓的对或错。但当这个行为是由自我意志所发动的，便有了基于私心的利益或无私的善意之分别。凡是在意志上图谋自利的行为就会造成自己对这行为的承受，而这个行为的后果就是"业"。

Behaviours, by themselves, are often not necessarily right or wrong. But when a certain behaviour is mobilized by self-will, then there is a difference between self-interest and selfless motivation. Any behaviour based on self interest will lead to consequences that we must accept. Such an effect due to a previous behaviour is referred to as Karma.

涅槃最上乐
Nirvana Is The Utmost Joy

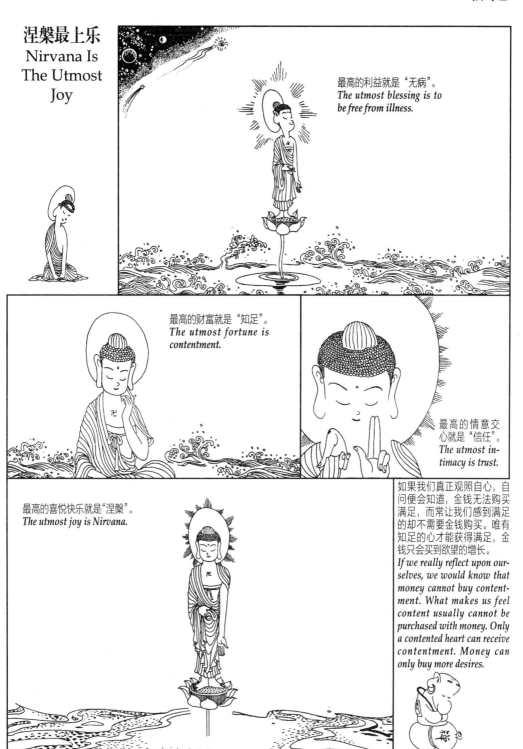

最高的利益就是"无病"。
The utmost blessing is to be free from illness.

最高的财富就是"知足"。
The utmost fortune is contentment.

最高的情意交心就是"信任"。
The utmost intimacy is trust.

最高的喜悦快乐就是"涅槃"。
The utmost joy is Nirvana.

如果我们真正观照自心，自问便会知道，金钱无法购买满足，而常让我们感到满足的却不需要金钱购买。唯有知足的心才能获得满足，金钱只会买到欲望的增长。
If we really reflect upon ourselves, we would know that money cannot buy contentment. What makes us feel content usually cannot be purchased with money. Only a contented heart can receive contentment. Money can only buy more desires.

淫欲
乐少苦多
Desires Bring Few Joys And Much Pain

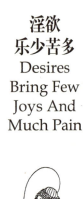

即使财富像雨一样不停地降临到人的身上，也不能满足人的贪欲之心。

Even if wealth keeps falling on our head like raindrops, our desires will not be satisfied.

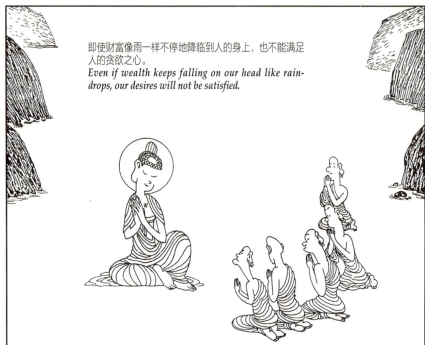

智者们知道追求外在的淫欲，到头来最终的结果一定是快乐的少，而痛苦的多。

The wise know that the pursuit of external desires will result in little joy and much pain.

从外在的掠取获得，永远不能满足内在的贪欲，它只会得到短暂的快乐，紧接着又会从这快乐引发了痛苦。为什么呢？因为我们冀求更好，得到的又怕失去。

Any gain from external grabbing of material goods will never satisfy our internal greed. It will only provide momentary pleasure. Immediately afterwards, this exact pleasure will induce further pain. Why is that so? It is because we will always look for something better and be afraid of losing what we have just gained.

善哉制一切
Self-discipline In Every Area Is A Virtue

最高的善就是能自我控制眼、耳、鼻、舌等感官的刺激。

The highest virtue is self-control over our response to sensory stimuli from our eyes, ears, nose, tongue, etc;

最高的善就是能自我控制自己的行为、语言和内心的意识。

The highest virtue is self-control over our behaviour, language and inner consciousness.

最高的善就是能自我控制身心的一切……

The highest virtue is self-discipline in every area of our body and mind...

能自我控制的人，他便能解除一切痛苦烦恼。

Those who can discipline themselves will be able to relieve themselves of all pains and worries.

不要看轻自己，也不要羡慕别人，如果我们羡慕别人，心便失去了和平寂静。
Do not look down on yourself or envy others. If we are consumed with envy, our mind will lose its peace and quiet.

虽然我们所得不多但自己却不嫌少，完全接纳这个事实，生活于清净不懈怠，这才是人人称赞的修行。
Although we do not own much, we do not need to feel deprived. Completely accept this truth and consistently live in purity—this is what everyone terms cultivation.

对于精神或物质的一切都不抱持我或我所有的观念……
Do not hold on to the concepts of "I" and "mine" in relation to everything mental or physical...

由于不是我或我所有，因此便没有我的痛苦、忧愁。这样的人才是真正的修行者。
There is no "I" and "mine". Therefore, there is no "my pain" and "my sorrow". People who hold such attitudes are true cultivators of spirituality.

人最爱自称"我"和"我所有"，但一个人他不能自我控制自己的生、死、健康、疾病，不能自我控制自己的感官、欲望、愤怒、恐惧、固执、贪欲，他怎么能称这个无能控制的自己为我的我呢？智者调心，首先要做到的是无我，于是慢慢他他便逐渐可以掌握这个我了。
People love to self-proclaim "I" and "mine". But we cannot personally control our birth, death, health and disease. Neither can we self-discipline our senses, desires, anger, fear, stubbornness and greed. How can we refer to the "I" that is not capable of controlling itself as "mine"? The wise ones discipline their minds—the first step is to be selfless. Gradually, we may come to discipline this "I".

无我所有
Nothing Belongs To Me

我们应该要做到身处在怨恨中而心无怨恨。
We should feel no hatred ever when physically surrounded by hatred.

身处于贪欲之中，而自心无贪欲。
...we should feel no sorrow even when physically surrounded by sorrow, and feel no greed even when physically surrounded by greed.

身处在苦恼中而心无苦恼。
We want to achieve the state where "not a single thing belongs to me." Live in quiescence without interference from external objects.

要做到"无一物是我所有"的观念，清静不受外物干扰地生活。
If we can achieve the state of "no I" and "nothing belongs to me", then none of the external hatred, sorrow and greed may be taken as my hatred, my sorrow and my greed.

如果我们能做到无我、无我所有的境界，那么外在的怨恨、苦恼、贪欲便没有一个我可以去取来作为我的怨恨、我的苦恼和我的贪欲。我都没有了，何来我的痛苦？
If there is not even an "I", where can "my suffering" come from?

爱别离为苦
Separation From Loved Ones Causes Suffering

我们的心要保持清静，不要去造成爱欲，也不要去造成憎恨……爱欲的对象离去消失会产生痛苦，面临憎恨的对象也会产生痛苦。

We want to keep our mind pure. Do not create affection or hatred... The departure of an object of our affection produces suffering. The appearance of an object of our hatred also produces pain.

因此，爱欲与憎恨是产生痛苦的原因，如果我们的心纯净不偏，没有爱欲和憎恨，即没有痛苦的束缚。

Therefore, affection and hatred generate pain. If our mind is pure and not biased, then we will not have affection and hatred. That is how we can be free from pain.

从喜爱产生了忧虑、恐惧，舍弃了喜爱之心，则忧虑、恐惧就无从产生。

From affection we generate worry and fear. If our mind abandons the thought of affection, then worry and fear can come from nowhere.

从贪欲产生了忧虑、恐惧，舍弃了贪欲之心，则忧虑、恐惧就无从产生了。

From greed we generate worry and fear. If our mind abandons the thought of greed, then worry and fear cannot come from anywhere at all.

我们的心如果有喜爱之心，憎恶的偏见也就产生了。我们如果对生活上的外在一切事物去心生分别，把其中某一部分划分为喜爱，那么另外一部分便成了憎恶。由于喜爱便会怕失去，憎恶便不希望它来临，于是痛苦便产生了。

If our mind has any preference, then the prejudice of hatred will also be created. Classification of certain objects as likes will automatically place the rest in the category of dislikes. We fear losing those we like. We avoid those we dislike. If our mind judges all external objects in life, the suffering will invariably be generated.

待己如敌
Treating Our-
selves As The
Enemy

人对待自己有如对待最痛恨的仇人一样。
People often treat themselves as if dealing with their most hated enemy.

任何敌人对我们的伤害，也比不上一个人自己的贪欲、瞋恨、无知对自己本身的伤害来得大。
No enemy can hurt us as badly as the harm we inflict on ourselves with greed, resentment and ignorance.

人对待自己有如对待最恨的仇人一样的残忍，躬身自省，想想造成我们最大痛苦的，往往是自己内心所引发出来的贪婪无知的自己。人是自己最大的敌人，对自己也最残忍。
People often treat themselves as cruelly as their most hated enemy. If we reflect on ourselves, we will find that we ourselves create our worst pain. The part of our inner self that manifests greed and ignorance is often responsible. People are their own worst enemy, and are the cruellest towards themselves.

自作自受
Face The Consequen-ces Of One's Actions

无知而愚蠢的人，对待自己好像仇敌一样。
Ignorant and foolish people treat themsel-ves like an enemy...

因为他行恶业，给自己身上带来了苦果。
...because they carry out evil acts that will invariably bear them bitter fruits in the future.

人的痛苦大都是来自自己，是自己的那颗永远不得满足的贪欲之心。与怨恨我们、仇视我们的敌人们比起来……我们自己那颗放逸的心，才是我们最大的敌人。

Most of our pains come from ourselves and are the result of our discontented heart. In comparison to our most heteful and hostile opponent... our own flighty heart is our biggest enemy.

191

得正法不流转
Proper Dharma Keeps Us From Spinning Our Wheels

失眠的人，夜长；疲乏的旅人，路长。
For those who cannot sleep, the night is long. For tired travellers, the road is long.

不知正法的愚者，则轮回流转长。
Fools who do not know proper Dharma keep spinning the same wheels in life after life forever and ever.

人因为追求妄念的达成而苦了现在，其实哪有什么未来的目的？生命的意义永远都在此时、此地、此人而已。

Humans often seek fulfilment of their fantasies and sacrifice the present moment for future goals. In fact, how can we control the future?

The meaning of life is always right now, right here, and for this very person.

192

远离诸恶
Distancing Ourselves From All Evils

如果知道应该爱惜自己的话，不可将自己与恶联结在一起。

If we know that we should cherish ourselves, we must not associate ourselves with any evil...

自己作，自己受，自己造恶业，自己承担苦果。我们要远离苦、渴、烦恼，首先得净化自己的生活，就是力行十善、不造十恶。这是获得安乐的第一步。

Whatever we do, we ourselves need to accept the consequences. When we create negative karma through our deeds, we must ourselves face bitter karmic fruits. If we want to distance ourselves from pain, thirst and worries, we should first purify our lives. That means carrying out only kind deeds and not generating any evil deeds. This would be the first step in gaining peace and joy.

因为，行恶业、做坏事的人们是得不到安乐的。

...because those who carry out bad karmic deeds will not attain peace and joy.

193

努力自救
Diligently Helping Ourselves

恶是由自己作的，
When we create evil,

苦是由自己受的。
the resulting suffering will be endured by us as well.

苦
suffering

恶
evil

恶要由自己去解除，净化是由自己去达成。
We must resolve evil by ourselves. Only we can accomplish our purification.

洁与不洁完全在乎于自己，
Our purity or pollution completely depends upon us,

没有人能净化他人。
Nobody can purify others.

狮吃兔子不觉得自己为恶，禾生稻米养人不觉得自己为善，人吃苦瓜不觉苦。每个人都是个案，每个人的苦只有他自己才知道，唯有努力自救，没有谁能救得了你自己。
Lions do not consider themselves evil when they prey on rabbits. Plants do not regard themselves as kind when they produce rice to feed humans. People do not think of themselves as suffering when they consume bitter squash as a favourite dish. Each one of us is a special case. Only we ourselves understand our own suffering. The only way out of suffering is to diligently help ourselves. Nobody else can bring us salvation.

善待自己
Treating
Ourselves
Well

无论任何人，如果他的行为所做的是恶行，他的话所说的是恶语，他的意所想的是恶念的话……
No matter who they are, those people with evil deeds, evil language and evil thoughts...

在身、口、意三业行恶的人，他们不是真正爱惜自己的人。
...do not really cherish themselves. They are building negative karma with their body, speech and mind, and will bring suffering on themselves later.

无论任何人，他们在所做、所说、所想的身、口、意三业行善的话……
No matter who they are, if they strive to practise acts of good karma in behaviours, words and thoughts ...

那么可以说，他们才是真正爱惜自己的人。
...then they truly cherish themselves.

我们最大的敌人就是我们自己，人生大多数的苦形成的原因也都来自我们自己。自己造的恶业只能由自己来承受，没有谁能代替得了我们。
We are our own greatest enemy. We create most of our suffering in life ourselves. All of the negative karma we accumulate can only be paid back by ourselves. No one can take our place.

195

自皈依
Seeking Refuge In Our-selves

我们自己才是自己的主，没有其他任何人是我们的主。
We are each our own master. Nobody else can be our master.

如果我们自己的身心能调御得很好，我们就得到了难得的主。
When we can finetune our body and mind to their best, we have found a rare master in ourselves.

我们所依靠的除了自己之外无别人，我们所凭借的除了正确的法以外别无他法，我自己就是自己的主，以我自己做我的依处。
We can depend only on ourselves and nobody else. We can rely only on the proper Dharma and no other methods. We are each our own master. The refuge we return home to is ourselves.

虽诵一千言
Reading One
Thousand
Verses

虽然念了一千句神圣的经句，但却不懂得其中的道理……

Although we have read one thousand verses from divine scriptures, we may not understand their meaning at all.

比不上只了解一句经典的句子……

To reach the goal of self-purification, it is better to understand only one verse...

并遵照着去实践，而达到净化自己的目的。

...and put it into practice.

经典的神圣在于它的神圣内容，在于实践这神圣的内容而使得自己转变成为神圣。食物是用来吃的；东西是用来使用的；音乐是用来听的；而经典是用来实践的。凡是错用经典，便是辱没了经典的神圣。

The divinity of scriptures stems from their divine contents. It is in practising these divine contents that we transcend to divinity.

Foods are for eating, utensils are for using, music is for listening, and scriptures are for practice. When the scriptures are misused, their divinity is insulted.

依教实行
Practise What Is Preached

如果我们诵咏的经典虽然不多，但能够遵照着去实践，并从中获得正确的见解，而断除内心的贪欲、不满、愚昧……

We may have read only a few scriptures, but we can still put them into practice. We can obtain proper points of view from them and cut away inner greed, dissatisfaction and delusion.

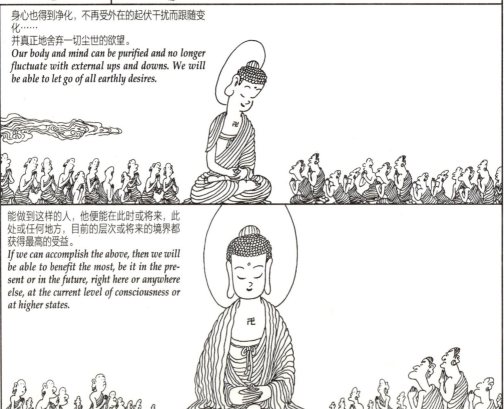

身心也得到净化，不再受外在的起伏干扰而跟随变化……
并真正地舍弃一切尘世的欲望。

Our body and mind can be purified and no longer fluctuate with external ups and downs. We will be able to let go of all earthly desires.

能做到这样的人，他便能在此时或将来，此处或任何地方，目前的层次或将来的境界都获得最高的受益。

If we can accomplish the above, then we will be able to benefit the most, be it in the present or in the future, right here or anywhere else, at the current level of consciousness or at higher states.

如果我们喜欢，我们也可以阅读少许的文字，讲少许的教义，但要根据正确的道理来行为。真理不是用来诵唱咏吟的，真理是用来实践的，唯有实践才能获得真理的果实。

We can also choose to read only a few scriptures and discuss only a few principles. The most important part is to act properly according to the teachings. Truth is not for singing or chanting. Truth is to guide our practice in life. Only in practising Truth can we achieve fruitful results.

百岁不如一日励行精进
Living One Hundred Years Is Not As
Good As Being Vigilant For One Day

与其不道德、不自制地活了一百年……
*Instead of living 100 years in immorality
and self-indulgence ...*

还不如有道德和不放逸地活一天。
*...it is better to live one single day
in morality and vigilance.*

生命不在于长短，而在于是否善用
生命。人不能自制，哪能说自己是
自己的主？纵然活上百岁却虽生犹
死，因为他被内心的欲望和外在的
变化所控制，他的人生比起能自我
调御做自己的主而活一天还短促。
*Whether our life is long or short,
the value is in making the best
use of it. If we cannot discipline
ourselves, how can we claim to
be our own master? Although
we may physically live to be 100
years old, spiritually we are like
the living dead. Only those who
can achieve self-discipline are
their own true masters. When we
are controlled by inner desires
and changes in our external environment, the value of our whole
life is less than one day's vigilance.*

199

如舌尝汤味
Like The Tongue Tasting Soup

愚笨的人虽然一生都与智者相处在一起，
Fools may spend their whole life with wise ones,

但他如果不能因此而正确了解经典中的真谛，就有如汤匙不能感受汤的美味。
But if they are not able to grasp the truths in scriptures, they are like a spoon not able to appreciate a delicious soup.

聪明的人分分秒秒都亲近智者，
Smart people stay close to wise ones every minute...

他能因此而贯通经典中的真谛，
...and learn to master the truths...

就好像喝汤的舌头能尝到汤味的鲜美。
...just as the tongue is able to appreciate a delicious soup.

凡夫误用经典，只是把它拿来念诵，他只是得到文字的表皮而没有掌握到真谛。凡夫误用经典的章句，只是把它拿来说说，而无身体力行。他只是得到章句的表皮，而放弃了真髓。
Ordinary people often misuse scriptures by only chanting and reading them. This way they only understand the superficial meanings of words but do not grasp the true essence of the scriptures. Ordinary people often misuse verses from scriptures by talking about them and not practising them physically. They only understand the superficial meanings of verses and abandon their real essence.

牧数他牛
A Herder Counting Others' Cattle

我们如果只是口中诵念经文，而身心放纵行为不按经文所说的内容去实践……

If we only read scriptures verbally and indulge our body and mind in self-will without practising the principles of the scriptures ...

这就像牧童替别人牧牛，虽然口中数念着牛只的数目，再怎么数……牛只也不会变成自己的。

...this is like a herder taking care of the cattle of others. No matter how often the herder counts the number of cattle, the cattle will never belong to him.

不论我们读了多少神圣的文字，说了多少神圣的话……如果我们不遵照这些话来行动，它们对我们会有什么好处呢？

只要表征而不要实质，这就像我们，只要文凭不要知识，只要地契不要土地，只要存折的数字不要现金一样的愚昧。

No matter how many divine scriptures we have read, how many divine words we have quoted...

...if we don't act according to these teachings, what good can they do for us? This is as foolish as if we only want a diploma without knowledge, a deed of ownership without land, or the amount in a bank statement without cash. All of these are only superficial representations without any real substance.

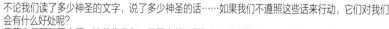

色美而无香
Pretty In Appearance, But Without Fragrance

我们如果只说而不做，只是明白道理，而不实行……
If we only give lip service without carrying it out, or only know the principles without practising them ...

那么就像一朵造型色彩美妙而无香味的花朵……
...then it is like a gorgeous flower without any fragrance.

只是说善语而不实行，就有如只会开花而不结果。
Only talking about kind deeds without carrying them out is like a blooming plant that can bear no fruit.

如果我们只是唱诵经典而不实行，那只是掌握文字而失去实质。就好像我们只爱文凭而不爱知识，只爱床铺不爱睡眠，只爱婚姻不爱幸福，只爱形式不爱实质。
If we only chant and read scriptures without practice, then we are only grasping the language and losing the real substance. It is like loving a diploma and not enjoying knowledge, loving the bed and not enjoying sleep, loving the marriage and not enjoying happiness. We end up loving the formality without being able to enjoy the real substance.

非裸行结发
Not By Walking Around Naked

裸体、结发、白泥涂身、绝食、卧地用尘涂抹全身、蹲踞不立不坐的苦行，以上种种都不能使人克服疑惑而成就净化。

Walking around naked, knotting hair in a particular way, pasting the body with white mud, fasting, lying on the ground and covering the body with dust, squatting without standing or sitting...

...all these acts of self-mortification cannot enable people to conquer their doubts and achieve purfication.

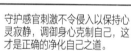

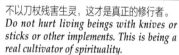

守护感官刺激不令侵入以保持心灵寂静，调御身心克制自己，这才是正确的净化自己之道。

Protecting ourselves from the invasion of sensory stimuli, keeping our heart serene, disciplining our body and mind ...these are the correct ways to purify ourselves.

不以刀杖残害生灵，这才是真正的修行者。

Do not hurt living beings with knives or sticks or other implements. This is being a real cultivator of spirituality.

能反躬自省而自制的人，是世上少有的，他擅长于避开会造成自我羞辱的行为，如良马避开被鞭打的错误行动。

Very few people in this world are capable of reflecting and self-disciplining. They are good at avoiding behaviours that bring themselves shame, just like fine horses avoid mistakes that lead to being whipped.

我们要勤于自我观照自心，勇往直前地迈向修行的终极目标。

We must be vigilant in self-reflection and be courageous in marching towards our final goal of cultivation.

完全清楚正确的真理，也完全明白自己的行动，知与行双管齐下，最后终将消灭所有的无穷痛苦。

We want to understand proper principles and our own behaviours completely. If we can combine understanding with practice, we will eventually extinguish all kinds of endless suffering.

心灵的净化完全属于自己，而不是来自于形而上的父权神祇的赐予，更不是那些徒具形式祀祭或身体行为。

心灵的净化在于完全清楚真理与真理的实践，我们只能通过正确的方法观照自己以达成净化，不让自己的心存有任何造成痛苦的因素来净化自己。

When we develop knowledge and behaviour in tandem, we will eventually extinguish all kinds of endless suffering.

愉快
JOY

佛陀说：
愉快是所有觉悟者开启智慧的起源。
佛就是觉悟的意思，觉悟出宇宙的真实相貌并开启智慧。
然而在找到智慧之前得先找到快乐，找到快乐之前得先找到自己。
人要寻求最高的觉悟，得先明白自己和自己与时空的关系。
修行之道就是寻求通往最终的智慧的道路，
而悟出最终的真理有两种形式，
一种是在极大痛苦之中顿悟；另一种则是在愉快中体会出生命的意义。
但如果是以痛苦而得到的顿悟，
当痛苦消失之后，这个顿悟也会随着痛苦的不存在而慢慢地消失。

Buddha once said:
"Joy is the source of all enlightened ones who open up to wisdom."
Buddha means "awakening"—
awaken to universal truths and unlock wisdom. However, before we find wisdom we must first find joy, and before we find joy we must first find ourselves. In order for us to seek the highest level of enlightenment, we must first understand ourselves and our relationship with time and space.
The path of spiritual cultivation is to seek the road leading to ultimate wisdom.
We will come to understand that there are two forms of ultimate truth:
one form is to gain enlightenment amidst suffering; the other form is to appreciate the meaning of life in joy.
However, if enlightenment was attained in pain, it is likely to slowly disintegrate when the pain disappears.

唯有能在生活中体会生命美好的特质，
在愉快中慢慢体会出实质的美妙生命，
这种顿悟觉知才能长久永存。
我们不能在痛苦中强说生命是美好的，
唯有在愉快中才真能感受愉快……
佛陀说：
愉快是觉悟的开始。

Only when we can appreciate the beautiful qualities of life in our daily existence, and slowly comprehend with joy the concrete realities of living, can this type of enlightenment last forever.

We cannot insist that life is beautiful when we are in pain; only when we are in joy can we feel the joy...

...therefore, Buddha taught:

"Joy is the beginning of enlightenment."

我等实乐生
We Real-
ly Live
Joyfully

我们愉快地生活……
生活于充满不满的尘世中而无不满；
生活于病态的社会之中而能无病；
生活于贪欲的世界之中而能无贪欲。

We live joyfully...
living without dissatisfaction in a mortal world
filled with dissatisfaction;
living without illness in a society with sickness;
living without greed in a greedy world.

我们愉快地生活，不
被物质条件所迷惑，
精神的快乐是我们的
原动力，就有如生活
于光的世界之人。
We live joyfully and are not confused
by the material world. Spiritual joy is
our motivator, just like those living in a
world of light.

我们是什么全因为我们自己，
不随着外在的条件而改变自
己。就像一朵莲花不因为它
的环境而使得白莲变污莲。
We are entirely what we
make of ourselves. We do not
change our true selves accor-
ding to the external environ-
ment. It is like a white lotus
blossom that is not tarnished
by its environment.

若人常正念
If We Keep Proper Mindfulness

如果常正确地观察，净心观照，看清感官输入所引起的心识作用，看清这颗心由快乐逐渐变成贪著，又由贪著逐渐变成痛苦，又由痛苦逐渐忘怀而消失……

If we often correctly reflect upon ourselves, we can observe clearly how sensory input causes reactions in our consciousness. We will observe clearly how our heart changes gradually from joy to greed, then from greed to pain, and then the pain is slowly forgotten...

如果我们真能看清苦的形成和苦的消失，那么我们便不会再受制于苦，而达到没有苦的生与苦的消失的境界。

If we can observe clearly the formation and disappearance of suffering, then we will no longer be controlled by suffering. We will be able to reach a state without formation and disappearance of suffering.

智慧的修行者们都知道守护自己的感官和知足，因此他的心远离了痛苦。

All wise cultivators of spirituality know how to protect their senses and be satisfied. This is how their heart stays far away from suffering.

智慧的修行者都知道依正确的生活方式：态度要诚恳，行为要端正。
Wise cultivators all know how to live proper lifestyles. They maintain sincere attitudes and upright behaviours.

因此他生活于愉快之中，也在愉快中得到智慧的觉悟。
Therefore, they live in joy and also attain enlightenment of wisdom in joy.

在愉快中消灭了所有的痛苦。
In joy, they extinguish all suffering.

我懂了。
I understand.

如果我们能看清"苦"的真相，看出苦由何处而生，由何处消逝，那么便容易做到不令苦形成，也就能够控制苦。痛苦大都是来自于心的不满，如果我们能知足常乐，不借助于外在的满足，苦就不容易生成。
If we can see clearly the true nature of "suffering", then it will be easy to control suffering by preventing it from happening. We need to see where suffering is born and where suffering is disappearing to. Sufferings most often come from mental dissatisfaction. If we can be content with what we have, stay in serenity, and not seek satisfaction from external stimuli, then suffering is not likely to take form.

我真安乐
I Am So Serene

别人都互相结怨，而我无怨结，所以我安详快乐。
Other people are entangled in resentment towards others, while I have no resentment. Therefore, I am serene

别人有苦恼，而我无苦恼，因此我安详快乐。
Other people have worries while I have none. Therefore, I am serene.

别人有贪欲，而我无贪欲，因而我安详快乐。
Other people have greedy desires while I have none. Therefore, I am serene.

我无烦恼无忧虑。食法喜食如光音天食。
I have no troubles and no worries. I feast on Dharma joy as if I were in seventh heaven already.

当我们内心中再也没有"自我"、"我所有"的想法，就不会再有因为"我"而生出的苦恼忧患，故能平静安详而生法喜充满之乐。
When we no longer have the concept of "I" and "mine" inside us, we will no longer have the pains and sufferings generated by the ego-self. Therefore, we will be able to stay serene and fulfilled.

211

度难度魔境
Overcoming Difficult Challenges Of Evil

能够真正了解真理的人，并能够真正地依据真理所说的方法去实行的人，他便能够抵达彼岸。

Those who can really understand truths, and can really practise according to the principles of truths, will be able to reach the other shore of tranquillity.

他能克服重重难关，克服身心的贪婪、欲望、固执、无知、愤怒、恐惧等障碍，净化自己的心以达到心灵的永远寂静安详。

They can overcome layer upon layer of difficult challenges, including obstacles of the body and the mind, such as greed, longings, stubbornness, delusion, anger and fear. They are able to purify themselves to reach the mental state of eternal tranquillity and peace.

真理的言语是指引我们走向永恒幸福为最后目标的工具，因此佛陀的神圣语言、神圣经典被称为"圣道迹"。真理的言语，一句一句就像一个一个脚印。我们可以随着一个个脚印向前走，必将有如佛陀一样地抵达当初他所到达的目的地。

Words of truth are the tools that guide us to the final goal of eternal joy. Therefore, the divine words and scriptures of Buddha are referred to as the "trail to the divine path". Every single sentence of divine words is like one footstep after another for us to follow. Marching forward this way, we will eventually reach the same destination as Buddha once did.

机缘难寻
It Is Rare To Find Such Unique Opportunities

得人身难，
It is rare to reincarnate into a human body,

人间活命难，
It is rare to survive for years after years in this world,

闻妙法难，
It is rare to hear the amazing Dharma,

值佛出世难。
It is rare to be present in the same era with the Buddha.

生命可贵，能活在这世间更可贵。能听到至高的真理是可贵的，正巧又碰到与佛活在同一时代更是难啊！

Being born into life is precious, while being able to continue living in this world is more precious. Being able to hear the utmost truth is precious, while being present in the same era with the Buddha is even more rare!

213

寂静最乐
Quiescence Is The Utmost Joy

最炽热的烈火，莫大于贪欲之火。
The hottest of fierce fires is the fire of greed.

最大的恶莫大于瞋恨，
The worst of all evils is resentment,

而人生中最至高无上的安乐，莫乐于寂静！
...from the five aggregates* of our own existence...while the utmost joy in life is quiescence!

最大的痛苦莫大于身心五蕴之苦……
The worst of all sufferings is physical and mental suffering...

贪欲是火能焚身，瞋恨是恶能害身，痴是无明能引起五蕴炽盛而苦了身心。要终止苦而达至安详快乐，唯有消除"我"、"我所有"的意识，令妄念不生才能获得身心止息的寂静之乐。
Greed is the fire that can burn our body, resentment is the evil that can injure our body, and delusion can cause us suffering through an imbalance, among the five aggregates of existence. The only way to end suffering and reach joy is to extinguish the consciousness of "I" and "mine". Not allowing the generation of any illusory thoughts is the only way to attain the quiet joy of body and mind.

**the five aggregates of existence are the material world, sensations, perceptions, decisions and consciousness.*

忍辱最难
Patience In Adversity Is Most Difficult To Achieve

罪大莫过于愤怒。
There is no greater crime than anger.

难能莫过于忍辱。
There is no greater difficulty than endurance in adversity.

故应努力习忍辱，种种方便作观修。
Therefore, we should make great efforts to learn endurance in adversity and adopt various strategies to cultivate ourselves.

对自己身心害处最大的就是愤怒，一个人最难办到的就是忍辱，所以我们应该要努力勤学忍辱这件事，利用人生中种种方法及运用生活中所遭遇的事，来修行忍辱的精神。

Anger holds the greatest harm for our body and mind. Endurance in a adversity is the most difficult to achieve for a person. Therefore, we should put our effort diligently into developing such capability. Apply all possible strategies to any opportunity that challenges us in life to cultivate the spirit of endurance.

善行者自御
Good Practi-
tioners Culti-
vate Self-dis-
cipline

灌溉农田的农夫擅长于引水；
Farmers who irrigate their fields are good at leading water to wherever they want it;

造箭的弓匠擅长于调直弓箭；
Makers of bows and arrows are good at straightening their arrows.

木匠擅长于取材切木；
Carpenters are good at picking the right lumber for specific types of wood.

修行净化自己的心灵首先要学会自我控制感官的入侵，能自我控制感官便容易自我控制内心的各种情绪，观照自己的心就是学习观察心识的运作，以达成心随意行。

In spiritual cultivation, the first step in purifying out mind is to learn to control the invasion of our senses. Once we are able to have self-control over out sensory input from the environment outside, we will find it easier to have self-control over our emotions inside. Reflecting on our mind is the way to learn to observe the dynamics of our consciousness. This is how we achieve a carefree state of mind that can go anywhere without losing its discipline.

智者擅长于自我控制身心。
The wise ones are good at self-discipline of both body and mind.

智者调心，如匠搦箭
Wise Ones Discipline The Mind Like Bow Makers Straightening Arrows

贤人自正其心，犹如造弓箭的人削箭矫正一样，慢慢将箭修直。
Virtuous ones discipline their own mind, just like the bow makers who slowly work on arrows until they are straight.

我们的心是很难抑制的……
Our mind is difficult to inhibit...

它无时无刻动念轻躁，难以调御……
It is constantly squirming and restless. Indeed, it is hard to tame...

但我们得先调御这颗心，然后才能一劳永逸地永远安详快乐。
But we must discipline this mind first, then we will be able to stay in peace and joy once and for all.

人的一切痛苦烦恼全都来自于自己的一颗心！一个呼吸间，心识就起了很多念，心一动念，人就随念而转，于是大苦则聚成了……
All of human suffering comes from our own mind. Just within the time of one breath, our consciousness has already generated many thoughts. Once the mind starts pursuing one thought, our whole being wraps around that thought. That is how great suffering starts taking form...

217

如鱼离水栖
Like Fish Living Without Water

就如同箭工将箭调直一样，智者也会将自己走偏的思想像箭工调箭般地调正。

Similar to bow makers straightening arrows, wise ones also control their deviant thoughts.

就好像一条脱离水搁浅在岸上颤抖的鱼一样急迫的心情，去摆脱心灵的魔境。

With the same anxiety as a wiggling fish on the bank seeking to return to the water, the wise anxiously rid themselves of spiritual nightmares.

如果让心随自己的欲望摆布，我们便会意志狂乱而无法自我掌握……心控制得当，能够自我主宰就能够得到安详快乐啊！

If we allow our mind to be manipulated by our desires, our mind will go crazy and we will completely lose control of ourselves. On the other hand, proper control of the mind will indeed allow us to be our own master and attain serenity!

木匠擅于以规、矩取方圆，造屋者擅于以墨绳取直曲，而智者擅以观照自己的心，守护感官不让欲望入侵而受其摆布。我们如果要主宰自己，得要学会控制自己的感官，净化自己的心不让它受外在的影响，这样我们才可能成为自己的主。

Carpenters are good at using appropriate instruments go make squares and circles. Home builders are good at using appropriate instruments to make straight and curved lines. Similarly, wise ones are good at reflecting upon their own mind. They protect their senses from invasion and manipulation by desires.

If we want to be our own master, we have to learn how to control our senses well. Purify the mind and protect it from environmental influences—this is how we are always able to be our own master.

胜败两俱舍
Let Go Of Both Victory And Defeat

征战无法达成愉快和圆满……
Bellicosity cannot bring happiness and perfection...

因为胜利会产生更大的仇恨和不满，
失败时则将坠落痛苦的深渊。
...because victory will produce even more hatred and dissatisfaction. On the other hand, failure will shove us into the depths of suffering.

唯有放弃胜利和失败两端，
才能获得真正的寂静安详。
Only when we let go of both the extremes of victory and failure, can we attain true serenity.

我们的行为不要落入于征战和争辩，一旦落入于净，一生便落入于纷争，我们的心也将随之起伏，烦恼痛苦也就紧随着我们。
Refrain from bellicosity and disputes. Once we fall into such conflicts, our life will be trapped in strife. Our mind will go up and down with victory and defeat. Worries and sufferings will be hot on our heels.

人同此心
People Share The Same Mentality

所有的人都战栗于被别人惩罚，所有的人都害怕死亡。
All humans tremble when being punished by others.
All humans are fearful of death.

将心比心，将别人比自己……
Put yourself in others' shoes. Treat others the way we treat ourselves.

我们不希望别人加诸于我们的，我们也不加诸于别人。
Do not do unto others what you do not wish done to you.

一个不杀害别人的人，就不会造成别人杀害他的原因。
Those who do not kill others are less likely to create reasons for others to kill them.

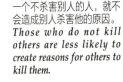

与乐曰慈，拔苦曰悲；同体大慈，无缘大悲。给予快乐叫做慈，替对方解决痛苦叫做悲。将心比心感同身受叫大慈，不分亲属、敌人同样看待地帮助叫大悲。为恶将遭恶所报复，不作恶者遭受到恶的机会自然就少。

To bring joy to others is kindness. To relieve others of suffering is compassion. Have great kindness towards others, as if we were all of the same body. Have great compassion towards others with whom we have no direct association. Put yourself in others' shoes. Be it our family or enemy, always help others with no discrimination. Those who do carry out evil deeds will receive evil deeds in return. Those who do not carry out evil acts are naturally less likely to encounter evil deeds.

一切皆
不可执著
Avoid Atta-
chment

因为有迷惘，所以才有觉悟。如无迷惘，何来觉悟
呢？离开迷惘，即无觉悟，离开觉悟，也无迷惘。
*Because there is illusion, there is enlightenment. If
there were no illusion to be enlightened to, where
is enlightenment coming from? Without illusion,
there would be no enlightenment. Without enlightenment, there would be no illusion.*

因此，执著于觉悟也是一种障碍。
*Therefore, attachment to enlightenment is also a
kind of obstacle.*

我们的心执著于什
么，那个所执著的
就成囚牢，如果我
们执著于觉悟，那
么觉悟就是一种囚
牢。因此，一切都
不可以执著。
*Whatever our mind
is attached to will
become our prison.
If we are attached to
enlightenment, then
enlightenment itself
can also become a
prison. Therefore,
we must not be at-
tached to anything.*

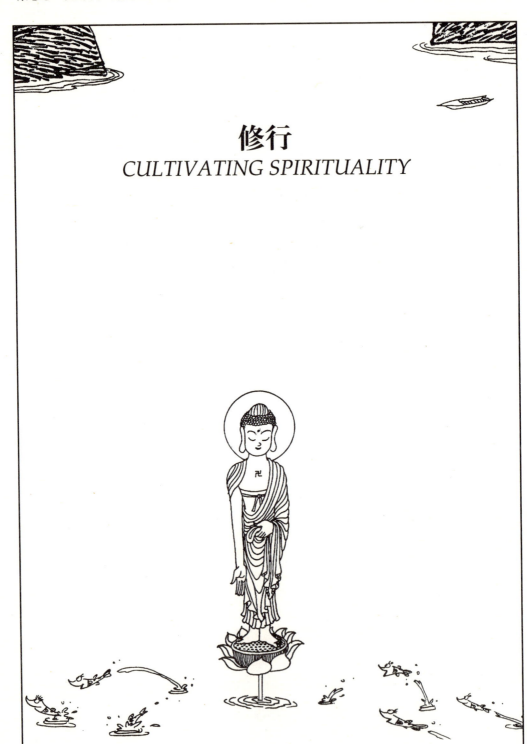

修行
CULTIVATING SPIRITUALITY

修行是净化自己心灵的过程……
净化自己完全在于自己，别人无法代替，
但是心要怎么净化呢？
佛陀说：
诸恶莫作，
众善奉行，
自净其意，
是诸佛教。
我们的心有很多种作用，
有一部分是坏的作用，
不利于自己也不利于别人。
有一部分是好的作用，
利于自己也利于别人。
什么是内心坏的作用呢？
就是贪欲、瞋恨、无知、爱欲、固执、
愤怒、恐惧、自大、骄傲、恶意、不满、
忧虑、焦躁等等。
什么是好的作用呢？
就是爱、慈悲、容忍、毅力、
无私、公正、善意……等等。

Spiritual cultivation is the process of purifying our consciousness...
Buddha once said:
"Purifying ourselves depends completely upon each of us. No one else can take our place."
But how are we supposed to purify our consciousness?
REFRAIN FROM ANY EVIL DEEDS.
DO ONLY GOOD DEEDS.
PURIFY YOUR OWN CONSCIOUSNESS.
THESE ARE THE TEACHINGS OF BUDDHA.
*Our mental activities have many kinds of effects. Some are negative and
benefit neither ourselves nor others.*
Some are positive and benefit both ourselves and others.
What are the negative effects of our conscious mind?
*They are greed, resentment, delusion, desire, stubbornness, anger, fear,
arrogance, pride, hostility, dissatisfaction, worry, anxiety and so on.*
What are the positive effects of our conscious mind?
*They are love, compassion, patience, endurance,
selflessness, justice, kindness and so on.*

过去的觉悟者们通过观照自己的心的修行，
了解人会产生痛苦、烦恼完全是来自于自心的那部分不好的作用。
因此过去的觉悟者们教导我们：
别让内心不好的作用兴起造作，
要让内心好的作用施展出来：
自己观照自己的心……
将心净化到完全没有不良的痛苦因子。
如果内心不再有坏的作用那一部分，
我们便不再会从其中引起痛苦、烦恼而达到永恒的愉快、安详。
修行即是净化心灵的过程，
能做到内心完全没有杂质、不造作，
我们便抵达了没有痛苦循环轮转的彼岸，
而永享快乐安静的寂静之境。

Through the spiritual cultivation of self-reflection, enlightened ones of the past realized that all human sufferings and worries arose completely from the negative effects of our mind.

Therefore, enlightened ones of the past taught us: do not ever allow internal negativity to get started, encourage your mind's positive effects to become manifest.

We are the ones who take care of our own minds...

We should purify our minds completely, so there will be no negativity to cause suffering.

If our minds no longer contain negative effects, then we will never again be led to suffering and worries. This is how we will attain eternal joy and peace.

Spiritual cultivation is the process of purifying our consciousness.

If we can achieve the state devoid of impure qualities and unnatural pretensions, then we will have arrived at "the Other Shore" that is without further cycles of suffering.

This is the place of quiescence where we can experience eternal joy.

诸恶莫作
Refrain From Any Evil Deeds

任何的恶都不可以作。
We should not do any kind of evil deeds at all.

所有的善都应该努力遵行。
We should diligently carry out all kinds of good deeds.

自己净化自己的心，使它纯清无染。
Purify your own mind to keep it clear, without pollution.

我们的心有很多种作用：贪念、欲望、愤怒、敌意、不满、骄傲、自大、恐惧、善意、慈悲、爱、容忍等等，这些作用有一半是属于对自己有害也不利于别人，有一半则是有利于自己与一切生灵。净化自己的心就是去除内在不好的心识作用，不令恶质的作用生出来。
Our mind has many types of effects: greed, desire, anger, hostility, dissatisfaction, arrogance, pride, fear, as well as kindness, compassion, love, tolerance and so on. About half of these effects are harmful for both ourselves and others, while the other half are beneficial for both ourselves and all living beings. Purifying our mind means eradicating the harmful effects of our inner consciousness and keeping negativity from even getting started.

以上这些……
就是了悟了真理的觉悟者们所教导我们的。
The enlightened ones, who have realized truths, taught us the above principles.

盖屋不密
必为雨浸
A House Built Sloppily Will Definitely Leak

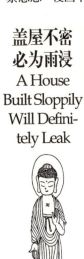

屋顶盖得粗率，房子会遭雨水浸漏……
A house with sloppily built roof will be soaked through by rain and leak water.

未经修养调御的心，欲望贪念会入侵……
A mind that is not cultivated and disciplined will be invaded by desires and greed.

懈怠是死路，努力精进才是生路。
Complacency is a deadend road. Vigilance is the only path for living.

人的心像一间有六个孔洞的屋子，贪、瞋、痴、渴、受、欲无时无刻地侵入，故欲得清净得先修缮自己的心。
The human mind is like a house with six openings. Greed, resentment, delusion, longing, attachment and desire are constantly infiltrating through these holes. Therefore, spiritual cultivation is the ultimate step for attaining purity of the mind.

有智慧的人常努力精进修缮他的心。
Wise ones often work diligently at improving their mind.

如来唯说者
Buddha Is
The Only
Lecturer

每个人要努力自求解脱，如来只是提供了修行的次第方法。
We all need to strive for our own salvation. Buddha only offered us the sequential methods for spiritual cultivation.

就从禅定开始着手，遵照我所说的方法真切地去做。
You can start by cultivating towards "centredness through meditation". Follow the methods I have taught you and implement them in life realistically.

最后终将获得解脱一切外在的束缚，心便得到了自由。
Eventually, you will attain mental freedom and release from all external bondage.

心的净化完全要靠自己，无论是多么神圣的人、多么神圣的经典，他们也仅仅能提供正确的方法指引出道路。净化自己的心完全在于自己，无人可以替代你。
The purification of our mind depends completely upon each of us alone. No matter how divine the teacher or the scripture, they can only offer proper methods to guide you onto the road. Purifying your own mind is totally up to your own self. Nobody else can play your role.

净心而苦灭
Purify The Mind And Suffering Ends

比丘们！要专心于致力令心永葆清净。
My fellow monks! Focus your best efforts on keeping your mind pure at all times.

谁能够不懈地遵行我所说的教理，谁就能够远离痛苦的轮转，而令苦完全消失。
Whoever can follow the principles of my teaching vigilantly will be able to free themselves from the cycles of suffering and make suffering disappear completely.

净心是远离痛苦最好的方式。我们若能守护六种感官，不让欲望去影响我们的心，心不造作行为，痛苦便无从升起。
Purifying the mind is the best method to distance ourselves from suffering. Protect your six senses and do not allow desires to influence your mind. When the mind has no room for misconduct, suffering will have no place from which to arise.

228

犹如猛
火烧去
大小结
Like A
Fierce
Fire That
Burns
Up All
Confi-
ning
Ropes

修行者留意自己的心，
不让思想任意奔流而无法
自我控制。
Spiritual cultivators pay great
attention to the mind. They do
not allow thoughts to freely
gallop without self-control.

他用警觉之
火烧去所有困住
他的大小烦恼。
They use the
fierce fire of great
caution to burn
up all worries,
both big and
small.

修行者留意自己的心，
不让它混乱堕落。
Cultivators watch their own
mind and do not allow confusion or indulgence to enter.

由于这样，他找到了内
心的宁静之道。
This is how they
find the way to inner
quietness.

我们唯有舍弃内心
中的不良杂质，如贪欲、
不满、固执等因子，才
能解开它们对我们的
系缚，心得以自由。
净化自己的心才能找
到内心安详的道路。
We must abandon
the impure qualities
inside us, such as
elements of greed,
dissatisfaction, stub-
bornness and so on.
Only after we release
ourselves from their
bondage, will we
be free spiritually.
Purifying the mind
enables us to find the
way to inner peace.

譬如蜂采蜜
Like Bees Collecting Nectar

修行者进入尘世化缘接受供养时……
When spiritual cultivators enter the ordinary world of mortals to solicit offerings of food...

应该要像蜜蜂采蜜一样。
...they should be like bees collecting nectar.

不损伤花的色与香……
They do not hurt the beauty and fragrance of flowers...

轻盈地采取蜜汁，无害于花本体。
They collect nectar gently without damaging the flowers.

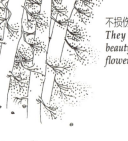

我们一生所需如果只是为了达到维生所需，其实需要的并不多，就像一只鸟、一条虫，天地其实提供的足以满足它们的需求。人为了维生所需，千万别伤了天地，也别伤了自己的心，养成了无尽的贪欲。

If all we need is to achieve a basic level of life support, we do not really need that much. Just like a bird or an insect, the universe actually provides enough to satisfy our survival needs. When we humans try to make a living, we definitely must not damage the surrounding environment. We should also not compromise our integrity and give in to endless greed.

默然为人诽
Quietly Accept Slander From Others

现在和从前一样，无论我们怎么做，都会有人批评。
Now, as well as in the past, no matter how we do things, there will always be people who criticize us.

默默不语，别人也批评！
Even if we stay quiet without a word, we will be criticized!

讲得多，也受到批评；讲得少，别人也批评。
When we talk a lot, we get criticized! If we talk very little, we still get criticized.

自古以来都一样，无论我们怎么做，都会有人批评。
Since ancient times, it has always been the same. No matter how we do things, there will always be people who criticize us.

因此，别在意别人的批评，更别由于别人的批评而影响自己的心。
Therefore, do not mind others' criticisms. Furthermore, do not allow others' criticisms to affect our consciousness.

我们的好或坏全因为自己，我们修正自己是为了要舍弃坏而趋向好的方向，而不是因为别人的批评。无论我们怎么做，总有一半的人反对，因此我们怎么做是为了善恶，而无关于别人的批评。

Whatever direction we take is completely for our own purpose in life. We change ourselves because we want to abandon our character defects and develop more character strengths. We do not change direction because of others' criticisms. No matter how we do anything, usually half of the crowd will be against it. Therefore, how we do things is based on our moral principles of good versus evil. Our decision has nothing to do with others' criticism.

231

心灵的主人
Master Of The Consciousness

如果有人毁谤我，毁谤我的教义或是毁谤我的弟子……
If someone slanders me, my teachings, or my disciples...

千万别因此而沮丧或心情烦乱。
...never become depressed or disturbed by it.

因为这样的反应无济于事，只会造成更大的损害。
This kind of response will not help anything and will only create more damage.

如果有人赞美我，赞美我的教义，或赞美我的弟子……
If someone praises me, my teachings, or my disciples...

不要因而过分欢喜或得意，因为这样的反应会妨碍正确的判断。
...do not become carried away by happiness or pride. This kind or response will interfere with proper judgements.

我们是我们的心灵的主人。
We are the master of our consciousness.

不因为外在的毁誉顺逆而影响自己的心。
Do not allow external slander, praise, success, or adversity to influence your consciousness.

我们也能忍受别人对我们的辱骂和敌视。
We will also be able to endure abuse and hostility from others.

坦然地接受事实的自己就会得到平静。
Those of us who calmly accept facts will attain peace of mind.

坦然地去接受外在，去克服愤怒。
Calmly embrace life on its terms and we will conquer our anger.

以爱去克服不满和怨恨。
Use love to overcome dissatisfaction and resentment.

愚人的心攀缘外在，随着外在的变化起伏，他怎能称自己为自己的主？
智者保有自己，不因为别人的评断与态度而改变自己的心，因此他是自己的主。
The minds of fools are attached to external things and fluctuate with environmental changes. How could they claim to be their own master? Wise ones protect themselves and keep their integrity intact. They do not change their mind due to others' judgements and attitudes. Therefore, they are indeed their own master.

如象在战阵
Like An Ele-
phant On A
Battlefield

我们要像一只大象一样，在战场上能承受箭的毒害而继续奋战不已……

We want to be like an elephant on a battlefield, enduring the pain of poisonous arrown and continuing to fight on and on.

我们也能忍受别人对我们的侮辱和敌视，而能保持自己内心的安详寂静。

We can also endure insult and hostility from others, and retain our inner peace and quiet.

心的不纯净是引发痛苦的来源！什么使得心不净呢？顽固、骄傲、自大是心理的杂质，由于这些杂质引出了错误的思想和行为，于是痛苦也因而产生于此。

Impurity of the mind is the origin of suffering. What makes the mind impure? Stubbornness, pride and arrogance are the mental impurities. These impurities lead to wrong thoughts and conduct and, in turn, the creation of suffering.

以恶止恶只会引来更大的纷争，唯有以完全坦然的善意才能平息恶的施展。
况且我之为我完全是因为自己才是什么，而不因为别人改变自己。
一朵芳香的花朵不因为憎恶的人到来而改变芳香的本质而发臭。

To stop evil with evil only invites more discord. The spread of evil can only be diminished with totally open kindess. Besides, I am what I am entirely because of my nature. I do not change my nature for others' sake. A fragrant flower does not change its natural fragrance to a foul smell just because of the arrival of a person it dislikes.

是故真实
This Is Real

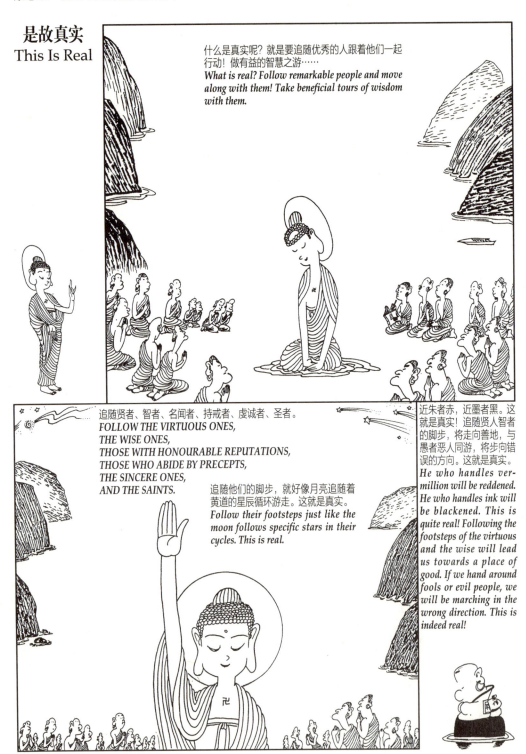

什么是真实呢？就是要追随优秀的人跟着他们一起行动！做有益的智慧之游⋯⋯

What is real? Follow remarkable people and move along with them! Take beneficial tours of wisdom with them.

追随贤者、智者、名闻者、持戒者、虔诚者、圣者。

FOLLOW THE VIRTUOUS ONES,
THE WISE ONES,
THOSE WITH HONOURABLE REPUTATIONS,
THOSE WHO ABIDE BY PRECEPTS,
THE SINCERE ONES,
AND THE SAINTS.

追随他们的脚步，就好像月亮追随着黄道的星辰循环游走。这就是真实。

Follow their footsteps just like the moon follows specific stars in their cycles. This is real.

近朱者赤，近墨者黑。这就是真实！追随贤人智者的脚步，将走向善地，与愚者恶人同游，将步向错误的方向。这就是真实。

He who handles vermillion will be reddened. He who handles ink will be blackened. This is quite real! Following the footsteps of the virtuous and the wise will lead us towards a place of good. If we hand around fools or evil people, we will be marching in the wrong direction. This is indeed real!

恶友比猛兽可怕
Evil Friends Are More Frightening Than Fierce Beasts

猛兽可以不再怕，但恶友可不能不畏……
We do not have to be afraid of fierce beasts, but we must be fearful of evil friends...

因为猛兽只会伤害我们的身体，
...because fierce beasts can only damage our physical body,

而恶友则会带坏了我们的心灵。
...while evil friends will bring harm to our spirit.

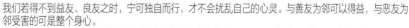

我们若得不到益友、良友之时，宁可独自而行，才不会扰乱自己的心灵。与善友为邻可以得益，与恶友为邻受害的可是整个身心。
When we cannot find beneficial and helpful friends, it is better to walk alone than to bring chaos to our spirit. Clearly we gain much from being around good friends. Being around evil friends will harm our whole body and mind.

不与愚人作伴侣
Do Not Keep Company With Fools

如果得不到比我们优秀的人作为朋友……
If we cannot find friends who are more spiritual than we are...

连和我们同一程度的人也找不到时……
...or even friends who are about as spiritual as we are...

宁可一个人独自修行，也不要和愚人相伴一起修行。
...it is better to cultivate alone. Do not cultivate in the company of fools.

宁可孤独修行，孤独地生活，也不要与愚人恶者为伍，因为他们会败坏了我们的心灵，增长感官的追寻。
We would much rather cultivate spirituality alone and spend our life alone than to be in company of fools or evil people. They will ruin our spirit and encourage harmful pursuits.

238

不与愚为友
Do Not Be-
friend Fools

宁可一个人独自走修行之道，也不
要和愚昧的人为友同行。
It is better to walk the road spiri-
tual cultivation alone than to
befriend fools along the way.

独自修行远离欲望的入侵，
Cultivating alone enables
us to distance ourselves
from the invasion of
desires,

独自观照修行，
犹如一只象勇猛地在
森林中独行。
Take the opportunity
of cultivating alone
to reflect on yourself.
Think of yourself as
an elephant bravely
marching on alone in
a forest.

走向心灵净化的修
行之道时，宁可一
个人孤独而行，也
不与恶友、愚友同
行。因为他们不但
无助于我们的修
行，还会由于他们
错误的观念引来了
更多烦恼，有害于
正确的净心。
On our path of
cultivation to-
wards purifying our
spirit, it is better to
march alone than
to walk with evil
or foolish friends.
Not only are they
of no help to our
cultivation, their
improper concepts
will bring us more
worries. They are
literally harmful to
the proper purifica-
tion of our mind.

如象独行林
Like An Elephant Marching In A Forest

修行之路，如果有同伴相行时，应善用智慧思虑，互相关照，克服困难。

If we have companions walking along the road of cultivation, we should make good use of our wisdom, care about each other, and overcome obstacles together.

没有同伴时，也应善用自己的智慧思虑，有如一位国王放弃了他的王位和国家，有如一只大象勇猛地在森林独行。

In the case that we have no companions, we should also make good use of our wisdom. Imagine yourself as a king who has given up status and kingdom, but bravely marches through a forest like a forceful elephant.

人有两个我，一个是别人心目中的我，另一个是心灵中的我。而在孤独的时候，那个心灵中的我最容易显现出来，不要害怕孤独，因为这个时候也是最容易与自己沟通，是最好的净化自己的心的时候。

Humans have two different "I's". One is the "I" as seen by others; the other is the "I" in our own spirit. When we are alone, that is the best time for that "I" in our spirit to appear. Do not be afraid of being alone—this is the easiest time to communicate with ourselves and the best time to purify our mind.

240

象师调象
Like The Ele-
phant Trainer
Disciplining
An Elephant

从前我的心随着感官的刺激纵情恣欲，我的身随着欲望的追寻而无止息。

In the past, my mind used to follow sensory stimuli and indulge in seeking pleasures. My body used to follow the pursuit of desires without rest.

而现在我知道要切除外在感官的诱惑，静心地观照自己，使自己成为身心的真正主人。

Right now. I know I need to abandon temptations from external stimuli, quietly reflect on myself, and make myself the true master of my own body and mind.

就像象师持着钩在训练大象一样，调御大象使它听从主人的心意。

This is just like the elephant trainer using a hook to discipline an elephant, which will learn to listen to its master's wish through training.

怎么样调御自己的身心呢?
就是在处于感官快乐的情境时，静心观照守护自己的心，别让感官刺激侵入。
What is the correct way to train our body and mind? Calmly observe and protect our mind even when we are in a state of sensory pleasure. Do not allow sensory stimuli to invade our quiet mind.

把自己从外在的诱惑中救出来，犹如一只跌落泥坑的大象，奋力冲出泥坑。
Save ourselve from external temptation, just like an elephant charging out of a mudhole after a fall.

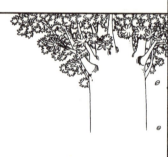

如果我们不能守护自己的感官，像士兵守护各个城门一样，那么感官所接收而来的刺激将影响我们的心，而这颗心将随着外在的各种不同变化而变化。外在顺随我们的心时我们就快乐，外在不如我们的意时，我们就不满而悲伤。人要守护自己的感官，调御自己的心如象师驯象一般。
We need to protect our senses like soldiers who guard every gate of a castle. Otherwise, sensory stimuli will influence our mind, which in turn will fluctuate with all sorts of external changes...We thereby become dependent on the external world, being happy when things go our way and upset when things do not. Therefore, humans must protect their senses and modulate and manage their mind just like an elephant trainer disciplining an elephant.

智者
WISE ONES

修行净化自己的心，有三个次第步骤：
就是戒、定、慧三学。
我们观照自己的心，了解引起痛苦的真正原因，
就是由于我们的心起了心识作用，
而去行有害于自己和别人的行为，乃至引发了烦恼、痛苦。
因此针对这个心开始做起……
首先守护感官不令刺激进入心灵，
也不做会引起内心激动、不安的错误行为，
巩固自己的心有如卫士守护城门一样，
这就是"戒"——行为与心灵的守护。

There are three sequential steps in spiritual cultivation and the purification of our mind: they include the study of precepts, settling down to concentration through meditation, and the development of wisdom.

If we reflect on ourselves, we will understand the real causes of suffering: because our mind starts manifesting behaviours that hurt ourselves and others. That is how worries and sufferings are created.

Therefore, we begin by focusing on this mind...

First, we protect our senses to keep improper stimuli from entering our consciousness.

We then refrain from carrying out improper behaviours that lead to inner excitement and anxiety.

We strengthen the defence of our mind just like soldiers protecting the gates of their castle.

This is the meaning of "precepts" — the guidelines for protecting our behaviours and our consciousness.

由于戒而心生安定，
再加上正确的禅定，
将心止于一处，平静不令它生起杂想妄念……
这就是"定"——心识安定寂静，不造作诸端混乱。
由于心安定了，便能像一池清潭一样照见一切，
加上明白正确的真理，了解生命的真实样子，
如实正确地看待一切，
这种没有自我执着、没有偏见的观点，
便能更清楚地去看清真实。
于是由"定"而生"慧"，智慧便自然地开展而来。
修行者通过正确的修行，
便能由戒生定，由定生意，成为一个智者。
他在愉快中品尝修行过程所得的甜美成果，
愉快地享受着生命真正美好的一面，
在愉快中觉悟出生命的真正意义。
正如佛陀听说，
智慧的行持，
将获得甜蜜的果实。

Abiding by precepts allows the mind to settle down.

We then add correct meditation to centre the mind at a calm place without any random thoughts...This is referred to as "centredness through meditation" — the conscious mind is peaceful and quiet, not creating any kind of confusion.

Because the mind is at peace, it will be able to mirror everything like a clear pond. In addition, if we understand proper truths and realize the true nature of life, we will be able to see everything correctly as it truly is.

This point of view, devoid of attachment to self and prejudice, will enable us to see truths ever so clearly.

Therefore, we develop wisdom based on centredness of mind.

This is how wisdom begins to spontaneously unfold within us.

Through correct methods of cultivation, we can achieve centredness through meditation by following precepts. This centredness gives rise to wisdom.

This is how spiritual cultivators become wise ones.

In joy, they taste the delicious fruits of the cultivation process, experience the truly magnificent aspects of life, and are enlightened to the real meaning of life.

Just as Buddha once said:

"Wise conducts in life will lead to sweet fruits."

觉知之道
The Way To Realization

智者不依凭学说，
Wise ones do not rely on theories,

智者不捆缚自己。
Wise ones do not tie themselves up.

他们只是仔细地看，仔细地听。
They only watch carefully and listen carefully.

如果我们的心执取什么，心就为其所困。智者无心，因此他没有固执不移的偏见，他不自困于不变，而是随着变化而变化。
Whatever our mind is attached to will trap our mind. Wise ones have their mind set on nothing. Therefore, they have no prejudices that they stubbornly adhere to, they do not trap themselves by not accepting change, and they just adapt to change.

246

智者自为洲
Wise Ones Are Islands Above The Flood Waters

智者很清醒地随时观照自己的心，反躬自省……
Wise ones constantly observe their own mind and reflect on themselves with clarity...

他很克己地小心注意自己的行为……
They carefully pay attention to their own behaviours with great discipline...

他遵照经典所说的正确方式生活……
They follow the proper lifestyles as prescribed by scriptures...

他奋勉地自制不放纵自己，调御自己的身心……
They refrain from indulging themselves and train their own body and mind diligently...

于是他使自己成为一个岛屿高地，洪水不能淹没他。
Therefore, they turn themselves into high islands which flood waters cannot submerge.

如果我们放纵自己的身心行为而无能自制，那么欲望、贪婪、愤怒、恐惧等便如洪水一样地吞没了我们。人要自我克制自己的身心行为，使自己变成一座岛屿、堡垒，这时才能成为一个真正属于自己的完整之人。
If we indulge our body and mind without self-control, then we will be engulfed by the flood of desires, greed, anger and fear. We humans need to self-discipline our own behaviours and enable ourselves to become castles on high islands. Then our complete self will truly serve us.

犹如
坚固岩
Like
Sturdy
Rocks

就像坚固结实的岩石，不会被风吹动一样……
Blowing wind cannot move solid and sturdy rocks...

毁谤、赞誉、批评、恭维，
Whether it is slander, praise, criticism or flattery,...

智者不会因这些外在的顺逆而动摇自己的心。
...all external adulation or adversities cannot shake the mind of the wise ones.

智者守护自己的心，如实地坦然接受真正的那个自己，不因为别人的毁誉而沮丧或得意。智者像一座岩石，八风吹不动，他屹立于风中而不移。
Wise ones protect their own mind and calmly accept the terms of the real self. They do not become depressed or proud because of others' slander or praise. Wise ones are like sturdy rocks standing up to all kinds of emotional winds. They just stand tall in the wind without moving an inch.

善人
离诸欲
Virtuous
Ones
Leave All
Desires

智者的心就像一池清净的湖水一样清澈澄净。
The mind of wise ones is clean and pure, just like the water of a clear lake.

智者完全了解生命的真理，他的心有如湖水般的清净。
Wise ones completely realize the truths in life, and their mind stays pure like lake water.

智者擅于净化自己，不被欲望、苦、乐所动，因此，智者的心非常平静，远离忧喜。
Wise ones are skilful at purifying themselves. They are not moved by desires, suffering or pleasures. Therefore, the mind of wise ones is quite calm and far away from worries and happiness.

雁过寒潭，雁去潭不留影；风吹疏竹，风过竹不留声。智者的心像一池清潭，像一面明镜。它只是如实地反映变化，而自己不被变化所改变。
When geese fly over a pool of water, they do not leave any shadows in the water. Similarly, when wind blows through thickets of bamboo, it does not leave any sound in the thicket. Wise ones' mind is like a pure pond or a clear mirror. It only reflects changes as they truly are, and does not fluctuate with the changes.

非过思为过
Taking Non-errors As Errors

智者了解自己，也了解宇宙的实相，并按照真实的样子去看待它……凡夫不了解实相，也常因错看生命的本质，而活在痛苦之中。

Wise ones understand themselves and the truths of the universe. These people of wisdom also treat all things according to their true nature...
Ordinary people do not understand the truths and frequently have misperceptions about the nature of life. As a result, such earthly humans often live in suffering.

不应该羞愧而羞愧，应该羞愧而不知羞愧……

Feeling shame when there is no need to, not feeling shame when one should...

这样的人将走向痛苦烦恼的境地。
Such people will walk towards the state of suffering and worries.

不应该恐惧而恐惧，应该害怕的而不自知害怕……
这样的人终将走向痛苦、烦恼的境地。

Feeling fearful when there is no need to, not feeling fearful when one should...
Such people will eventually walk towards the state of suffering and worries.

不是过失误以为是过失，而真正的过失却不自知是过失……这样的人将走向痛苦烦恼的境地。
Believing correct behaviours to be mistakes, not recognising mistakes when real mistakes are made...
Such people will walk towards the state of suffering and worries.

智者对一切如实知，并按真实的样子去看待一切。
Wise ones know all things as they truly are. These people of wisdom also treat all things according to their true nature.

过失时自知过失，没有过失时自知没有过失……
Wise ones know their own mistakes when they make them, and believe they have made no mistakes when they have not...

因此，他一步一步地走向完美的层次。
Therefore, one step at a time, they walk towards the level of perfection.

我们痛苦，是因为我们无知，是因为我们固执。智者了解自己，对外在的一切也都如实知。因此智者没有迷惘，因为智者了解真实。
We suffer because of our ignorance and because of our stubbornness. Wise ones understand themselves and know all external things as things really are. Therefore, because they realize truths, wise ones have no confusions.

智者弃小乐
Wise Ones Abandon Small Pleasures

舍弃一己之私、点点滴滴小小满足的追寻，才能得到永恒的安详宁静。智者舍弃小乐，因此他得到了大乐。

Only when we abandon pursuing small drops of satisfaction for our own sake, can we attain eternal peace and quiet.
Wise ones obtain ultimate joy because they can abandon small pleasures.

如果为了达到个人的满足而使得别人受苦……
If we make others suffer because of our personal satisfaction...

他便被憎恨、不满所纠缠，怨恨憎恶将紧紧地跟随着他而不得解脱。
...then we will be entangled by others' hatred and resentment. We will be closely followed by animosity and never be free.

应该做的没有做，不应该做的却做了……自傲而放纵自己行为的人，他便会增加自己的烦恼。

Not carrying out dèeds that should be done, and carrying out deeds that should not be done...Those arrogant people who do as they please will add to their own worries.

智者常观照自己的身心，不行不应行的恶，而行该要行的善。

Wise ones often reflect on their own body and mind. They avoid doing things that they should not do, and do things that they should do.

由于他经常观照自己，因此所有的烦恼便不会发生，而得到身心的宁静。

Because they reflect on themselves often, worries are no longer generated. They therefore attain peace of body and mind.

人无法由感官获得真正的满足，我们愈是供给它的需求，它们要求得愈多。假使我们肯静下感官，而不纵情恣欲，这时我们的心将逐渐清醒过来，慢慢地将了解生活的目的，而不再作盲目的感官满足的追寻。

Humans cannot gain real satisfaction from sensory pleasures. The more their demands are met, the more they ask for. If we are willing to calm down our senses and not indulge ourselves in seeking pleasures, then our consciousness will gradually awaken. Then, little by little, we will come to realize the deeper meaning of life and no longer foolishly pursue sensory satisfaction.

智者防护心
Wise Ones Guard Their Mind

如果我们的心臣服于欲望，它便显得捉摸不定，这颗瞬息变化的心任谁也无能掌握。

If our mind is submissive to our desires, then it will appear to be unpredictably chaotic. This kind of fickle mind, which changes from instant to instant, cannot be managed by anyone.

智者防护自己的心，能完全地驾驭它，而获得宁静快乐。

Wise ones guard their mind and are capable of controlling it completely. This is how they attain peace and joy.

智者调御自己的心，无论它想得远还是近，或是无想无形，都在自己的控制之中，由于智者是心的主人，所以他找到了自由。

Wise ones train their minds and discipline their own thinking process, whether it involves deep pondering or brain-storming or being quiet without a thought. Because wise people are the master of their own mind, they find freedom.

我们不是自己的主人，我们是外在的奴隶。我们的苦与乐不是由自己做主，而是随着外在的顺逆而起伏。智者自我控制自己的心，因此他是自己的主。

We cannot claim to be our own master when we are slaves to the external world. When we fluctuate up and down with external events that go our way or against us, we are not in charge of our own joy and suffering. Wise ones self-control their own mind, and therefore are their own master.

不观他人过
Not Watching Others' Faults

智者用心的重点，不在于观察别人有没有过错，也不在于观察别人造不造恶行。

Wise ones do not focus their minds on whether others have made mistakes or have acted in evil ways.

智者用心的重点在于反躬自省自己的身心有没有过失……

Wise ones focus their minds on reflecting upon themselves. They self-examine their bodies and minds for any errors.

自己本身该做到的善有没有做到？不该造的恶自己是不是没有做？

They ask themselves: "Have I accomplished the good deeds as I should have? Have I avoided the evil deeds as I should have?"

修行的第一步得先做到对修行有益的要做到，有害于自身修行和有害于别人的千万不要做，不观他人过，只观自己该做的有没有做，不该做的又有没有做。

The first step in spiritual cultivation is to do everything possible that benefits cultivation. At the same time, we must make absolutely sure that we refrain from doing anything that harms our own cultivation or other people. Do not watch others' faults. We should only observe ourselves to examine whether we have done everything as we should and whether we have avoided everything we need to.

255

易见他人过
Seeing Faults In Others Is Easy

别人的过错我们很容易发现，但要发现自己的过失则很困难。
It is so easy to see others' faults and yet quite hard to discover our own shortcomings.

我们要舍去自己的过失如同舍去糟糠一样地自我净化……
We must get rid of our character defects and purify ourselves, just like husks of rice are discarded in the milling process.

已经犯过的错误绝不再犯。
No matter what, do not repeat the same mistake over and over again.

正如下棋的人绝不再下出曾经犯过的恶手。
Be a chess player who never makes the same fatal error twice.

看到别人的过失就生气，这样的人只会增加烦恼，他离开净化自己的道路愈来愈远了。

Some people get upset whenever they see others' faults. This kind of attitude will only increase their own problems. They will depart further and further from the road of personal purification.

天空没有可以走的道路，错误的修行方法抵达不了觉悟的终极目际。

The sky offers no road for walking. Improper methods of cultivation will never lead us to our final goal of enlightenment.

人们喜欢追寻虚妄不实的事物，觉悟了的智者看清真实，不被虚妄所迷惑。

People often like to pursue illusory ideas that have no firm base in reality. The wise ones who are enlightened can see the truths and are not confused by illusions.

人看不到真实，他看到的只是站在一己立场的偏见。
智者无我，他不以自己的立场看事物。
由于智者的心中没有我和我所有的观念，因此他看到的不是局部的偏见，而是全部。

Humans usually cannot see truths. Rather, they only see personal prejudice from their own perspective. Wise ones have no ego-self and do not see things from their own point of view. Because the minds of wise ones do not even have the concepts of "I" and "mine", they see the whole picture instead of one part based on their bias.

莫嗜爱欲乐
Do Not Luxuriate In Hedonistic Pleasure

愚蠢的人沉溺于放任，因此成为欲望的奴隶。智者不放任自己，留意观照自己的心，因为他知道那是自家的珍宝。

Fools indulge in doing as they please; therefore, they become slaves of desires. Wise ones do not allow themselves to do as their desires wish and keep a close eye on their own mind. They know well that the mind is the most precious possession.

别耽溺于外在的一切而放任自己啊！别嗜爱外在的欲望所得来的快乐啊！

Do not indulge in external stimuli and allow yourself to luxuriate in heeding wishes! Do not gloat over external pleasures motivated by personal desires!

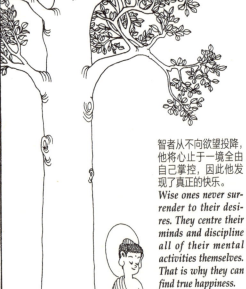

智者从不向欲望投降，他将心止于一境全由自己掌控，因此他发现了真正的快乐。

Wise ones never surrender to their desires. They centre their minds and discipline all of their mental activities themselves. That is why they can find true happiness.

人为了维生，必须取其所需。但人由于无知，在他取其所需的过程中学会了贪欲，于是渐渐地他的心便被外在的利益所控制而成为欲望的奴隶。我们要向一只蜜蜂学习，它为了生活采蜜时，既不伤害花也不伤害自己。

In order to make a living, humans must take what they need from the environment. However, because of their ignorance, they learn to be greedy in the process of meeting their needs. Therefore, they gradually become controlled by external profit and turn into slaves of desires. We have a lot to learn from bees, which never harm flowers or themselves when gathering nectar.

**舍恶取善
乃为牟尼**
Giving Up Evil
And Taking
Up Goodness
To Become
A Tranquil
Buddha

愚昧无知的人，他虽然也是默然不语寂静的样子，但智者不会误以为他们是圣人啊！
Foolish and ignorant people may be quiet, but wise ones will definitely not mistake them for saints!

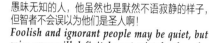

能调服身心，知晓内在外在的才是真的圣人。
Only those who can discipline their body and mind as well as understand their inner and outer worlds are true saints.

圣洁的人不因为他默然不语或满口真理，圣洁的人是因为他的心能舍弃恶而取其善，能自我控制自己，因此他才称为牟尼。
Saints are saints not because they are quiet or talk about truths. Saints are saints because their minds can abandon evil and adopt goodness. They are capable of keeping themselves to be quiet in body, mouth and consciousness. That is why they are respectfully referred to as the tranquil Buddhas.

能舍弃一切的恶，而取一切的善才是真正的圣人。
Only those who can give up all evil and embrace all goodness are real saints.

259

彼岸
THE OTHER SHORE

佛陀说：
通往世间的利益是一条路，
通往智慧的彼岸又是另一条路。
以佛为师的佛弟子们啊！
不要贪图世间的利益，
应该要远离满足贪欲的那条路啊！
无论我们的生命还有多长，
我们只能活在当下的这一时，
无论世界有多广大，
我们只能站立于目前所站的这一处。
无论世界上的路有多少条，
但我们只能走在目前正在前进的这条路。
我们无能同时活在过去、现在、未来，
我们也无能同时踩在这里、那里、此处、他处。
我们的一双脚更不可能同时走两条路，
更何况这两条路的终点
又是完全相反的目的地，
不属于同一个层次。

Buddha once said: "One road leads to earthly profits, while another separate road leads to "the Other Shore" of wisdom.

My Buddhist disciples!

If you honour Buddha as your teacher, then do not long for earthly profits.

You should distance yourselves from that road of never-ending desires.

No matter how long our life is, we can only live in this present moment.

No matter how wide the world is, we can only stand right here at this spot right now.

No matter how many roads there are on this planet, we can only walk on the very road that we are marching on here and now.

We are just not capable of living in the past, the present, and the future, all at the same time. Neither can we be standing here, there, this place and that place, at the same time.

It is entirely impossible for our two feet to be walking two separate roads at the same time — not to mention that the destination of these two roads are completely opposite in direction and elevation of consciousness.

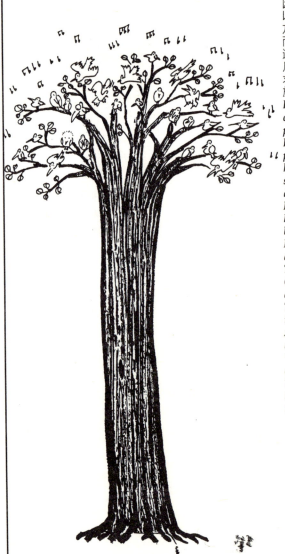

生而为一个有思、有想、有自我意识的人，
当然很自然地会追求个人的快乐。
什么才是对自己最有益、最久远的快乐呢？
人在尚未知晓什么是永恒的快乐之前，
通常都是追求世间的个人利益与感官上的刺激，以获得
个人欲望的满足。
而佛陀说：
当一个人追求外在欲望的快乐之时，这个快乐就是痛苦
的来源。
人无法从欲望的获得而满足，
因为欲望满足了之后会增长更大的欲望，
以致永远填不满，唯有追求心灵的满足才是永恒的快乐
方式。
而追求世间的利益是一条路，
追求心灵永恒的快乐又是另外一条路。
凡是在此岸追求世间利益的就是凡夫众生，走向彼岸追
求心灵圆满的就是修行者，而抵达彼岸完全获得心灵解
放的觉悟者们就是"佛"。

Born as a human being with ideas, thoughts and consciousness of the self, it is natural for us to seek personal happiness.

But, what is the most beneficial and longlasting happiness for the self? Before humand realize what eternal happiness is, we usually pursue personal profit and sensory stimuli to achieve the satisfaction of personal desires in this world.

However, Buddha taught us: "When a person seeks happiness from external desires, this happiness will become the source of suffering."

Humans cannot gain satisfaction from desires, because our desires always grow bigger after they are satisfied.

Therefore, we can never fill up the bottomless pit of desires. Only pursuit of spiritual satisfaction is the way to eternal joy.

The road that takes us to eternal joy of the spirit is entirely different from the road leading to earthly profit.

All of those who seek earthly profit on "This Shore" are ordinary living beings. Those who move towards "the Other Shore" to seek spiritual perfection are the cultivators.

The enlightened ones who have reached "the Other Shore" and attained complete spiritual salvation are the Buddhas.

262

达彼岸者少
Few Can Reach "The Other Shore"

世界上这么多人当中，能净化自己的心而达至彼岸的人很少。

Out of so many people in the world, very few can purify their mind to reach "the Other Shore."

大多数的人都是在追求个人的利益以满足贪欲，徘徊在痛苦轮转的彼岸。

Most people are busy pursuing personal profit to satisfy their greedy desires. Therefore, they continue to cycle through sufferings on "This Shore".

人有两种状态，一是睡，一是醒。有多少人是真正清醒地正确过他的一生？大多数人都只是随着别人与客观环境的步骤而活，不自知自己，也不自知自己要去哪里？他的行为只是跟随着世风而行，这样的人怎么能说是清醒？

Humans have two states to being — being asleep and being awake. How many people are really awake and live their life to the fullest? Most people only live passively, according to the presumed sequence of events as prescribed by other people and the immediate environment. They do not know who they are or where they want to be. Their actions only follow the societal trends surrounding them. How can this kind of person be considered to be awake at all?

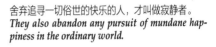

自为
自依陪
Self As
Self's Re-
fuge

身静、语静、心静，身心止于寂静之境。
Tranquil saints calm down the body, lips and mind in a state of quietness...

舍弃追寻一切俗世的快乐的人，才叫做寂静者。
They also abandon any pursuit of mundane happiness in the ordinary world.

以自己为保护者，自我保护，以自己为依靠处，自我依靠。我们应该要自我驯服自己的身心，就像驯马师在调教良马一样。
These saints are their own guards in self-protection. Their self-reliance is their own refuge.

静心就是让心休息不工作，不以自我的立场去心生判断，更不以个人的利益心生出种种对未来的期盼而纷扰不安。心不动不思不行为，但保有不以自我观点出发的敏捷。
To quiet the mind means to allow the mind to rest instead of work. A resting mind does not judge from the ego-self's point of view. In addition, this mind does not generate all sorts of expectations for the future based on personal profit. Therefore, the mind is not chaotic, not volatile, not thinking, and not commanding. At the same time, the mind remains sharp because it is not attached to the ego's perspective.

众睡独醒
Being Awake Within A Sleeping Crowd

在别人都沉溺于身心的放任而独他调驭自己的身心的人，就像别人都在做梦而独他是清醒一样……
When other people are drowning in the indulgence of body and mind, only cultivators are working at disciplining the body and mind. It is as if the others are all dreaming and only they are awake.

智者就像原野中奔驰的马一样，控制自如，自由自在。
Wise ones are like galloping horses of the plains. They can run fast and stop short, completely at will. Therefore, they are carefree.

不能自我控制心识的人，他被欲望所控制，怎么能称为清醒的人呢？
智者调伏自己的心，像个优秀的骑士自如地控制自己所骑的马匹一样，这才是真正清醒驯服自心的人。
Those who cannot control their conscious mind are going to be controlled by their desires. How can such people be considered "awake"? Wise ones tame their own minds like remarkable riders who control their horses with ease. These people can tame their minds with the same ease and are truly awake.

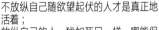

无逸不死道
Avoilding Indulgence Is The Way To Stay Alive

不放纵自己随欲望起伏的人才是真正地活着；
放纵自己的人，犹如死尸一样，哪能保有自己？
不随着世间的韵律起舞的才是真正的存在；
随世间节奏而行的，由于放纵而被世间吞没。

Only those who do not allow themselves to fluctuate up and down with desires are fully alive.

People who indulge themselves in their lives might as well be dead. How can they possibly keep their integrity?

Only those not dancing to earthly melodies are truly human beings.
People who march to worldly rhythms will invariably be engulfed by their indulgences.

觉悟了的智者们深知这个道理，他了解清醒地保有自己，不随欲望情绪起伏……
The enlightened wise ones deeply realize this principle in their hearts. They know well how to protect their integrity by keeping their consciousness awake. Their mind is not subjected to the ebb and flow of desires and emotions...

因此他成为自己的主人、生命的主人，他变成真正快乐的人啊！
Therefore, they become their own masters, the masters of their lives. They turn into completely joyous people.

如果我们放纵欲望奔驰，我们便失去了自主，而随着欲望起舞，变成它的奴隶虽生犹死。
智者观照自己，他很清醒地保有自己，因此他很自由自主，也因此而清心快乐。
If we allow desires to run around as they wish, we will then dance along with desires and lose our autonomy. Once we become slaves of desire, we might as well be dead. Wise ones reflect upon themselves and protect their integrity with full consciousness. Therefore, they are carefree and autonomous, and at the same time pure and joyous.

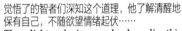

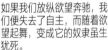

正信而具戒
Believing In Truths And Abiding By Precepts

知晓人生真谛并遵照着去做的人，他有七种特质：
People who realize the truths of life and practise these principles have seven characteristics:

一、信：坚信正确的道理。
二、进：一心精进不懈怠地去实行。
三、戒：守护感官，不纵情恣欲。
四、惭愧：不对不起别人，不对不起自己。
五、闻：对不懂的尽力求知。
六、舍：舍弃爱憎之分别心。
七、定慧：观照自己的身心。

1)Faith: believing in correct principles.
2)Diligence: focusing on practising whole-heartedly without complacency.
3)Precepts: protecting senses from indulgence in desires.
4)Sense of shame: doing nothing shameful against others or themselves.
5)Learning: seeking as much understanding of truths as possible.
6)Equanimity: calmness without the dualism of likes versus dislikes.
7)Wisdom through centring the mind: reflecting upon one's body and mind in a meditative state.

这样的人……无论他走到哪里处处都受人尊敬。这样完美的人，他名扬远方，犹如喜马拉雅山一样，很远也看得见。
Such people will be respected by others wherever they happen to be present. These people of perfect virtue cannot help but have their reputation known far and wide. Just like the Himalayan Mountains that stand out to attract our attention even at a great distance.

而不善的人就像我们在夜间打猎，明明他在我们前面也看不见他的存在。

People who do not have remarkable virtues remain invisible to cultivators. Spiritual seekers are like night hunters who cannot see unremarkable people even in front of their eyes.

他独坐、独卧、独行而融入于孤独，在孤独中观照自己、调御自己的身心，他高高兴兴地融入于当下的生活。

They are capable of immersing themselves in solitude, whether sitting, sleeping or walking. They reflect upon themselves and discipline their body and mind while being alone. They joyfully become one with the mountain and the forest in their daily lives.

智者为了修行而过着孤独的生活，并能乐在其中……

Wise ones maintain simple lifestyles for the benefit of spiritual cultivation. They could be alone and thoroughly enjoy themselves in the process...

实践是抵达真理的唯一方式，真理不是用来念的，也不是用来空口言说，而是用来指引走上真理、通往真理的地图。

智者了解真理，因为他遵循真理所指的道迹而行，因此智者可以说是了解真理的两种用意，一是真理的含义；一是真理的实践之理。

The only path to the truth is through practice. The truth is not merely to be chanted or to be paid lip service but to be practised in daily life. The wise understand the truth for they follow the path as pointed out by the truth. They truly comprehend the two purposes of truth:

1)The meaning of truth.

2)The principle of putting the truth into practice.

269

涅槃最上
Nirvana Is The Utmost Goal

身心清净不受俗世所束缚的涅槃之境，是智慧的觉悟者所追求的最高目标。

The state of Nirvana means purity of body and mind free from the bondage of the mundane world. This state is the utmost goal pursued by the enlightened wise ones.

能忍辱不为所动才是最高的苦行。

All of the forms of selfmortification are not as difficult as patience and equanimity in adversity.

为害外在的不能称为出家者……

Those who harm their external world cannot be referred to as ordained ones.

被外在所牵绊而苦恼不得自由的，没资格叫做沙门。

Those who are entangled in their external world without freedom from worries cannot qualify as monks.

当我们的心洁净没有一切不良的因子，没有自我、愤怒、贪欲、骄傲、自大，这样便不会为害外在，也不被外在所为害，这样的心才是自在无拘，才是自己的主。

When our mind is pure, it does not have any negative components, such as ego-self, anger, greed, arrogance and pride. This way we will neither harm the external world nor be harmed by it. This kind of mind is indeed carefree without bondage. Then we will be our own true master.

寂静最乐
Quietness Is The Sweetest Joy

最好的功德莫过于慈悲心；
最甜蜜的快乐莫过于心灵的宁静；
最清净的真理莫过于了解无常的真谛；

There is no more virtuous merit than loving-kindness of the heart;
There is no sweeter joy than quietness of the mind;
There is no purer truth than realizing the essence of impermanence;

最崇高的宗教莫过于智慧的开展；
最伟大的哲理莫过于教导我们如何在当下证实得到了成果。

There is no more noble religion than the development of wisdom;
There is no greater philosophy than the teaching of the way to test truths for ourselves in the present moment.

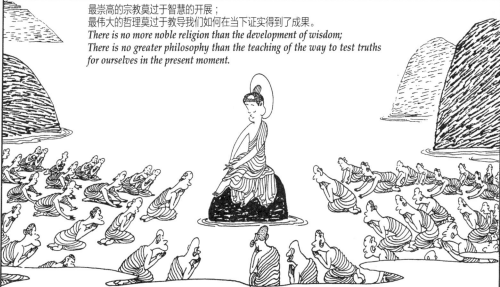

了解正确的道理而付诸行动。这就是真实！
观心自净以达永恒的安详宁静。这就是真实！
寻求智慧的开展品尝成果的甜美。这就是真实！
只是表面地念诵经典，象征性地外在行为，都不能正确地净化自己的心，得到成果。
这就是错看真实！

Understanding proper principles and carrying them out in actions this is reliable truth! Reflecting upon ourselves and purifying our mind to reach eternal peace and quiet — this is reliable truth! Seeking the development of wisdom and tasting its sweet fruits — this is reliable truth! Superficial acts of chanting scriptures and symbolic rituals, without the proper purification of one's mind and without proper attainment of the final result — these are totally unreliable.

后记
CONCLUDING NOTES

两千五百年前，佛陀于临终涅槃之前，
仔细地对阿难叮咛：
不要担心我的不存在，
我所有的法都已经教给你们了，完全没有保留。
将来你们要以法为师，以法为庇护所，庇护你们自己。
你们要做自己的一盏明灯，指引自己的道路。
守护自己的感官，观照自己的心，努力精进千万不可懈怠。
《法句经》是佛陀一生所说的话摘录成册，
佛弟子们应该要像阿难一样，
面对着佛陀的一声声叮咛，
遵循佛陀的最后交代用心去实行。
虽然，我们不能从几则精辟的话语里面，
就能获得真正的顿悟。

About 2,500 years ago, just before the Historical Buddha left this world for the Ultimate Nirvana, he repeatedly instructed his disciple Ananda with great care: "Do not worry that my physical body is no longer present in this world. I have taught you all of my Dharma and held nothing back.
In the future, you must regard the Dharma as your teacher.
You should also use the Dharma as your refuge to protect yourself.
You need to serve as your own bright beacon to guide you on the road of cultivation.
Guard your own senses and reflect upon your own mind.
Focus on marching towards your goals diligently.
Never allow yourself to become complacent."

This Dharma Sutra is a compendium of Buddha's most famous words in his lifetime, as edited by his disciples.
Buddhist practitioners should model themselves on
Ananda—talking Buddha's instructions to heart and
following Buddha's last words attentively in daily
practice.

Of course, even from these concise words of wisdom
we are not able to attain real enlightenment instantaneously.

但至少我们应该可以将其中所说的真理付诸行动，遵照着去实行。
由实行而慢慢地得到观照、净化自心所得的甜味。
佛陀说：
我们愉快地生活，不去恨那些恨我们的人。
我们没有烦恼、没有贪婪，因此我们愉快地生活。
虽然，我们生活于贪欲的世界里，
但我们都能像莲花一样出于污水而不染，
出于贪欲而本身过着没有贪欲的生活，
因此我们没有烦恼，我们很愉快地生活。
我们要坦然地面对自己、接受自己、保有自己。
我们要接受事实去克服愤怒；
以爱去克服不满；以净化自己的心，去克服内在的欲望；顺服于宇宙的自然定律。
佛陀说：
凡是存在的必然变化；
凡是无变化的，必不存在。
我们存在于世，除了自然变化了我们的身之外，
我们也应该自主地变化自己的心，
由凡夫变化为一个觉悟的智者。

But at least we should be able to act upon the truths, as taught by Buddha, in our personal practice.

Slowly we will taste the sweetness of reflecting upon ourselves and purifying our own minds.

Buddha once said: "We live joyously. We bear no resentment towards those who hate us. We have neither worries nor greed. Therefore, our life is full of joy. We live within a world of greedy desires. Like the lotus blossoms remaining pure within muddy water, we grow among greed and yet live without greed. Therefore, we have no worries and live in joy daily."

We must calmly face ourselves, accept ourselves, and protect ourselves. We must accept realities to overcome anger, use love to overcome dissatisfaction, and purify our mind to overcome inner desires. We have to obey the natural laws of the universe.

Buddha taught us: "Everything that exists must surely change. Anything that does not change must not exist." Living in this world, in addition to nature's imposition of our own physiological change, we should also independently regulate our mind for the better. "Change from an ordinary person into an enlightened one of wisdom!"

274

...End...

此部分为本书图画页的延伸阅读，各段首所示的页码与图画页对应。

P157 一 诸法意先导，意主意造作。若以染污意，或语或行业，是则苦随彼，如轮随兽足。

二 诸法意先导，意主意造作。若以清净意，或语或行业，是则乐随彼，如影不离形。

三 "彼骂我打我，败我劫夺我"，若人怀此念，怨恨不能息。

四 "彼骂我打我，败我劫夺我"，若人舍此念，怨恨自平息。

五 在于世界中，从非怨止怨，唯以忍止怨；此古（圣常）法。

P158 六 彼人不了悟："我等将毁灭"。若彼等如此，则诤论自息。

七 唯求住净乐，不摄护诸根，饮食不知量，懈惰不精进，彼实为魔服，如风吹弱树。

八 愿求非乐住，善摄护诸根，饮食知节量，具信又精进，魔不能胜彼，如风吹石山。

九 若人穿袈裟，不离诸垢秽，无诚实克己，不应着袈裟。

一〇 若人离诸垢，能善持戒律，克己与诚实，彼应着袈裟。

P159 一一 非真思真实，真实见非真，邪思惟境界，彼不达真实。

一二 真实思真实，非真知非真，正思惟境界，彼能达真实。

一三 如盖屋不密，必为雨漏浸，如是不修心，贪欲必漏入。

一四 如善密盖屋，不为雨漏浸，如是善修心，贪欲不漏入。

P160 一五 现世此处悲，死后他处悲，作诸恶业者，两处俱忧悲，见自恶业已，他悲他苦恼。

一六 现世此处乐，死后他处乐，作诸善业者，两处俱受乐，见自善业已，他乐他极乐。

P161 一七 现世此处苦，死后他处苦，作诸恶业者，两处俱受苦，（现）悲"我作恶"，堕恶趣更苦。

一八 现世此处喜，死后他处喜，修诸福业者，两处俱欢喜，（现）喜"我修福"，生善趣更喜。

P162 一九 虽多诵经集，放逸而不行，如牧数他牛，自无沙门分。

二〇 虽诵经典少，能依教实行，具足正知识，除灭贪嗔痴，善净解脱心，弃舍于世欲，此界或他界，彼得沙门分。

《南传法句经 · 双品》

P163 二一 无逸不死道，放逸趣死路。无逸者不死，放逸者如尸。

二二　智者深知此，所行不放逸。不放逸得乐，喜悦于圣境。
二三　智者常坚忍，勇猛修禅定。解脱得安隐，证无上涅槃。

P164　二四　奋勉常正念，净行能克己，如法而生活，无逸善名增。
二五　奋勉不放逸，克己自调御，智者自作洲，不为洪水没。
二六　暗钝愚痴人，沉溺于放逸，智者不放逸，如富人护宝。

P165　二七　莫沉溺放逸，莫嗜爱欲乐。警觉修定者，始得大安乐。
二八　智者以无逸，除逸则无忧，圣贤登慧阁，观愚者多忧，如登于高山，俯视地上物。
二九　放逸中无逸，如众睡独醒。智者如骏驰，驽骀所不及。

P166　三〇　摩伽以无逸，得为诸天主。无逸人所赞，放逸为人诃。
三一　乐不放逸比丘，或者惧见放逸，犹如猛火炎炎，烧去大结、小结。
三二　乐不放逸比丘，或者惧见放逸，彼已邻近涅槃，必定不易堕落。

《南传法句经·不放逸品》

P167　三三　轻动变易心，难护难制服。智者调直之，如匠搋箭直。
三四　如鱼离水栖，投于陆地上，以此战栗心，摆脱魔境界。
三五　此心随欲转，轻躁难捉摸。善哉心调伏，心调得安乐。
三六　此心随欲转，微妙极难见。智者防护心，心护得安乐。

P168　三七　远行与独行，无形隐深窟。谁能调伏心，解脱魔罗缚。
三八　心若不安定，又不了正法，信心不坚者，智慧不成就。
三九　若得无漏心，亦无诸惑乱，超越善与恶，觉者无恐怖。
四〇　知身如陶器，住心似城廓，慧剑击魔罗，守胜莫染著。

P169　四一　此身实不久，当睡于地下，被弃无意识，无用如木屑。
四二　仇敌害仇敌，怨家对怨家，若心向邪行，恶业最为大。
四三　（善）非父母作，亦非他眷属，若心向正行，善业最为大。

《南传法句经·心品》

P170　四四　谁征服地界，阎魔界天界，谁善说法句，如巧匠采花？
四五　有学克地界，阎魔界天界。有学说法句，如巧匠采花。
四六　知此身如泡，觉悟是幻法，折魔罗花箭，越死王所见。

P171　四七　采集诸花已，其人心爱著，死神捉将去，如瀑流睡村。
四八　采集诸花已，其人心爱著，贪欲无厌足，实为死魔伏。
四九　牟尼入村落，譬如蜂采华，不坏色与香，但取其蜜去。

P172　五〇　不观他人过，不观作不作，但观自身行，作也与未作。
五一　犹如鲜妙花，色美而无香，如是说善语，彼不行无果。

五二 犹如鲜妙花，色美而芳香，如是说善语，彼实行有果。

五三 如从诸花聚，得造众花鬘，如是生为人，当作诸善事。

P173 五四 花香不逆风，栴檀多伽罗，末利香亦尔。德香逆风熏，彼正人之香，遍闻于诸方。

五五 栴檀多伽罗，拔悉基青莲，如是诸香中，戒香为最上。

五六 栴檀多伽罗，此等香甚微。持戒者最上，香熏诸天间。

P174 五七 成就诸戒行，住于不放逸，正智解脱者，魔不知所趣。

五八 犹如粪秽聚，弃著于大道，莲华生其中，香洁而悦意。

五九 如是粪秽等，盲昧凡夫中，正觉者弟子，以智慧光照。

《南传法句经·华品》

P178 六〇 不眠者夜长，倦者由旬长，不明达正法——愚者轮回长。

六一 不得胜我者为友，与我相等者亦无，宁可坚决独行居，不与愚人做伴侣。

六二 "此我子我财"，愚人常为忧。我且无有我，何有子与财？

P179 六三 愚者（自）知愚，彼即是智人。愚人（自）谓智，实称（真）愚夫。

六四 愚者虽终身，亲近于智人，彼不了达摩，如匙尝汤味。

P180 六五 慧者须臾顷，亲近于智人，能速解达摩，如舌尝汤味。

六六 愚人不觉知，与自仇敌行，造作诸恶业，受定众苦果。

六七 彼作不善业，作已生后悔，哭泣泪满面，应得受异熟。

P181 六八 若彼作善业，作已不追悔，欢喜而愉悦，应得受异熟。

六九 恶业未成熟，愚人思知蜜；恶业成熟时，愚人必受苦。

七〇 愚者月复月，虽仅取（少）食——以孤沙草端；（彼所得功德），不及思法者，十六分之一。

P182 七一 犹如搆牛乳，醍醐非速成。愚人造恶业，不即感恶果，业力随其后，如死灰覆火。

七二 愚求知识，反而趋灭亡，损害其幸福，破碎其头首。

七三 （愚人）骛虚名：僧中作上座，僧院为院主，他人求供养。

P183 七四 "僧与俗共知——此事由我作，事无论大小，皆由我作主"，愚人作此想，贪与慢增长。

七五 一（道）引世利，一（道）向涅槃。佛弟子比丘，当如是了知，莫贪著世利，专注于远离。

《南传法句经·愚品》

P184 七六 若见彼智者——能指示过失，并能谴责者，当与彼为友；犹如知识者，能指示宝藏。与彼智人友，定善而无恶。

七七 训诫与教示，阻（他人）过恶。善人爱此人，但为恶人憎。

七八 莫与恶友交，莫友卑鄙者。应与善友交，应友高尚士。

P185 七九 得饮法（水）者，心清而安乐。智者常喜悦，圣者所说法。

八〇 灌溉者引水，箭匠之矫箭，木匠之绳木，智者自调御。

八一 犹如坚固岩，不为风所摇，毁谤与赞誉，智者不为动。

P186 八二 亦如一深池，清明而澄净，智者闻法已，如是心清净。

八三 善人离诸（欲），不论诸欲事。苦乐所不动，智者无喜忧。

八四 不因自因他，（智者作诸恶），不求子求财、及谋国（作恶）。不欲以非法，求自己繁荣。彼实具戒行，智慧正法者。

P187 八五 于此人群中，达彼岸者少。其余诸人等，徘徊于此岸。

八六 善能说法者，及依正法行，彼能达彼岸，度难度魔境。

八七 应舍弃黑法，智者修白法，从家来无家，喜独处不易。

P188 八八 当求是（法）乐。舍欲无所有，智者须清净，自心诸垢秽。

八九 彼于诸觉支，正心而修习。远离诸固执，乐舍诸爱著，漏尽而光耀，此世证涅槃。

《南传法句经·智者品》

P189 九〇 路行尽无忧，于一切解脱，断一切系缚，无有苦恼者。

九一 正念奋勇者，彼不乐在家。如鹅离池去，彼等弃水家。

九二 彼等无积聚，于食如实知，空无相解脱——是彼所行境，如鸟游虚空，踪迹不可得。

P190 九三 彼等诸漏尽，亦不贪饮食，空无相解脱——是彼所行境，如鸟游虚空，踪迹不可得。

九四 彼诸根寂静，如御者调马，离我慢无漏，为天人所慕。

九五 彼已无愤恨，犹如于大地，彼虔诚坚固，如因陀揭罗，如无污泥池，是人无轮回。

P191 九六 彼人心寂静，语与业寂静，正智而解脱，如是得安稳。

九七 无信知无为，断系因永谢，弃舍于贪欲，真实无上士。

九八 于村落林间，平地或丘陵，何处有罗汉，彼地即可庆。

九九 林野甚可乐；世人所不乐，彼喜离欲乐，不求诸欲乐。

《南传法句经·阿罗汉品》

P192 一〇〇 虽诵一千言，若无义理者，不如一义语，闻已得寂静。

一〇一 虽诵千句偈，若无义理者，不如一句偈，闻已得寂静。

一〇二 彼诵百句偈，若无义理者，不如一法句，闻已得寂静。

P193 一〇三 彼于战场上，虽胜百万人；未若克己者，战士之最上！

一〇四 能克制自己，过于胜他人。若有克己者，常行自节制。

一〇五 天神乾闼婆，魔王并梵天，皆遭于败北，不能胜彼人。

P194 一〇六 月月投千（金）——供牺牲百年，不如须臾间，供养修己者，彼如是供养，胜祭祀百年。

一〇七　若人一百年——事火于林中，不如须臾间，供养修己者，彼如是供养，胜祭祀百年。

P195　一〇八　若人于世间，施舍或供养，求福一周年，如是诸功德，不及四分一，礼敬正直者。

一〇九　好乐敬礼者，常尊于长老，四法得增长：寿美乐与力。

P196　一一〇　若人寿百岁——破戒无三昧，不如生一日——持戒修禅定。

一一一　若人寿百岁——无慧无三昧，不如生一日——具慧修禅定。

一一二　若人寿百岁——怠惰不精进，不如生一日——励力行精进。

P197　一一三　若人寿百岁——不见生灭法，不如生一日——得见生灭法。

一一四　若人寿百岁——不见不死道，不如生一日——得见不死道。

一一五　若人寿百岁——不见最上法，不如生一日——得见最上法。

《南传法句经·千品》

P198　一一六　应急速作善，制止罪恶心。怠慢作善者，心则喜于恶。

一一七　若人作恶已，不可数数作；莫喜于作恶；积恶则受苦。

一一八　若人作善已，应复数数作；当喜于作善；积善则受乐。

一一九　恶业未成熟，恶者以为乐。恶业成熟时，恶者方见恶。

一二〇　善业未成熟，善人以为苦。善业成熟时，善人始见善。

P199　一二一　莫轻于小恶！谓“我不招报”，须知滴水落，亦可满水瓶，愚夫盈其恶，少许少许积。

一二二　莫轻于小善！谓“我不招报”，须知滴水落，亦可满水瓶，智者完其善，少许少许积。

一二三　商人避险道，伴少而货多；爱生避毒品，避恶当亦尔。

P200　一二四　假若无有疮伤手，可以其手持毒药。毒不能患无伤手，不作恶者便无恶。

一二五　若犯无邪者，清净无染者，罪恶向愚人，如逆风扬尘。

一二六　有人生于（母）胎中，作恶者则（堕）地狱，正直之人升天界，漏尽者证入涅槃。

P201　一二七　非于虚空及海中，亦非入深山洞窟，欲求逃遁恶业者，世间实无可觅处。

一二八　非于虚空及海中，亦非入深山洞窟，欲求不为死魔制，世间实无可觅处。

《南传法句经·恶品》

P202　一二九　一切惧刀杖，一切皆畏死，以自度（他情），莫杀教他杀。

一三〇　一切惧刀杖，一切皆爱生，以自度（他情），莫杀教他杀。

一三一　于求乐有情，刀杖加恼害，但求自己乐，后世乐难得。

一三二　于求乐有情，不加刀杖害，欲求自己乐，后世乐可得。

P203　一三三　对人莫说粗恶语，汝所说者还说汝。愤怒之言实堪痛；互击刀杖可伤汝。

一三四　汝若自默然，如一破铜锣，已得涅槃路；于汝无诤故。

P204 一三五　如牧人以杖，驱牛至牧场，如是老与死，驱逐众生命。

一三六　愚夫造作诸恶业，却不自知（有果报），痴人以自业感苦，宛如以火而自烧。

一三七　若以刀杖害，无恶无害者，十事中一种，彼将迅速得。

P208 一三八　极苦痛失财，身体被损害，或重病所逼，或失心狂乱。

一三九　或为王迫害，或被诬重罪，或眷属离散，或破灭财产。

一四〇　或彼之房屋，为劫火焚烧。痴者身亡后，复堕于地狱。

P209 一四一　非裸行结发，非涂泥绝食，卧地自尘身，非以蹲踞（住），不断疑惑者，能令得清净。

一四二　严身住寂静，调御而克制，必然修梵行，不以刀杖等，加害诸有情，彼即婆罗门，彼即是沙门，彼即是比丘。

一四三　以惭自禁者，世间所罕有，彼善避羞辱，如良马避鞭。

P210 一四四　如良马加鞭，当奋勉忏悔。以信戒精进，以及三摩地，善分别正法，以及明行足，汝当念勿忘，消灭无穷苦。

一四五　灌溉者引水，箭匠之矫箭，木匠之绳木，善行者自御。

《南传法句经·刀杖品》

P211 一四六　常在燃烧中，何喜何可笑？幽暗之所蔽，何不求光明？

一四七　观此粉饰身；疮伤一堆骨，疾病多思惟，绝非常存者。

一四八　此衰老形骸，病薮而易坏；朽聚必毁灭，有生终归死。

P212 一四九　犹如葫芦瓜，散弃于秋季，骸骨如鸽色，观此何可乐？

一五〇　此城骨所建，涂以血与肉，储藏老与死，及慢并虚伪。

一五一　盛饰王车亦必朽，此身老迈当亦尔。唯善人法不老朽，善人传示于善人。

P213 一五二　寡闻之（愚）人，生长如牡牛，唯增长筋肉，而不增智慧。

一五三　经多生轮回，寻求造屋者，但未得见之，痛苦再再生。

一五四　已见造屋者！不再造于屋。椽桷皆毁坏，栋梁亦摧折。我既证无为，一切爱尽灭。

P214 一五五　少壮不得财，并不修梵行，如池边老鹭，无鱼而萎灭。

一五六　少壮不得财，并不修梵行，卧如破折弓，悲欢于过去。

《南传法句经·老品》

P215 一五七　若人知自爱，须善自保护。三时中一时，智者应醒觉。

一五八　第一将自己，安置于正道，然后教他人；贤者始无过。

一五九　若欲诲他者，应如己所行，（自）制乃制（他），克己实最难。

P216 一六〇　自为自依怙。他人何可依？自己善调御，证难得所依。

一六一　恶业实由自己作，从自己生而自起。（恶业）摧坏于愚者，犹如金刚破宝石。

一六二　破戒如蔓萝，缠覆裟罗树。彼自如此作，徒快敌者意。

P217　一六三　不善事易作，然无益于己；善与利益事，实为极难行。

一六四　恶慧愚痴人，以其邪见故，侮蔑罗汉教，依正法行者，以及尊者教，而自取毁灭，如格他格草，结果自灭亡。

P218　一六五　恶实由己作，染污亦由己；由己不作恶，清净亦由己。净不净依己，他何能净他？

一六六　莫以利他事，忽于己利益。善知己利者，常专心利益。

《南传法句经·自己品》

P219　一六七　莫从卑劣法。莫住于放逸。莫随于邪见。莫增长世俗。

一六八　奋起莫放逸！行正法善行。依正法行者，此世他世乐。

一六九　行正法善行。勿行于恶行。依正法行者，此世他世乐。

P220　一七○　视如水上浮沤，视如海市蜃楼，若人观世如是，死王不得见他。

一七一　来看这个世界，犹如壮严王车。愚人沉湎此中，智者毫无执著。

一七二　若人先放逸，但后不放逸。彼照耀此世，如月出云翳。

P221　一七三　若作恶业已，覆之以善者。彼照耀此世，如月出云翳。

一七四　此世界盲暝。能得此者少。如鸟脱罗网，鲜有升天者。

一七五　天鹅飞行太阳道，以神通力可行空。智者破魔王魔卷，得能脱离于世间。

P225　一七六　违犯一（乘）法，及说妄语者，不信来世者，则无恶不作。

一七七　悭者不生天。愚者不赞布施。智者随喜施，后必得安乐。

一七八　一统大地者，得生天上者，一切世界主，不及预流胜。

《南传法句经·世品》

P226　一七九　彼之胜利无能胜，败者于世无可从，佛（智）无边无行迹，汝复以何而诳惑？

一八○　彼已不具于结缚，爱欲难以诱使去，佛（智）无边无行迹，汝复以何而诳惑？

一八一　智者修禅定，喜出家寂静，正念正觉者，天人所敬爱。

一八二　得生人道难，生得寿终难，得闻正法难，遇佛出世难。

一八三　一切恶莫作，一切善应行，自调净其意，是则诸佛教。

P227　一八四　诸佛说涅槃最上，忍辱为最高苦行。害他实非出家者，恼他不名为沙门。

一八五　不诽与不害，严持于戒律，饮食知节量，远处而独居，勤修增上定，是为诸佛教。

一八六　即使雨金钱，欲心不满足。智者知淫欲，乐少而苦多！

一八七　故彼于天欲，亦不起希求。正觉者弟子，希灭于爱欲。

一八八　诸人恐怖故，去皈依山岳，或依于森林，园苑树支提。

P228　一八九　此非安稳依，此非最上依，如是皈依者，不离一切苦。

一九○　若人皈依佛，皈依法及僧，由于正智慧，得见四圣谛。

一九一　苦与苦之因，以及苦之灭，并八支圣道，能令苦寂灭。

一九二　此皈依安稳，此皈依无上，如是皈依者，解脱一切苦。

一九三　圣人极难得，彼非随处生；智者所生处，家族咸蒙庆。

P229　一九四　诸佛出现乐，演说正法乐，僧伽和合乐，修士和合乐。

一九五　供养供应者——脱离于虚妄，超越诸忧患，佛及佛弟子。

一九六　若供养如是——寂静无畏者，其所得功德，无能测量者。

《南传法句经·佛陀品》

P230　一九七　我等实乐生，憎怨中无憎。于憎怨人中，我等无憎住。

一九八　我等实乐生，疾病中无病。于疾病人中，我等无病住。

一九九　我等实乐生，贪欲中无欲。于贪欲人中，我等无欲住。

二〇〇　我等实乐生，我等无物障，我等乐为食，如光音天人。

P231　二〇一　胜利生憎怨，败者住苦恼。胜败两俱舍，和静住安乐。

二〇二　无火如贪欲，无恶如瞋恨，无苦如（五）蕴，无乐胜寂静。

二〇三　饥为最大病，行为最大苦；如实知此已，涅槃乐最上。

P232　二〇四　无病最上利，知足最上财，信赖最上亲，涅槃最上乐。

二〇五　已饮独居味，以及寂静味，喜饮于法味，离怖畏去恶。

二〇六　善哉见圣者，与彼同住乐。由不见愚人，彼即常欢乐。

P233　二〇七　与愚者同行，长时处忧悲。与愚同住苦，如与敌同居。与智者同住，乐如会亲族。

二〇八　是故真实：

贤者智者多闻者，持戒虔诚与圣者，从斯善人贤慧游，犹如月从于星道。

《南传法句经·乐品》

P234　二〇九　专事不当事，不事于应修，弃善趋爱欲，却羡自勉者。

二一〇　莫结交爱人，莫结不爱人。不见爱人苦，见憎人亦苦。

二一一　是故莫爱著，爱别离为苦。若无爱与憎，彼即无羁缚。

P235　二一二　从喜爱生忧，从喜爱生怖；离喜爱无忧，何处有恐怖？

二一三　从亲爱生忧，从亲爱生怖；离亲爱无忧，何处有恐怖？

二一四　从贪欲生忧，从贪欲生怖；离贪欲无忧，何处有恐怖？

P236　二一五　从欲乐生忧，从欲乐生怖；离欲乐无忧，何处有恐怖？

二一六　从爱欲生忧，从爱欲生怖；离爱欲无忧，何处有恐怖？

二一七　具戒及正见，住法知真谛，圆满自所行，彼为世人爱。

P237　二一八　渴求离言法，充满思虑心，诸欲心不著，是名上流人。

二一九　久客异乡者，自远处安归，亲友与知识，欢喜而迎彼。
二二〇　造福亦如是，从此生彼界，福业如亲友，以迎爱者来。

《南传法句经·喜爱品》

P238 二二一　舍弃于忿怒，除灭于我慢，解脱一切缚，不执著名色，彼无一物者，苦不能相随。
二二二　若能抑忿发，如止急行车，是名（善）御者，余于执缰人。
二二三　以不忿胜忿。以善胜不善。以施胜悭吝。以实胜虚妄。

P239 二二四　谛语不瞋恚，分施与乞者；以如是三事，能生于诸天。
二二五　彼无害牟尼，常调伏其身，到达不死境——无有悲忧处。

P240 二二六　恒常醒觉者，日夜勤修学，志向于涅槃，息灭诸烦恼。
二二七　阿多罗应知：此非今日事，古语已有之。默然为人诽，多语为人诽，寡言为人诽；不为诽谤者，斯世实无有。

P241 二二八　全被人诽者，或全被赞者，非曾有当有，现在亦无有。
二二九　若人朝朝自反省，行无瑕疵并贤明，智慧戒行兼具者，彼为智人所称赞。
二三〇　品如阎浮金，谁得诽辱之？彼为婆罗门，诸天所称赞。

P242 二三一　摄护身忿怒，调伏于身行。舍离身恶行，以身修善行。
二三二　摄护语忿怒，调伏于语行。舍离语恶行，以语修善行。
二三三　摄护意忿怒，调伏于意行。舍离意恶行，以意修善行。
二三四　智者身调伏，亦复语调伏，于意亦调伏，实一切调伏。

《南传法句经·忿怒品》

P246 二三五　汝今已似枯焦叶，阎魔使者近身边。汝已伫立死门前，旅途汝亦无资粮。
二三六　汝宜自造安全洲，迅速精勤为智者。拂除尘垢无烦恼，得达诸天之圣境。

P247 二三七　汝今寿命行已终。汝已移步近阎魔。道中既无停息处，旅途汝亦无资粮。
二三八　汝宜自造安全洲。迅速精勤为智者。拂除尘垢无烦恼，不复重来生与老。

P248 二三九　刹那刹那间，智者分分除，渐拂自垢秽，如冶工锻金。
二四〇　如铁自生锈，生已自腐蚀，犯罪者亦尔，自业导恶趣。
二四一　不诵经典秽，不勤为家秽，懒惰为色秽，放逸护卫秽。
二四二　邪行妇人秽，吝啬施者秽。此界及他界，恶法实为秽。

P249 二四三　此等诸垢中，无明垢为最，汝当除此垢，成无垢比丘。
二四四　生活无惭愧，卤莽如乌鸦，诋毁（于他人），大胆自夸张，傲慢邪恶者，其人生活易。
二四五　生活于惭愧，常求于清净，不著欲谦逊，住清净生活，（富于）识见者，其人生活难。

P250 二四六　若人于世界，杀生说妄语，取人所不与，犯于别人妻。

284

二四七　及沉湎饮酒，行为如是者，即于此世界，毁掘自（善）根。

三四八　如是汝应知：不制则为恶；莫贪与非法，自陷于永苦。

二四九　若信乐故施。心嫉他得食，彼于昼或夜，不得入三昧。

P251　二五○　若斩断此（心），拔根及除灭，则于昼或夜，彼得入三昧。

二五一　无火等于贪欲，无执著如瞋恚，无纲等于愚痴，无河流如爱欲。

二五二　易见他人过，自见则为难。扬恶如颺糠，已过则覆匿，如彼狡博者，隐匿其格利。

P252　二五三　若见他人过，心常易忿者，增长于烦恼；去断惑远矣。

二五四　虚空无道迹，外道无沙门。众生喜虚妄，如来无虚妄。

二五五　虚空无道迹，外道无沙门。（五）蕴无常住，诸佛无动乱。

《南传法句经·垢秽品》

P253　二五六　卤莽处事故，不为法住者。智者应辨别——孰正与孰邪。

二五七　导人不卤莽，如法而公平，智者护于法，是名法住者。

二五八　不以多言故，彼即为智者。安静无恐怖，是名为智者。

P254　二五九　不以多言故，彼为持法者。彼虽闻少分，但由身见法，于法不放逸，是名持法者。

二六○　不因彼白头，即得为长老。彼年龄虚熟，徒有长老名。

P255　二六一　于彼具真实，具法不杀生，节制并调伏，彼有智慧人。除灭诸垢秽，实名为长老。

二六二　嫉悭虚伪者，虽以其辩才，或由相端严，不为善良人。

二六三　若斩断此（心），拔根及除灭，彼舍瞋智者，名为善良人。

P256　二六四　若破戒妄语，削发非沙门。充满欲与贪，云何为沙门？

二六五　彼息灭诸恶——无论大与小，因息灭诸恶，故名为沙门。

二六六　仅向他行乞，不即是比丘。行宗教法仪，亦不为比丘。

P257　二六七　仅舍善与恶，修于梵行者，以知住此世，彼实名比丘。

二六八　愚昧无知者，不以默然故，而名为牟尼，智者如权衡。

二六九　舍恶取其善，乃得为牟尼。彼知于两界，故称为牟尼。

P258　二七○　彼人非圣贤，以其杀生故。不害诸众生，是名为圣者。

二七一　不以戒律行，或由于多闻，或由证三昧，或由于独居。

二七二　谓"受出家乐，非凡夫所能"。汝等漏未尽，莫生保信想！

《南传法句经·法住品》

P259　二七三　八支道中胜，四句谛中胜，离欲法中胜，具眼两足胜。

二七四　实唯此一道，无余知见净。汝等顺此行。魔为之惑乱。

二七五　汝顺此（道）行，使汝苦灭尽。知我所说道，得除去荆棘。

二七六　汝当自努力！如来唯说者。随禅定行者，解脱魔系缚。

P263 二七七　"一切行无常"，以慧观照时，得厌离于苦。此乃清净道。

二七八　"一切行是苦"，以慧观照时，得厌离于苦。此乃清净道。

二七九　"一切法无我"，以慧观照时，得厌离于苦。此乃清净道。

P264 二八〇　当努力时不努力，年虽少壮陷怠惰，意志消沉又懒弱，怠者不以智得道。

二八一　慎语而制意，不以身作恶。净此三业道，得圣所示道。

二八二　由瑜伽生智，无瑜伽慧灭。了知此二道，及其得与失，当自努力行，增长于智慧。

P265 二八三　应伐欲稠林，勿伐于树木。从欲林生怖，当脱欲稠林。

二八四　男女欲丝丝，未断心犹系；如饮乳犊子，不离于母牛。

二八五　自己断除爱情，如以手折秋莲。勤修寂静之道，善逝所说涅槃。

P266 二八六　"雨季我住此，冬夏亦住此"，此为愚夫想，而不觉危险。

二八七　溺爱子与畜，其人心感著，死神捉将去，如瀑流睡村。

二八八　父子与亲戚，莫能为救护。彼为死所制，非亲族能救。

二八九　了知此义已，智者持戒律，通达涅槃路——迅速令清净。

《南传法句经·道品》

P267 二九〇　若弃于小乐，得见于大乐。智者弃小乐，当见于大乐。

二九一　施与他人苦，为求自己乐；彼为瞋系缚，怨憎不解脱。

二九二　应作而不作，不应作而作，傲慢放逸者，彼之漏增长。

二九三　常精勤观身，不作不应作，应作则常作，观者漏灭尽。

P268 二九四　杀（爱欲）母与（慢）父，杀刹帝利族二王，（破）王国杀其从臣，趋向无忧婆罗门。

二九五　杀（爱欲）母与（慢）父，杀婆罗门族二王，杀其虎（将）第五（疑），趋向无忧婆罗门。

P269 二九六　乔达摩弟子，常善自醒觉，无论昼与夜，彼常念佛陀。

二九七　乔达摩弟子，常善自醒觉，无论昼与夜，彼常念达摩。

二九八　乔达摩弟子，常善自醒觉，无论昼与夜，彼常念僧伽。

P270 二九九　乔达摩弟子，常善自醒觉，无论昼与夜，彼常念于身。

三〇〇　乔达摩弟子，常善自醒觉，无论昼与夜，常乐不杀生。

三〇一　乔达摩弟子，常善自醒觉，无论昼与夜，心常乐禅定。

P271 三〇二　出家爱乐难。在家生活难。非俦共住苦。（轮回）往来苦。故不应往来，随从于痛苦。

三〇三　正信而具戒，得誉及财者，彼至于何处，处处受尊敬。

三〇四　善名扬远方，高显如云山。恶者如夜射，虽近不能见。

三〇五　独坐与独卧，独行而不倦，彼独自调御，喜乐于林中。

《南传法句经·杂品》